BOY BAND SUMMER

SARA WEALER

1

"Here are the basics," Violet says as she cues up a video for my first Boy Band 101 lesson. "Emilio is the hot one. Landon is the funny one. Karsten is the serious one, and Chase is the sweet one. Avery, you're not paying attention!"

She shakes her phone in my face, pulling my focus back to the screen, where four guys are dancing and singing in leather pants.

"Sorry," I say as I squint at the video. "The smoldering sincerity was so powerful I had to look away for a minute."

"If you're going on tour with these guys, you should at least know their names."

I flop onto my bed, taking her phone and holding it above my head so the four guys hover over me. Each one is attractive in a safe, shiny way, and as the camera pans across their faces they sing into the lens as if I am the only girl in the world.

"I don't know for sure if I'm going," I tell Violet. "Maybe I'll stay home and get a babysitting job instead."

She rolls her eyes and nudges me with her foot.

"God, why?" she says "You have a chance to go on tour with True Meaning. I don't get why you aren't more excited."

"Probably because up until four days ago I had no idea who or what True Meaning was."

Until last week, I was blissfully boy band ignorant—just hanging out with my show choir friends, cruising through the last semester of sophomore year, waiting for my boyfriend Hunter to ask me to Prom. Things weren't perfect; my parents were still separated, and my mom had lost her job as school nurse thanks to budget cuts at the district. But other than that, my life was pretty much OK. Normal.

Then Mom got a call from her best friend from college, who works for Calliope, the kids' network. They have a band going on tour that needs a nurse because one of the members has diabetes and another has potentially deadly food allergies. Mom put her name in, thinking nothing would come of it. But that first call led to a phone interview, and then a call where they gave her the job. From Memorial Day to Labor Day, she'll be cris-crossing America, standing ready with insulin and epi-pens while also tending to the bumps, scrapes, sunburns and stomach bugs of the rest of the band and its roadies.

"It pays as much as I'd make in almost two years as a school nurse," she told me. "When I get home, I can take some time off, maybe go back to school and start a new career."

Then she told me there was another job—one I could have if I wanted it. This great opportunity, which, according to Mom, is sure to look super-impressive to colleges, comes with the title of "Unpaid Intern," which basically means I would run around fetching drinks, emailing stuff, posting on social media, maybe selling tee-shirts or whatever other grunt work needs to be done.

"They have room on a bus, and Brynn's positive she can get you in," Mom said. "Think how much fun it would be. You'll get a chance to see something besides Cincinnati."

I don't despise the idea of going on the tour. Traveling *does* sounds like fun. But I don't love it, either. I guess you could say I've been ambivalent, which is why Violet is giving me a crash course in all things True Meaning, or TM as they're known to fans.

She leans over to tap the phone screen and a new video comes on, a slow song with a lot of harmonies. When the camera pans wider I can see it's a live performance. The four of them sound amazing, even without autotune and backing instrumentals.

I swing my foot to the beat. "They're actually really good. Why haven't I heard them anywhere?"

"Most of their stuff is from their show," Violet explains. "True Meaning was put together by Calliope to try and follow the K-Pop bandwagon. They're not K-Pop, but they do have a ton of fans. We're talking ridiculously devoted fans. TM fans make all other fans in the history of fandom look tame."

"Awesome." I give Violet back her phone. "You're making my decision a whole lot easier."

"No! Forget I said anything," she scrambles. "True Meaning fans are the best! Come on, Avery. This is a once-in-a-lifetime chance. And besides..."

She trails off without saying what I know she's thinking: *It's not like you have anything better to do.*

Up until three days ago, I had plenty—or at least I thought I did. I was supposed to get into Choraliers, the top show choir at our school, which would have meant spending the summer learning new routines for competitions in the fall. But then the audition results were posted.

I didn't make it.

So now my summer is probably going to consist of entertaining myself while my other friends are at rehearsals, and then avoiding them in the evenings while they talk about all the fun they're having without me. Normally I would just hang out with Violet, except she has a packed schedule with tennis, which means she won't be able to spend much time at the swim club.

That doesn't mean I'm completely without options, though.

"Hunter is here," I say.

"Mm hm."

More silence, until I'm tempted to knock the phone out of her hand and stomp on it. Two days ago, Hunter and I decided to spend some time apart because we were arguing and in a rut and basically just needing to be away from each other for a while. But I know he misses me. And Prom is coming up. He'll need a date. So of course he'll ask me, and we'll get back together in time to have an incredible summer, just like last summer when we started dating and realized we were perfect for each other.

"Hunter is here," I repeat. "And he is way hotter than..." I wave my hand at the guy on the phone screen—the quote/unquote *hot one*. "What's his name? Eli?"

"Emilio."

"Yeah." I get up and wander over to my closet, choosing something cute to wear tomorrow just in case I run into Hunter. We might be on a break, but I still want to look nice.

And I do appreciate that Violet is concerned. There's a reason she's my best friend—the person I'd do anything for and who I know would do the same for me. Violet has had a front-row seat to all my anguish this past week. She wants me to be happy.

And I will be. I may have had a couple of setbacks, but I'm not ready to pack my bags and leave town because of them.

"I love you for looking out for me," I say as a I pull down a new sundress and hold it up to see how it fits. "But I'll be fine. I don't need to go on tour with a boy band to have a great summer. I can make it epic all on my own."

2

I am a show choir girl. I love to sing, dance and perform, and I love everything that goes along with singing, dancing and performing. Stuff like Broadway musicals, sparkly dresses, and TV shows with celebrity judges where dreams get made or broken by votes from the viewers at home. I realized I was a show choir girl in fifth grade, when Mom got her job as the nurse at Oak Park Senior High. One of the first things she did was take me to a Choraliers concert.

The Choraliers are the top show choir in the state. Most years, they're among the best show choirs in the country. Our school pumps a ton of money into the group, and people work their butts off every year to get in. That means Choraliers is world-class. It also means the competition is extremely fierce.

I didn't think I'd have to worry, though, because I've always been one of the top performers at school. I might not be the absolute best dancer, and sometimes I'm a little *too* enthusiastic, but I am, without a doubt, right up there when it comes to dedication and what Ms. Zebari, the head of the music department, calls "dazzle." I made it into Pops Choir, the group just below Choraliers, as a freshman, which is impressive in its own right. I take a ton of voice lessons and dance classes, plus I volunteer at all the local invitationals. For the past two years I have invested every ounce of my energy and passion into show choir excellence.

So naturally I saw myself joining Choraliers as a junior, like all the top performers do. Auditions were just a formality; I'd sail through, take my place with the rest of the elite, and be on my way to glee club glory.

Then, Monday happened.

When people describe a nasty shock as a kick to the stomach, they're right, because that's exactly what it felt like when I saw the audition results. I read the list quickly at first and thought I'd just missed my name. I read it again, and the breath went right out of me.

The worst part was that Hillary Hamilton was standing directly to my left. Hillary, who's been my closest music friend since Freshman year, but always one or two maddening steps ahead, *did* get into Choraliers.

"Oh no, Avery!" she said. "Oh my God, I'm so sorry!"

"It's..." I looked around for an escape through the crowd that had gathered outside the choir room door. "It's OK."

"No it's not, you deserved to get in."

"Uh huh."

"But they only take six of each voice part, so the spaces were limited."

"I know." The crowd was too tight, and more people were joining as everybody jostled to see the bulletin board. I couldn't get out without busting my way through, and then it would be obvious I was upset.

"There were so many strong performers this year." Hillary shook her head sorrowfully.

"Right," I said.

"It was probably the choreography. You had problems with the Taylor Swift mashup, remember?"

"Yep." People were starting to look at me with pity. Most everybody had read the list by now, and the whispering about who'd been chosen and who'd been left behind had started.

"Plus the sight reading," Hillary continued.

Tori Roszkowski, a soprano who thought she was amazing but had never had any realistic chance of making Choraliers, had started to cry openly about not seeing her name on the list. She sobbed as her friends led her away and I swore that, at the very least, I would have more dignity.

"There's always next year," Hillary told me. "You'll get in then for sure."

"Right," I repeated, thinking with growing bitterness that maybe there wouldn't be a next year. Do I really want to stay in the second-best group when everybody else will be moving up? Do I want to stick around, knowing Ms. Z didn't think I was good enough to be at the top?

If I'm not going to be in Choraliers, do I even want to be in show choir?

"You're taking this really well," Hillary said, almost like she was disappointed, which sort of perfectly sums up our friendship. It seems to be based on her getting everything and me always coming in second.

Or in this case, dead last, because not making Choraliers, for someone who's as big a show choir geek as me, is probably the most humiliating thing that could possibly happen.

Hillary tried to pull me in for a hug but I stepped away, out the side door and into the back parking lot. I wasn't going to give her the satisfaction of comforting me while I cried. No, I kept my composure until I got to Violet's, then I cried for two hours straight. And Violet didn't say anything except, "I know it hurts," and "I'm sorry," and "I ordered Indian food and called your mom that you're staying over, OK?" Because Violet is a true friend. Plus, she's a 3-star recruit in tennis, so she's got real, serious stuff riding on whether she wins or loses. When Violet says, "I know it hurts," she really does know. Not like Hillary, who's probably never even lost a sock in the laundry.

It's Friday now, and I've had some time to get over the initial shock. Then this morning, I made the mistake of talking to Ms. Z.

"The scores were very close," she told me. "Work on choreography and brush up on your sight reading. There's always next year, right?"

There it was again: next year. I didn't tell her I was considering dropping out of choir. And I guess she thought I'd take it as a compliment that I just barely missed getting cut. But it only makes me feel worse. Especially since I have to keep going to Pops Choir, where people either can't look me in the eye or can't stop talking about how excited they are to be moving up. Just now, Hillary told me her parents might not renew their swim club membership because none of them has time to go anymore.

"I'm really going to miss it, but the new Choraliers have so much material to learn if we want to be ready for fall," she says. "I'm sure I'll be the one who drags everybody down."

"Actually..." I say, scraping for something to take the look of faux concern off her face, "I won't be at the pool this summer, either. I'm probably going on tour with True Meaning."

"Who?"

"They're a band? They have a show on Calliope."

"The kids' channel?"

"Yeah..." Now I feel stupid. They sound like a group for toddlers. "My mom got a job as the tour nurse and I'm invited to intern, so it's going to be a bunch of concerts and parties and stuff like that."

"Oh," Hillary says. "Well, that sounds like fun."

The last bell rings and I stand, waiting for her to follow. Our lockers are next to each other, so we always walk over together after choir. But today, she stays in her seat.

"There's a meeting," she tells me. "The new Choraliers are supposed to throw a party for the outgoing Choraliers. It's tradition. We have a lot of planning to do."

"Oh, right," I say. "I knew about that. No problem."

I gather up my backpack and put my music folder away at the front of the room. To get there I have to walk past other people who, like Hillary, are staying behind. Before leaving I turn and say, "Bye!" brightly, to show I really don't care and that I hope they have a wonderful time planning their party without me.

But when I get out to the hall, a hollow feeling over-whelms me, paired with surprise tears, so that I have to duck into a bathroom and hold a wad of paper towels to my eyes. The tears pass. I take a deep breath, and I tell myself to stop freaking out. Yes, I'm disappointed, but disappointed doesn't mean devastated. All I have to do is get through the rest of the school year, then summer will be just as great as I'd always planned.

~

THE HOLLOW FEELING settles in my chest as I walk through the halls. All around me, people are getting ready for track, softball and other after-school things. Everybody is right where they belong, while I am starting to experience a sickening sense of déjà vu that threatens to undo the pep talk I just gave myself. Suddenly I'm back in grade school. Back to being the girl in the corner. Not good at sports. Not good at social stuff. Invisible.

Except to my mom and dad.

Dad called me "Beautiful" and took me on hikes through the woods near our house. Mom introduced me to scary movies, listening in between old-school horror flicks as I talked about how I felt like the odd one out everywhere I went. At home, I sang at the top of my lungs, dressed up in their old formalwear, danced along with videos online, and they loved it. I thought I'd never find another place where I could be myself that way.

Until I found show choir.

Sitting in the school auditorium, 10 years old, watching the Choraliers for the first time, it was everything that had ever captivated me wrapped up in one glittery package. And as soon as I discovered this, the world seemed to open up. Violet moved to town—a new girl, also lonely, who also had an all-consuming passion. Freshman year, she made Varsity tennis, I made Pops Choir, and the world opened even more. People in Pops didn't think I was weird for wanting to belt out show tunes or choreograph a Disney villain-themed number. Those people became my friends.

Now, they're all moving on without me.

And my mom and dad aren't together anymore.

On my way out of school, I pass the nurse's office. I used to stop in and say hi to Mom every day, but I haven't since Dad moved out. I can't shake the memory of him sitting on my bed, crying as he tried to explain that they were separating. I remember Mom sitting in the living room with a mug of coffee while he packed, then icily asking me whether I had any homework to do. For three weeks after that, I spoke as little to her as possible, even when she lost her job.

Walking past now, I can see her through the open door, boxing up her things. She catches me peeking and dusts her hands off on her scrubs.

"Hey, Avery," she says. "Headed home?"

I slow to a stop, embarrassed at getting caught. It's not like this whole thing was a surprise; the district has always had money problems, and we knew they were thinking about cutting back the nursing staff. Still, nobody likes to think about their parent getting laid off. Parents are supposed to have a plan, which is why I'm glad Mom has this tour lined up for the summer.

"I was thinking about going for something to eat, but Violet's at tennis." I step to the door and look around at the newly bare walls, the piles of books that used to line the shelf above her desk. "Why are you packing already? We still have weeks left of school."

She picks up a clipboard and checks something off a list.

"They want me in L.A. before the tour starts," she says. "For meetings and onboarding."

I wander over to the box she's packing and look inside. The lumpy bowl I made in ceramics is there, next to a teddy bear in an old-fashioned nurse's uniform. Underneath it is a framed photo of her and Dad and me.

Mom wraps an *I'm a nurse, what's your superpower?* mug in some tissue paper and puts it in the box.

"You could get out a week early, too," she tells me.

"Is that a hint?"

"Maybe." She rummages around in another box, then pulls out a spiral-bound notebook with a black cover studded in silver dots. "A student gave me this last year and I never used it. I thought you could take it on the tour and keep a diary of all the cool stuff that happens."

"I can write on my phone. Besides, it's kind of premature to be talking about cool stuff when I haven't even decided if I'm going."

She tugs open my bag and slips the notebook inside.

"Take it anyway. I just figured a fresh start—different people, different scenery—would help you feel better."

I want to say, *What would make me feel better is having my family back the way it was.* Everything is different from what I'd planned: My parents, the Choraliers, Hunter...

Actually, no. Nothing's changed with Hunter. I've just been giving him a few days' space, and now a few days are over. By this point, he has to have realized that this stupid break is just that: stupid.

"I'll think about the tour," I tell Mom. "But right now I'm going to Hunter's."

"Be home by 6:30," she says. "There's a nursing student coming about renting the house while I'm gone. I want you to meet her."

"Why would someone be renting the house if I'll be there?"

"You're not going to live by yourself all summer. If you stay in Cincinnati, you'll be at your dad's."

My father's been living in an apartment half as big as my bedroom. I love him, but there's no way we'd be able to exist together in a space that small. Now that Mom's brought it up, though, I don't really know what I was visualizing for the summer. I guess I was thinking I'd stay at our house and Dad would come check on me. Or, really, what I was thinking about was a time, not long ago, when Dad was always at the house. I still can't picture him not being there.

"We'll make it work either way," Mom says. "I just need

to know you're safe—plus, the rent is extra money that could be used for shopping. Or me going back to school. Or shopping!"

She smiles hopefully.

"I'll be home by 6:30," I tell her. "Promise."

And then I hurry out, because I want to cry again. She thinks a boy band tour is going to take my mind off everything. But I don't want my mind taken off it—I want my world the way it's supposed to be.

Starting with getting my boyfriend back.

3

Hunter is washing his truck when I arrive. He turns when I slam my car door, and I ache all over at the sight of him smiling with that adorable chipped tooth, those big brown eyes, and the sandy hair that always looks like it needs a cut. He and Violet are my two non-choir people—each more than willing to be a music-free island when I need it.

I never thought I'd need it as much as I do right now.

"Avery," he says. "What's up?"

I think about making up a story about how I just happened to be in the neighborhood, but what would be the point? We've been together almost a year. We should be able to tell each other the truth.

"I wanted to see you," I say.

"Oh." He smiles again. "OK."

We lean against his fender, side by side. I want to nudge up next to him, cuddle into that warm spot where his shoulder meets his neck and feel him put his arm around me, but there's something between us still, thick and invisible. It's hard to put a finger on what sparked it. I was preparing for Choraliers auditions and he had a big Physics project, so we didn't see each other as much. Underneath that were a bunch of inexplicable, tiny shifts. We started having misunderstandings that went beyond the occasional petty argument. All of a sudden it was hard to know what to say.

But maybe being apart for the past couple of days has fixed all that.

"I heard about Choraliers," he says. "I'm really sorry."

I hold my breath a heartbeat.

"Me, too."

It stings knowing he heard, but then why wouldn't he? Choraliers is such a big deal that news gets out quickly once a new group is selected.

I push the question of why he didn't text or call out of my head. I'm sure he had a good reason.

We chat about meaningless things—the weather, the grade he got in Physics, a movie we both want to see—until finally I blurt out, "So my mom got a summer job. She's going on tour with a band."

"A band?" he says. "As in being a roadie?"

I tuck my hair behind my ears and shrug.

"Mom's the tour nurse. Her friend helped set it up, and there's an internship for me if I want it. It's three months on the road."

"So a rock band tour?"

"I guess you would technically call them a boy band. They have a streaming show and a ton of fans. But nobody else seems to know much about them. It's probably going to be really lame."

"You should do it."

"Excuse me?"

I expected him to act surprised when I told him I might leave—to tell me he wants me to stay. I study his face for an indication he's joking.

"You should absolutely go," he says.

"But we wouldn't see each other for three months."

"I'll be here when you get back."

That punched-in-the-gut feeling hits again. "You want me to go?"

"I just think you might have a lot of fun. Don't give up something like that for me."

"I wouldn't be giving it up for you, I'd be giving it up for us."

"Avery." His voice has an edge I've heard too many times these past few weeks. Maybe we still do need some time apart. But that doesn't mean we should give up the whole summer.

I start to backtrack.

"Forget I mentioned the tour. It's stupid I was even thinking of going. We'll have a lot more fun here."

"I think…" he starts, but before he can say anything else, his brother Hamish comes out of the house.

"Hey, Hunt," he calls. "You ready?"

Hunter motions for him to wait, then hauls himself to his feet.

"We're going to AutoMart and then dinner," Hunter tells me as he starts backing down the driveaway. "But I want to talk more, OK? I'll call you later. Seriously, Avery, do the tour."

He jumps into Hamish's car, leaving me alone in the driveway. I go back to my own car, where I sit until they've driven out of sight. I text Violet, then call, hoping she's done with tennis and can meet up for fro yo, but she doesn't answer. I get fro yo by myself and take it to my dad's apartment. It's near a strip mall next to the highway, a universe away from quiet, tree-lined Ramona Avenue where, up until a few weeks ago, he and Mom and I lived together in what I thought was a happy family.

I park in front of the building and stare up at the balconies that stick out like specimen drawers in a science lab. Something flashes in the corner of my eye. Mom's notebook peeks out of my bag, silver dots glinting in the sunlight.

I take the book out and flip through the blank pages. What would I write in it? Hillary and I have a show choir TikTok, but what can I say about my personal life—the one that has nothing to do with music? If I wrote about the past two weeks, it would be so pathetic I wouldn't be able to stand it, let alone let anybody else read it.

My phone rings while I'm putting the notebook away.

"I called as soon as I could," Violet says.

"Hunter said I should go on the tour," I tell her. "I told him about the internship, and he said I should take it."

She sighs. "Avery..."

I get out of my car, dump my half-eaten fro yo in a trash can, and wander over the fence surrounding the apartment complex's dinky pool.

"Why would he say that? He says I shouldn't give it up just for him, but doesn't he understand our relationship is more important to me than going on some stupid road trip with a cheesy boy band?"

"Avery."

The lump that lodged itself in my throat earlier this afternoon starts to grow. "That's three months we wouldn't see each other. Three months might as well be forever!"

"Avery!" Her sharp tone finally shuts me up.

"What?" I say, swiping an arm across my nose.

"Hunter asked Zosia Heron to Prom today."

And now I'm flat-out bawling. I knew it. I knew something like that was going on, but I didn't want to admit it. Violet doesn't even try to calm me down. She just sits quietly on the other end of the line.

Finally, I manage to sniffle out, "How do you know? Are people talking about this behind my back, too?"

"No! Zosia is best friends with Phoebe Nixon, and I heard them talking about it in the locker room after practice. Hunter wouldn't blab to other people before telling you first, and I honestly don't think Zosia would, either. Nobody else knows yet. Avery, I'm really sorry."

"Why couldn't he just tell me himself, though?"

Even as I'm saying it, I know why. He felt sorry for me, like everybody else does.

Violet says all the right supportive things, but I barely hear them because a gray car has just pulled into the lot. The door opens, and Dad gets out. It's almost 5—a little early for him to be getting off work, but not totally unheard of now that April 15 has come and gone. In past years, the end of tax season meant Dad making surprise appearances before dinner to take Mom and me out to eat or an early movie.

Now here he is, starting up the walk toward his apartment, alone. I hang up with Violet and go after him.

He turns when he hears my footsteps.

"Daddy." It comes out like a sob.

"Avery?" He opens his arms, and I rush into them, getting mascara all over his pressed blue shirt. "What's wrong?"

"Everything. Everything is wrong!"

He strokes my hair, calling me Avey – his pet name since I was a baby. But it only makes things worse because he smells different, he feels different—he *is* different in tiny, indescribable ways. It's frightening how quickly a person can start to feel like a stranger when they aren't a part of your everyday life.

He waits until the tears have slowed, then he says, "Come up to the apartment. I'll put a pizza in the oven, and we can talk."

"No." His apartment is so bare and impersonal—so *not home*. "I'm sorry, but I don't like it there."

He sighs. "I can't say I blame you. How about the gazebo, then?"

Near the entrance to the sad-looking swimming pool is a small patch of dirt with a few parched rose bushes. They surround a brown gazebo that is way too big for the space. It's our only option, so we sit on the bench at the center and try to talk over the sound of cars on the highway.

"Oh, Avey," he murmurs after I tell him about Choraliers and Hunter. "When it rains it pours, doesn't it?"

"This has been the worst week of my life," I shout at the stupid apartment building and the stupid depressing gazebo with its stupid roses that my dad's landlord obviously forgot to water. "It's like the Universe said, *Hey there's a person who's happy with lots of good things going on – we can't have that! Let's pull everything right out from under her. That'd be fun!*"

"I know the feeling," Dad says.

I lay my head on his shoulder. "When are you coming home?"

"I don't know."

"But you are coming home, right? Maybe at the end of the summer when Mom gets back from her tour?"

"Maybe," he says. "We'll see. Your mom and I have a lot

to work out. But I don't want that to be one more thing on your mind right now, OK?"

"Too late."

"Oh, Sweetheart…" He squeezes, smashing my cheek into his chest. I let myself be crushed, smiling just a little now. Because he didn't say he wasn't coming home. He sounded like he wanted to. That and the hug and the not-saying-no add up to a "maybe."

I'll take it.

"Are you sure you don't want to come up for dinner?" he says. "Or we could go out. Maybe get sushi?"

"I don't think I can. I told Mom I'd help her show the house to a nursing student."

"That's smart she's renting it for the summer. Tell her I approve."

"Or you could tell her yourself."

"Maybe I'll do that."

One last hug, then he walks me back to my car and watches as I pull away from his complex. But I don't go home right away. I drive back around school, past the swim club, past the baseball diamonds where Hunter will spend most of the coming months with his select team, and then by the Zip Dip where he and I used to meet after games before going to the bluffs overlooking the river until curfew.

There's nothing here for me anymore. If I stay in Cincinnati, I'll spend most of the summer by myself, bored and probably depressed. The more I think about the stretch of long, hot days ahead, the more I want to escape.

The clock on my dash pushes 6:45 by the time I turn for home. When I get there Mom is upstairs, showing the master bedroom to the potential renter. She turns, furious that I'm late, but then sees my face.

She excuses herself and pulls me into my room.

"Avery?" she says. "What's the matter? Have you been crying?"

I straighten under her gaze and take a shuddering breath. But I don't cry again. I'm done with that.

"I decided, Mom," I tell her. "I'm going on the tour with you."

4

The upside of doing the tour is that I get out of school a week early. The downside is that nobody except for Violet really cares. Hunter has been with Zosia ever since Prom, which I avoided because I couldn't see a good reason to go and torture myself. I did get asked, but by Bryson Wells, who wanted to double with Hillary and her Choraliers girlfriend, Mimi. So my best option was to continue getting my nose rubbed in the fact that I am *not* in Choraliers while watching my ex-boyfriend dance with a girl who, apparently, is the new love of his life.

No, thank you. I decided to stay home and experience Prom through Violet, who went with her tennis friend Ramesh, and who texted me photos all night of people acting dumb in tragic fashion choices. She tried to shade Hunter and Zosia, too, but it didn't help because Zosia is actually extremely nice, and it looks like Hunter really likes her.

He avoids me now. I guess you could say I'm doing the same to him by leaving town.

When I tell people about the tour, they do their best to act impressed. The idea is cool, but it becomes a lot less so when no one knows anything about True Meaning. The one person who does is a Freshman on the school paper. She interviewed me for an article, but I had no idea how to answer most of her questions, like which guy would I rather kiss, or who do I think is the hottest. So she ended up turning the story into a quiz on the website, asking those questions of everybody else. Only about four people participated, which shows what a not-big-deal True Meaning is.

And then I got a look at the tour schedule. Turns out it's almost entirely county and state fairs in places like Iowa and Wisconsin. So my summer of getting away from my boring Midwestern city is going to be spent visiting every other boring Midwestern city in the country.

Great.

It's too late to back out, though. Calliope already cleared a spot on a bus. Plus Mom keeps saying things like, "I'm so glad you're going, Avery. This will be a chance for us to spend some quality time together. I feel like we need it, don't you?" With the way she and I tiptoe around each other, I'm a little concerned that living together on a bus will be a powder keg. But my room at home has been rented, I've packed up all my summer outfits, and the swim club membership has not been renewed.

And so, on a Monday morning at the end of May, while the rest of my friends are getting ready for their last week of school, Mom and I are saying goodbye to her job of six years. Saying goodbye to Taco, my fat yellow cat. Saying goodbye to Dad, who slips me $300 so I'll have spending money on the road. And saying goodbye to Violet, who makes me promise to Instagram everything.

Then we drive to the airport and get on the plane for L.A. Just me and my mom, a couple of vagabond rejects, hitting the road.

LOS ANGELES TURNS out to be smoggy and gray. There are palm trees, and mansions on the hills, and the beach is nearby, but Mom and I won't be sunbathing or hanging out at the Pier. We land, get on the slow-moving freeway, and go straight to the bare-bones hotel where we'll spend the next couple of days until we fly out again to meet the tour at its first stop. The hotel isn't seedy or dirty, it's just all-business, located between a car repair place and an In-N-Out Burger.

We drop off our suitcases, then get an Uber to the Calliope studios. As soon as we're settled in the backseat, Mom reaches into her purse. She pulls out the black and silver notebook.

"You forgot to pack this," she says.

"I forgot it on purpose," I tell her.

"You don't want to keep a journal of our trip?"

"I've got my phone. And my laptop." Hillary's almost completely taken over our TikTok, but I'm thinking I'll start one of my own. Not many people get to experience what a real band tour is like. My stuff will be ten times more interesting than Hillary's stale *Glee* memes.

"I don't need a notebook," I tell Mom.

She slips it into my bag anyway. And since I'm not in the mood to fight, I shut my mouth and let it stay.

Sunset Boulevard is a lot more like I'd envisioned Hollywood would be. The Calliope studios are an enclave of buildings like you see in the movies, and we have to go through a security gate to get into the parking lot. Inside, though, everything is disappointingly corporate. Sure, it's more colorful than my dad's accounting firm, but it's not like we run into any film crews or actors in funky costumes. It's just a bunch of offices and people walking around in stylish-but-still-office-ish officewear.

The receptionist leads us to a conference room, where we meet a lady from human resources. She goes over our itinerary, which basically consists of training and paper-work. I'm signing my name for what feels like the 50th time when a woman comes squealing into the room.

"Brynn!" Mom cries, launching herself into the woman's arms. They laugh and hug and comment on how big I've gotten and how fast time went since they were roommates at Ohio State. Brynn can't stop apologizing for not having us stay at her place.

"They're replacing the sewer lines at my condo," she says. "It would have been a nightmare for you. Can you see the bags under my eyes? I'm lucky I even got a shower this morning."

"The hotel is just fine," Mom assures her. "We're not picky."

The door opens again, and we are joined by a young Black woman in a white pantsuit, all perfect teeth and eyebrows. She immediately homes in on my mother.

"Are you Jessica? I'm Eisha! Your busmate for the summer?"

Mom's face lights up again as she grips the woman's hand, gushing about how excited she is. Eisha can't be older than 25. She's super-polished, and every other sentence out of her mouth sounds like a question.

I'm next to get my fingers pressed by her French manicure.

"You must be Avery," she says. "I'm Eisha? The onsite publicity director? Brynn's told me so much about you. Are you so excited to be coming on tour with True Meaning?"

She beams, clearly expecting me to gush back, but there's something guarded in her eyes, like she's sizing me up. My stubborn instinct kicks in—the one that makes me want to do the exact opposite of whatever is expected of me.

"I didn't know we were having someone else on our bus," I say.

"Oh!" Mom jumps in. "I just found that out."

"Each bus has six beds," Brynn explains.

"So Eisha's boarding with us."

"You'll barely notice me," Eisha assures. "It's going to be fun, right?"

Mom tells her she's sure it will be wonderful, but all I've really heard is "six beds." If Mom and Eisha and I are taking three, then who's taking the other ones? I figured there would be some surprises this summer, but I was not planning on spending the next three months in a rolling dorm.

Then there are the tour rules, which are laid out in excruciating detail by the HR lady. There are the obvious things like, "*No alcohol or drugs,*" "*Nobody without proper credentials allowed backstage,*" and, "*Do not speak with members of the media, influncers, or anyone claiming to be covering the band. Direct all questions and requests to the onsite Director of Publicity.*" In other words, Eisha.

But the "*No social media*" rule makes me do an actual double take. Turns out nobody is allowed to post anything anywhere about the tour. We are not even supposed to say we're on the tour. Basically, anything that might even remotely hint that we might possibly be someplace with a band that may or may not be True Meaning is off limits.

"That one's important," Eisha says. She winks at me, and

suddenly I get why she was put with our bus. As far as I know, I'm the only real teenager on the tour. And as far as everybody here is concerned, I'm just one post away from starting a PR disaster. Eisha's job is to keep that from happening.

I slide my phone out of sight, glad after all that I've got Mom's black notebook. If I want to document the boy band experience, it looks like I'll have to do it the old-fashioned way. Maybe I can post everything after the tour. I'll write a book, become a best-selling author, and show everyone back home I didn't need show choir after all.

The HR lady slides the rule packet my direction. I sign, then push away from the table.

"Is that it?" I ask. "Am I done?"

"I think that's it for you for now," the lady tells me. "We still have a few things for your mom."

Eisha hands me a badge to wear around my neck. "This will let you in and out of the offices, and most places on the Calliope lot. It'll be pretty clear if there's someplace you're not supposed to be. If you have a question? Just ask."

"Why don't you stay close, though?" says Mom. "I'll feel better that way."

"There's a Peet's Coffee right up the street," Brynn offers. "Just outside the gate and up a block."

"Ooh! Get me a mocha," Mom says. "I'll text you when I'm done here."

And that's how I find myself nursing an Americano in a coffee shop that looks like any other coffee shop in the U.S., surreptitiously taking photos of people I think might be stars. But when I text them to Violet she says no, they're probably just production assistants. The closest I've come to spotting a celebrity is a girl I vaguely recognize from a tween show about a cheerleader who's secretly a robot. She's in sweatpants and a messy bun and so skinny she looks like she might actually be ill. The encounter is totally unglamorous and somewhat disturbing, just like the rest of my L.A. experience so far.

I take out the notebook and start to write.

WHAT NOT TO DO ON A BOY BAND TOUR

1. Talk about being on a boy band tour
2. Expect it to be glamorous
3. Be the only teenager in the room
4. Think too much about what you left behind

5

By day two in L.A., after an evening of pizza at Brynn's under-repair condo, I am ready for a little glamour. Today's main event is an "All Tour Personnel Meeting," which looks promising because if all tour personnel are required, then True Meaning might be there too. I may know next to nothing about them, but they're sure to be more exciting than the business-casual automatons I've met so far.

Mom and I arrive at the conference room to find it filled with people, all of whom exude varying degrees of official-ness. There are a couple of men who look like they lift heavy things for a living. There's a hipstery dude in a black tee-shirt and glasses. I see a couple of ladies in scarves and flowy skirts, and some guys in their 20s who look sort of tech-geeky.

I'm scanning the crowd, searching for faces that match the ones I've seen on Violet's phone, when Eisha appears. She sinks into the chair next to mine and says, "So... Avery? You're into show choir!"

I lean away from the scent of her expensive-smelling perfume.

"How did you know that?"

"I looked you up. I like your TikTok—the one you're doing with your choir friend, Hillary? You're not on X or Threads, I noticed, but you've got quite a bit on Instagram. I actually wanted to chat with you about those photos you posted flying out to L.A. The ones from on the plane? Could I ask you to take those down?"

"What? Why? I didn't say anything about True Meaning."

"No, but you alluded to a tour. And believe me, people will track you down and put two and two together. You'd be amazed."

"This is America, though. What about freedom of speech and all that?"

Eisha takes a sip from her Starbucks cup and checks her phone.

"It's free country, which means you can say what you want without the government bothering you," she says. "But this is a private tour? Put on by a private company? You're free to say what you want, but we are also free to not take you with us."

Wow. I've been here less than a full day and already I'm getting threatened with being fired.

Eisha continues, cheerful as ever. "Believe me, once you've been out for a few weeks with the tour, you'll appreciate why we have these rules."

Mom emerges and takes the seat on my other side. She hands me a danish from the pastry table.

"Everything OK?" she asks.

I consider telling her what Eisha just said, but then I get a vision of Mom packing up her office at school. She's happy now as she sips her orange juice, waiting for our meeting to start. This morning, we were able to get ready without the usual tension between us. She doesn't need me ruining this for her.

"It's fine," I say, and Eisha nods agreement as she responds to another text.

When everybody's helped themselves to breakfast, the tour manager, a guy who introduces himself only as Jack, comes to the front of the room. Jack is a big, extremely well-dressed guy with chapped cheeks and hair that appears to have gone prematurely grey. He radiates sensibleness and good humor—the kind of person you wouldn't dare mess with because, #1) he'd see right through it, and #2) nobody wants to get on the bad side of a sophisticated-looking Santa Claus.

"Good morning, friends!" he booms. "It's time to get this show on the road—literally! Many of us have done this before together, so if I haven't said a personal *welcome back* yet, just sit tight. For those in the room who are new, I'm looking forward to getting to know you. To that end, let's go around and have everybody share who you are and what you'll be doing with us this summer."

The introductions start, and it's eye-opening how many people are needed to make a tour like this happen. There's the wardrobe mistress and the head of security, the merchandising manager, the choreographer, a bunch of technicians, and other people whose jobs I can't even begin to remember. We'll be meeting up with the actual crew when we get to the first concert venue. Most of these people work behind the scenes, keeping the tour up to, as Jack puts it, "Calliope's high standards."

Thus begins a discussion of logistics and ticket sales and

a bunch of other stuff that probably should concern me but only makes my eyes glaze over.

Afterward, I get up the nerve to approach the HR assistant.

"Where's the band?" I ask. "Are we going to get to meet them?"

"They're rehearsing," she tells me as she hands a stack of papers to the hipster dude in black. "You'll meet them soon."

But two days later, I still haven't. And since we leave tomorrow, time is running out. I go to one last meeting where I finally get details on what the job of Unpaid Intern entails. (Basically, like I thought, it's doing whatever anybody asks me to do, for no money.) Then I go for one last stroll around the Calliope lot. By this time I'm getting bold, wandering to areas that may or may not be OK for me to visit. I'm checking out the back buildings when I come upon a group of people who look like they've been camped out for a while. They're on the other side of the parking lot gate, huddled over their phones or chatting with each other while a security guard stares over their heads, looking intimidating.

All of a sudden, one of the girls shrieks, "There's Karsten!" and they all rush the fence, screaming. I crane to see who they're shouting at. It's a guy in a red hoodie, young and undeniably hot, but he appears to be multi-racial with blue-tipped hair, and, if I remember correctly, the Karsten from True Meaning is Caucasian and blond.

"It's not him," another girl shouts. But that doesn't stop the yelling. Instead they shout, "Do you know Karsten? Can you bring him out here? Please?" The guy in the hoodie just waves and shrugs, holding up his hands like he'd like to help but can't.

These must be the fans Violet told me about.

I thought True Meaning's show was for kids, I text her. *Why are there people our age camped outside the studios?*

Technically the show's for tweens which you'd know if you'd watch it. Violet answers. *The music's much older tho. Have you SEEN these guys, Avery?!?!?*

I duck out of sight, not wanting to attract attention. But now the gears in my head are turning: if the fans are camped out here, then it must mean the band is somewhere in the building.

I sneak around to the back, flashing my badge at the door. It's cavernous inside, and oddly empty of people with coffee and clipboards. I venture down the nearest hallway, past a bunch of closed doors, until I hear music. A live band is playing somewhere nearby. I follow the sound of a wailing guitar to a set of double doors. The guitar riff is imitated by a guy's miked voice. Drums and a keyboard join in, playing a disco groove that clashes with the heavy metal guitar and vocals.

The music stops and I hear laughter—male laughter. I step closer and lean in until I've got my ear to the smooth, dark wood.

The door swings open, nearly smashing my nose. A guy comes out and stops, looking surprised to see me. He's lean, with dark hair in messy spikes and a faint scar near his eye where the brow meets the bridge of his nose.

I glance past him, and there they are: True Meaning. By now I've seen enough posters to recognize them. Karsten is the blond—I've already figured that out. Landon is Black and a little stocky. Emilio is Latino with movie star looks, and Chase looks like he just stepped out of a K-pop video. They look exactly like their photos, except without the leather pants, the popped collars, and the soulful camera stares. They're just hanging out, taking a rehearsal break. Landon is doing a freestyle rap about his favorite breakfast cereal while Chase and Karsten dougie and Emilio paces with his phone to his ear.

Up to now I've maintained a relatively blasé attitude, but in person... wow. I can feel my blood pumping faster as I start to understand what Violet meant. They are probably the hottest guys I've ever seen.

The rough-haired rocker guy examines the badge around my neck.

"Are you with Calliope?" he asks.

Before I can answer, a massive hand lands on my shoulder. I look up to see a guy in a "Security" tee shirt looming over me.

"You're going to have to leave, Miss."

I suddenly see myself through his eyes and realize I probably look like one of the fangirls from outside. I show him my badge, tell him I'm with the tour. The guy with the scar smiles, which I'm not sure how to interpret. Is he glad I'm with the tour? Is he relieved I'm not a stalker? Or does he just think I'm full of crap?

Whatever he thinks, it doesn't matter because Security Dude is the one to impress. And he does not look persuaded.

"Sorry, Miss. You'll have to go."

"OK," I say. "No problem." Then, since it seems rude to walk away without some sort of closing statement, I tell the guy with the scar, "See ya!"

His smile broadens, showing off teeth so perfect I can't help comparing them to Hunter's. Not a chip in sight.

"See ya," he answers back.

I turn to go, but this time, I leave through the front.

When I open the door, the fans snap to attention. They

wilt when it's clear I'm not with True Meaning, but they start yelling anyway.

"Hey! What's your name?"

"Do you know Emilio?"

"Can you bring Landon out, pleeeease?"

"Tell Chase I love him!"

They're straining against the fence, trying to wring out any information they can about what's going on inside with True Meaning. And even though I'm nowhere near the inner sanctum, I realize I am closer than they probably ever will be. My performer's instinct kicks in. I smile and shrug like the guy with the red hoodie did earlier. I wave, trying to look like I'd love to help them but it's out of my hands. Then I get out my phone and snap a photo to send to Violet.

I caption it *Fans in Captivity*.

But Violet doesn't answer. I make a mental note to save the photo for my blog-exposé-book—whatever, then I head back to the main building, back to where Mom is waiting. We have dinner plans for tonight, the last night before my boy band summer officially begins.

6

"So what do you think?" I twirl in front of the webcam, trying to let Violet see the outfit I picked out: Jeans and pumps with a babydoll tank under a pink cardigan. "Are the shoes too much? Should I put on sandals or flats?"

"You're friends with pop stars now," she says. "You should go all-out."

"I'm not friends with them, I heard them through a door."

"And you saw them up close, which is more than most people will ever do. It's about time things got exciting there. No offense, but if you're going to be boring, I'd rather have you be boring here with me. I finally got a free hour to go to the pool today and the only person worth hanging out with there was Hunter."

"Oh really?" I say in what I hope is a breezy tone.

"Yeah. He asked about you."

"Oh really?" That wasn't breezy at all. In fact, the idea of Hunter bringing me up in conversation makes my chest ache.

"I got the impression he's thinking about you," she tells me. "Maybe absence really does make the heart grow fonder."

Video chat pings and my heart jumps into my throat. "Oh my God, that's him right now. What is with today? I spent two months being nobody, now I'm suddenly in hot demand."

"You're giving off Pop Star BFF vibes. I bet he's having second thoughts about telling you to go on the tour now."

I groan. "Don't get my hopes up."

"Tell me what he says."

"Definitely."

I check the hotel room mirror before clicking over. Hunter has a baseball cap on backward. His nose is sunburned. I haven't seen him in more than a week, and it's been way longer since we actually talked.

"Hi," he says. "You look nice."

"Thanks." I touch my hair, hoping it hasn't frizzed out in the humidity. "The tour leaves tomorrow. There's a send-off dinner tonight."

"So you're really going?"

"It's kind of too late to back out now."

"I guess..." He glances over my shoulder, and I am gripped by fear of letting the conversation lag.

"What's up with you?" I ask.

"Nothing." He takes off his cap, ruffles his hair, then puts the cap back on. "I just didn't say goodbye before you left, and I wanted to tell you have a good summer. You know. Since I was the one who told you to go and all."

"Yeah. You did."

I am dying to ask about Zosia, but I don't know how to do it without sounding bitter and jealous. Better to let him think I've moved on.

"We're starting the tour in Utah," I say. "Doesn't that sound glamorous? And then the next day we're in North Dakota, which is, like, three states away. Then we go down to Arkansas. The schedule for this thing is totally screwed up."

"But you're coming to Columbus in July," he says. "A bunch of us are going to that show."

"You are?"

"Didn't Violet tell you? She and Hillary are planning it."

"Really?" I squint into the camera, suspicious. Out of everybody I know, Violet and Hillary are the most diametrically opposed. Hillary's the kind of person whose sweetness regularly spills over into passive aggressiveness, while Violet doesn't take crap from anybody. Violet sort of openly despises Hillary. Or at least I thought she did.

"They're buying a ton of tickets and we might even rent a party bus," Hunter tells me. "Or maybe just my mom's van. But it's going to be epic. Aren't you excited?"

"Absolutely! But you have to promise me Skyline. I'll be going through withdrawal by then."

"A three-way with hot sauce. Just like you like it."

"Now you're making me homesick!"

Mom, who can't help but listen due to the lack of privacy in our room, pokes her head into the screen.

"Guys, I hate to cut this short, but Avery and I need to go."

"Oh," says Hunter. "Well, break a leg, then."

"Technically, it's the band that needs to break a leg," I tell him.

"And I'll be there to fix it," Mom adds, which makes everybody laugh because we're all desperate to break the tension.

"See you later, Hunter," says Mom.

"See ya," says Hunter. "Don't forget the little people."

I don't tell him that, as an Unpaid Intern who spent the last two days lurking around back lots and getting kicked out of rehearsal studios, I am the very definition of *little people*. Instead I say, "I'll try to find you a souvenir from the road. Something to remember me by until I get back."

"Just have fun," he says. "I'll see you on the other side."

His face disappears from my screen, and it's all I can do to keep from telling Mom to go without me—not just to dinner but the entire tour. I told Hunter it was too late to back out, but that's not true.

"You coming?" Mom asks.

I hesitate, knowing every step forward is a step I can't take backward toward home.

I shut my laptop, shutting out temptation.

"Yes," I say. "Let's go."

DINNER IS on one of the soundstages where they shoot True Meaning's show. Since the show's over for the season, the sets have been packed away, leaving a big, black room filled with tables in white cloths and a buffet of fresh, organic food—miles different from Cincinnati's artery-clogging signature Skyline Chili. After filling our plates, we sit around the tables and get to know each other better. Mom and I are with Barry the merchandising manager and Claire, the head of wardrobe. Eisha's at our table, too, but ever since her not-so-veiled threat to fire me, I've been ignoring her as much as possible.

By now I've gotten used to True Meaning not attending these events, so I don't necessarily have my eye out for them. When I scan the room, I do find the guy who ran into me outside the rehearsal studio—the one with the dark hair and the scar above his eye. He sits at a table with some other guys I haven't seen before.

Catching me looking, he waves. Mom notices and raises an eyebrow.

"I met him this afternoon," I tell her. "I think he does something with the band."

For the first half-hour, dinner is little more than salads and small talk. Barry passes around photos of his kids. Claire tells stories about films she's worked on, which are actually pretty interesting. I think I'm going to like her.

Finally Jack, the tour director, taps his glass for attention and introduces the head of Calliope. Like everyone in charge around here, she's extremely polished, upbeat and intense. She tells us how excited she is to see the tour come together, she thanks us for the "important work" we do, and she wishes us luck on the road.

"I don't need to tell you we're looking for a real success story here," she says. "The guys have great fans, but we want to let the rest of the world know about True Meaning. To do that, we're relying on each and every one of you. And to let you know just how much you're appreciated, the boys would like to express their gratitude in person. Ladies and gentlemen, let's have a welcome for Emilio, Chase, Karsten and Landon!"

Finally! I am actually going to be in the same room with the four people around whom my life will revolve for the next three months. They come in through a side door as the rest of us stand and clap. They're dressed a lot nicer than they were this afternoon: blazers and jackets with dark jeans and expensive sneakers. They look fresh-scrubbed, but with enough edge to be intriguing. I find myself wondering how they ended up together, and what it's like to have an entire road show designed around you. Back at home, the Choraliers and Pops Choir have choreographers and designers who create the costumes and numbers we take to competitions, but it's nothing compared to all of this.

The guys motion for us to sit. Karsten, the "Serious One," steps forward.

"We just want to say thanks to all of you," he says. "This is our first major tour, and we can't think of anybody else we'd rather do it with. We're going to be family when it's all over. So we'll put on the best show we can, and we know you've got our backs."

As he speaks, the other guys nod and clap each other on the shoulder. They're so formal and professional—so different from the way they were in the practice room. When Karsten's speech ends, they don't stay to eat with us; I imagine they're savoring their last night of freedom before three months of back-to-back shows. But the guy with the scar does stick around. I catch myself glancing over as he laughs with his tablemates over pasta and grilled veggies.

Eisha side-eyes me when I pull out my phone.

"I'm just texting my friend Violet," I tell her. "She knows the rules. You can cyber-stalk us both if you don't believe me."

Her expression says she doesn't like it, but what does she expect? I'm not going back to the dark ages of no technology. Besides, it's not like there's anything interesting to take photos of anymore. Like always, the real stars of the evening have been whisked away to someplace else.

True Meaning has left the building. Again.

Bummer, Violet texts back. *What did Hunter say?*

Break a leg. That's pretty much it

She sends a frowny face. I reply with a thumbs down. Then I put my phone away, take Mom's notebook out of my bag, and add to my list of things not to do on a boy band tour.

WHAT NOT TO DO ON A BOY BAND TOUR

1. Talk about being on a boy band tour
2. Expect it to be glamorous
3. Be the only teenager in the room
4. Think too much about what you left behind
5. Lurk around back rooms and get kicked out in front of a cute guy
6. Have someone at home you can't forget

7

Our flight leaves at 8 a.m., so Jack set the airport all-call for 6. Eight of us are traveling from the L.A. team, in addition to the True Meaning guys, who will fly First Class while the rest of us go coach.

Our entourage creates a hurricane of activity in the departures area. A group of about 20 fans hang out around the perimeter, kept at bay by Calliope's security team. Then there's Mom, me, and a few others, just trying to make sure our luggage gets where it's supposed to be. At the center of the storm, Eisha bustles about in slacks and a buttondown, keeping everybody away from Karsten, Chase, Landon and Emilio. The guys cradle Starbucks cups and listen to music on their airPods. They're joined by four other guys, who, I've figured out by now, have got to be the back-up band.

The guy with the scar is among them. In his coffee-free hand, he grips the handle of a hard black case.

"Who's that?" I ask Claire, the wardrobe mistress. "The one with the spiky hair."

"Guitar player," she replies. "I think his name's Griffin. He's cute, isn't he?"

I blush and look away, because after Hunter's call last night, I can't get out of my head this idea that maybe he misses me. Maybe he wants to get back together. And if that is the case, then I definitely do not need to be confusing things by looking at other guys.

And yet. I glance over one last time, wondering if this Griffin person will wave like he did last night at dinner. Before he can notice me, Eisha ushers in a cameraman and a reporter. The guys clown around for the camera. They take a few photos with the fans. Then, when they're sure the reporter has what she needs, they go back to their earbuds and coffee. Soon, they're all whisked off through security.

The fans continue to scream, even after the guys have disappeared down the concourse.

"How did they know what time our flight was?" I ask Eisha as we go through bag check. "And how did they know what airline we were taking? I thought everything was supposed to be top secret."

She steps out of her black pumps and places them into one of the x-ray trays.

"I told you this was something you had to experience to believe," she says. "If they really want to, the fans can find us anywhere."

BY THE TIME we get on the plane, the guys and their band are all asleep in First Class. Passing them on our way back to coach, I'm struck again by how good looking they are, but also how normal. I think I even saw Chase drooling on his travel pillow.

Once we're in the air, I get on wifi and spend a half-hour stalking Hunter. He checked in two nights ago from the Zip

Dip. He also posted a video of him and his friends being dorks at the pool. There's no mention of Zosia, but then there's no mention that he's NOT with Zosia. It should be noted that there's no mention of me, either.

Good morning, I DM Violet. *I am on an airplane, torturing myself. FML*

She responds after a couple of minutes, during which I imagine her waking up in her own bed in her own room. I miss my bed. I miss my room.

Let me guess, Hunter?

I want to come home. This is ridiculous. I am on an airplane to Utah.

LOL Utah?

Like I said, FML

You're actually glad you're not here. Hillary says the Choraliers are all in a crap mood because they hate the new theme. It's this post-apocalyptic thing with 80s pop, which sounds dumb right?

I find myself squinting again, wondering how it is that Violet and Hillary have been discussing the theme for the upcoming show choir season. Was this while they were planning their Columbus road trip?

Plus, the music's hard. Lots of melismas (sp?) – she said you'd know what that means

I bite my fingers to keep from writing something snarky. The only time Hillary and Violet are ever really in the same place together is when I'm around, so it's more than a little weird to see Violet talking like they hang out all the time.

Don't remind me about Choraliers, I respond. *Did I mention I'm on a plane to Utah?*

OK, change the subject.

There's a boy band up in first class.

Squee!!!

Eh...

Does Karsten really have a receding hairline?

Which one is Karsten again?

Seriously Avery, learn something about them, OK?

Her next message contains a link. I open it, then sign off, because Violet is right. Now that I've seen True Meaning in person, I feel guilty I don't know more about them. The link goes to the Calliope website. I scroll past the banner ad for tour tickets and find their bios.

First up, Landon Baker. He's got a ton of acting and singing experience, starting when he was a baby in a diaper commercial. True Meaning is his first starring role.

Emilio Padilla has a lot of prior acting credits, too, almost all of them in shows that got canceled after a short run. Unlike Landon, his roles were all leads.

Karsten King never actually tried out for True Meaning. He's a classically trained guitar player turned garage band singer who just happened to accompany his buddy Landon to the audition. They asked him to read, then offered him a part on the spot.

And finally, Chase Yun. He grew up in Missouri and won his True Meaning spot by entering a nationwide talent search on YouTube.

There's nothing in the bios about the back-up band. I try to Google *Griffin* and *guitar*, but since I don't know his last name, I don't get much—just a couple photos of him playing duets onstage with Karsten.

Now that I've dipped my toe into the world of TM, I can't resist wading in a little deeper. From what I can tell there are two or three really big fan accounts that act as a sort of clearing house for information and discussion about the band. Then there are a ton of smaller, individual accounts. They're obsessive, with tags and threads discussing the smallest details of the guys' music, physical appearance, acting, personal lives, etc. There are even whole sections devoted to stories about the guys with each other, and by "with" I mean *with*. Some of the fans seem convinced that Chase and Karsten really are together. There are a ton of photos and videos analyzing how close they stand, how often they look at each other during press events, what they say about each other in interviews, and so on.

That one makes me laugh. Not that it would be a big deal if they were a couple, but the "evidence" seems pretty thin. Besides, my limited time with them so far was more up-close than most fan encounters, and I definitely didn't get a romantic vibe.

A rumor that does catch my eye is one about Emilio. According to "inside sources" he's dating Celia Nicholas. That is interesting because Celia is an amazing actress with what appear to be some pretty big personal problems. And it looks like she and Emilio are trying to keep their relationship a secret. They've been seen holding hands and kissing at private events, but they've never been photographed officially together, nor do they ever mention each other in the press. But the couple of grainy photos that exist of them definitely show two people who seem to have a real connection.

And this is where the fans get brutal. They mock Celia's stays in rehab and the movie shoots delayed due to "exhaustion." Some of the things they say are just over-the-top cruel, and I get the distinct impression that anyone who dates one of the True Meaning guys is going to be universally reviled.

So, dating a member of a boy band is another item for my list of things not to do.

Not that that seems even remotely possible, especially

when they're getting first-class treatment while I'm just another anon in coach. I'm one of the little people Hunter said not to forget, and right now I'm having a hard time forgetting about Hunter.

I surf back to his story to find something new posted: A photo of a plate of scrambled eggs at IHOP with a smiley face scrawled in ketchup. A girl laughs in the background. The image is blurry, but I can tell it's Zosia.

I turn off my phone and stash it in my bag. Mom's asleep next to me, her crosswords open in her lap. I swipe the book and start a new puzzle—anything to distract myself from thinking about home.

Right now, the #1 thing on my list of things not to do on a boy band tour is give a crap about boys at all.

8

"Here it is, home sweet home!"

Mom plops her suitcase onto blacktop and climbs the three steps just inside the door of our bus. When our plane landed, we were brought by van to where the first concert of the tour will take place. Or to be more accurate, we were brought to the parking lot behind where the concert will take place. This section is barricaded off by orange fencing on concrete blocks. I can see trees in the not-far-off distance, but here it's all asphalt and exhaust fumes. The crew has already started unloading equipment from semis that are backed up to the stage, which is really just a big platform framed by rigging in front of an amphitheater with hundreds of empty seats.

Here in our portable village, all the buses are shiny, black and identical. I'm pretty sure that was done on purpose so nobody from the outside can tell which one belongs to True Meaning. The four guys will travel together in one bus. Their band will ride in another. Then there are three other buses, each one housing 6 people. We'll stay in hotels whenever we get a day off or the drive between cities isn't too long. But with nightly shows that often are hours away from each other, we mostly will live in these buses.

At first glance, it's pretty amazing the way they've set it up. A kitchenette takes up the front section. Just past that are the sleeping bunks, three compartments on either side, stacked on top of each other. And beyond that is a lounge with lots of comfy-looking seating. In the middle of it all sits a miniscule bathroom with the tiniest shower I've ever seen.

"Where am I supposed to put all my clothes?" I ask, searching around for something resembling a closet.

"How much space do you need for shorts and tank tops?" Mom asks.

"You've seen my suitcase, right?" Before I left Cincinnati, Violet and I bought a bunch of cute new outfits. Since I'll be on the road with pop stars, we figured I should dress accordingly.

"If we need to ship some stuff back home, you'd better tell me now," Mom says, irritated.

"Suitcases go under the bus," Eisha cuts in. Somehow she managed to sneak onboard behind us, now she's tossing a chenille pillow down on the bottom right bunk. "There's plenty of room under there."

"Thanks, Eisha," Mom says. From under one of the beds she pulls a shallow drawer. "See? I knew we could find a solution. In the meantime, you can have some of my space in here, Avery. I'm planning on mostly wearing scrubs, anyway."

She heads to the front of the bus to sign for a box of supplies that's just arrived, leaving me and Eisha alone together.

"So? Avery," Eisha says. "First day of your internship. Are you ready?"

"Yes," I reply, a little too quickly and perhaps a bit defensive. The truth is I'm nervous. My job is to do whatever anybody needs, and since nobody's told me what they need, I basically have nothing to do.

"We'll be spending a lot of time together," Eisha continues. "Our attorney has informed us that internships must have an educational purpose, so Jack and I will be teaching you about the exciting world of entertainment marketing. Isn't that great? Everybody's being challenged to bring their A game here? So Calliope will be very interested in how you do."

"OK," I say, stepping to the kitchenette and opening the mini-fridge. I'm craving a soda, but all I see is bottled water, fruit, and yogurt.

"Plus you'll be working with the public. That's where your show choir skills will come in handy, I'll bet."

"Right." I peek into one of the cupboards, desperate for a Pop-Tart. Instead, I find granola bars and low-cal snack packs. Where are the chips and Oreos?

I pull down a bag of trail mix and shake some into a coffee mug. That's when Claire comes in, followed by a short woman in harem pants and lots of jingly bracelets.

"Hello, Roomies!" Claire trills. She puts an arm around the lady with the bangles. "Allow me to introduce June, our most brilliant stylist."

"Welcome!" says Mom, but June isn't paying attention. She's rummaging in the refrigerator.

"Where is the soy milk?" she demands. "I'm sorry, it's lovely to meet you all, but I was very clear about my dietary needs and soy milk is non-negotiable."

Eisha whips out her phone. "I'm sure we can get some delivered."

"If not, then one of us can pop out to a grocery store,"

Mom adds. "My daughter, Avery, is the tour intern. Maybe that can be her first job."

I smile extra wide, trying to let Mom know with my eyes that buying soy milk in a strange town is not a job I particularly want. Mercifully, Eisha secures a bottle, and Claire changes the subject.

"I have good news," she says. "I just confirmed that we're only going to have five on our bus instead of six like everybody else. We are the envy of the tour, let me tell you."

The bad news is that June, although small, appears to have a big enough personality to make up for the missing person.

"I have to say I'm relieved to be traveling with a nurse," she tells Mom after pulling no less than 10 herbal supplement bottles out of her purse and lining them up next to our kitchenette's tiny sink. "I have IBS, and the symptoms can be quite distressing."

"What is IBS?" I ask Mom under my breath.

"Irritable bowel syndrome," she whispers back.

I immediately think of the bus's tiny bathroom.

Oh boy.

"Also, I'm going to have to insist on taking the bigger sleeping area if we're to have fewer people," June continues. "I have apnea and need a variety of sleep aids."

"Certainly," chirps Eisha. "Whatever makes you the most comfortable."

Turning up the chipper seems to be Eisha's strategy for dealing with awkward situations. Meanwhile, Mom's in *let's get this over with* mode as she helps convert a single sleeping berth into a double. Claire has made herself scarce, which is what I decide to do, too.

"I need some fresh air," I announce. "I'm going to see if Jack's got any jobs for me yet."

Out in the parking lot, I wander, watching people move into their buses, catching glimpses of temporary mini-offices being set up in the bare rooms behind the stage. Rounding the corner, I see a figures on ATVs zipping around an open space between the buses and semis.

It's the guys. And not just Karsten, Chase, Emilio and Landon, but the back-up band, too, including Griffin, the guitar player with the scar. With no security guards hovering, no fans, and no cameras, they laugh and joke freely. The lack of those things also means that nothing but my own shyness stands between me and them.

And I definitely am feeling shy. If I wanted to approach them, how would I do it? Do I walk up and go, "Hi! I'm Avery the Unpaid Intern?" They look so relaxed with each other that I can't imagine trying to get in the middle of that. I find a spot near one of the trucks to watch them, unseen.

"Hey! You! Move it!"

A man with a giant cart of electrical equipment stands in front of me, bug-eyed, like I've just done the stupidest thing he's ever seen.

"Oh, I'm sorry!" I flatten myself against one of the giant trailer wheels, trying to get out of his way.

"Are you kidding me?" he barks. "Are you serious right now?"

"Um... Don't you need to get by?"

He gestures above my head, and I look up to see another guy preparing to lower a huge expanse of metal from the back of the trailer.

"What I don't need is to be responsible when your ass gets flattened by an 18-wheeler loading ramp," the man says. "I normally wouldn't give a crap since it's your decision to stand under the back wheels, but since I'm in charge of the crew it's apparently also my job to save you from yourself."

"Oh." I step away from the semi, cheeks burning. This wasn't covered in any of the meetings I attended. "I'm sorry. I didn't know."

"I'm sure you didn't. It involves work, so it doesn't involve you, huh?"

My stubborn streak flares up before I can get a grip on my mouth.

"Actually, I'm an intern. And I have as much right to be here as you do."

Whoops. Big mistake.

"You want to go there, Princess?" The guy is full-on shouting now, making me cringe because there is no way this is not going to be heard by everybody within a 20-yard radius. "We've got 48 shows on this tour, and some of us actually have to make that happen. While you're out fetching coffee and selling tee-shirts, I'm making sure the band has a stage to perform on. There wouldn't *be* a tour without me."

To my complete and utter humiliation, the ATVs have stopped zipping and the guys have noticed what's going on. Griffin, of all people, trots over.

"Hey there, Lenny," he says to the cart guy. "What's up?"

Lenny puts up his hands.

"It's cool, Griffin. You know me, man. I'm just trying to keep everybody safe. We don't have time for BS here."

Griffin slaps the guy on the shoulder. "Totally get that. And trust me we would be lost without you. I'm sure..." he looks at me, eyebrow raised in a silent request for my name.

"Avery," I say.

"I'm sure Avery will steer clear of the trucks from now on. Right?"

"Right."

I give a lame thumbs up, hoping it will appease this

Lenny person and make him go away. Thank goodness, he grabs his cart and rolls it up into the truck. I can hear him complaining about me to the guy inside.

"Sorry about that," Griffin says. "Lenny's our stage manager. He's mostly harmless."

"He seems mostly intimidating to me."

"He just takes his job really seriously. Stay out of his way and you'll be OK."

When Griffin smiles, I get to appreciate his perfect, non-Hunter-ish teeth again. He has sleepy eyes, and, of course, that little scar on his right eyelid.

"I take it you're not on the crew," he says.

"I'm interning. My mom's the tour nurse. I'm here with her, actually."

So far, the True Meaning guys haven't paid much attention to us, but now Chase shouts, "Hey, Griffin, tell your friend she can come over. We don't bite."

Griffin nods at me to follow him.

"You haven't met the guys yet, have you?" he asks.

"We've pretty much been segregated from them," I answer. "Unlike you, it appears."

"We've been in non-stop rehearsals, so it'd be hard to segregate us. Then, you know, we're on stage together every night."

And now, I am standing in front of four incredibly good-looking human beings who may not be famous with any of my friends, but who are more famous than anybody I've ever met before. Chase steps up first, offering his hand.

"You don't look like a roadie, and we would have met you already if you were PR," he says. "Let me guess... you won a backstage pass from Calliope."

"If she won a backstage pass she'd be surrounded by PR." That's Landon, the one with all the food allergies. He gives me a not-so-subtle once-over. "I'm thinking you're not a fan. Too quiet."

"I'm an intern," I say, blushing. "My mom's the tour nurse."

"Oh, right," says Landon. "She's here to make sure Chase takes his insulin."

Karsten, who's watched everything in silence up until now, suddenly smacks Landon on the arm. "Hey, does this mean now you can get that thing on your butt checked out, too?"

"Don't talk about his butt," Chase moans. "I have to sleep under his butt for the next three months."

"We're not always jerks like this," Landon says to me.

"Yes you are," says Griffin.

"OK, *I* am a jerk," Landon corrects. "These other guys are actually decent human beings."

He sweeps an arm out, referring to Karsten and Chase, and to Emilio, who's been on his phone this entire time. Emilio nods at us but doesn't stop talking.

The introductions continue. I meet Hank the drummer, Josh the bass player, and Yukon, who plays keyboard.

"These guys are like my brothers," Griffin tells me. "We've been through some pretty incredible stuff together."

"Everybody's got a horror story," Yukon agrees. "You'll have a few, too, by the time we're done."

"But here's the most important thing you need to know," says Karsten. "Never take a crap on the bus. Always do your business at the venue."

"Dude," Chase groans. "It really is all about poo with you, isn't it?"

And just like that, they are off on a five-minute toilet talk bender that makes the six-year-old neighbor I babysit at home look mature. Karsten, especially, appears to have one twisted sense of humor, and I find myself wondering what the fans would think. Isn't he supposed to be the "Serious One?"

Eventually, the talk of bodily functions dies down, and they ask things like where I'm from and why I decided to come on the tour. I'm dying to get a photo to show Violet, but I don't want Eisha to show up and start threatening my mom's job again. More than that, I don't want the guys to think I'm like the people at the airport.

Paranoid about overstaying my welcome, I tell them I need to get back to my job. I don't mention that I have no real idea what my job is, just that I have one, and that it is waiting for me.

"I'll walk you back," says Griffin.

We leave the others to their ATVs and head toward my bus.

"Thanks for rescuing me back there," I tell him. "I'm pretty sure that Lenny guy hates me."

"If you think he's edgy now, wait until we're two months in."

I shudder.

"Sounds terrifying."

"No more terrifying than how bloated you get after weeks of eating catered food and junk from a mini-fridge. Or when you realize you have absolutely no idea what side of the country you're on. Tour isn't for the weak—are you sure you're up for it?"

He says this like it's a joke, but the truth is that I'm starting to wonder what I've gotten myself into. Forty-eight shows, a different city almost every day—it's nearly impossible to get my brain around it.

"I think I'm ready. Are you?"

"This is what I love," he says. "I toured with Selena

Gomez over the winter. Last summer I was with Billie Eilish."

I've been sneaking glances this entire time, trying to figure out how old he is. I can't just come out and ask, so I say, "You went on tour during the winter? What about school?"

"I do it online. I'm four courses away from graduating. What about you?"

"It's summer break right now."

"Ah yes. I've heard of it."

Up ahead, I see Eisha poke her head out the door of our bus, probably looking for me.

"That's my boss," I tell Griffin.

"I need to get back anyway," he says. "We haven't checked out our own buses yet, and I'm superstitious about which bunk I sleep in. I'll see you around, OK?"

"Right."

He turns for his bus, I turn for mine. I hear him call my name and look back over my shoulder to see him wearing a somewhat sheepish but deadly serious expression.

"What Karsten said about not, um... doing you know what on the bus? Well, he's right. The number one rule of the road is only go number one on the road."

"Oh, OK..." I stammer. "Thanks, I think."

"I just thought you might want to know that."

He smiles a smile that manages to be both kind and devilish at the same time, then turns again, and pretty soon he's swallowed up in the crush of people rushing to prepare for the first concert of the tour.

9

The merchandising company screwed up its staffing plan, so it looks like my first official job as Unpaid Intern will indeed be selling tee-shirts. But not before Eisha gives me a little lesson on how tours make money by charging people tons for stuff they can't get anywhere else. The work I will be doing tonight, she tells me, directly impacts the Bottom Line.

"That's extremely important?" she says in that way of hers that always sounds like a question. "Merch is a big money maker."

First, though, she wants me to help at the VIP tent. That's where fans who paid extra get to go before the show for a meet-and-greet with True Meaning.

I've got about an hour or so before everything starts, so I grab a turkey wrap and some chips from catering. Then I sneak around to where I can get a glimpse of the stage while also steering clear of Lenny and his temper. The set for the concert isn't elaborate—mostly lights on the rigging and fog machines and stuff. But putting them up appears to take a lot of climbing and testing to make sure everything works like it's supposed to. Down below, there are three levels of risers where True Meaning and the backup band will perform, plus a big trampoline at the center of it all. I can only imagine what they're planning to do with that thing.

While I'm watching, the band goes on for sound check. A piece of scaffolding blocks my view, but I can hear the bits of songs, the harmonies, the joking as they adjust their mics. At one point, a guitar riff screams out. That has to be Griffin. He sounds great; they all do.

The opening act, a local group called Sock Drama, goes on for their sound check just as the VIP fans start showing up. By this point, True Meaning is hidden away, either on their bus or in one of the rooms backstage. The whole thing is expertly timed. There's the manic-yet-controlled set-up phase. Then, the technical sound check. Then things go quiet while everybody gets cleaned up, ready to face the public.

I figure I'd better get ready, too, so I dash back to our bus and put on one of the outfits Violet helped me pick out: a sundress with lace-up wedges. I squeeze into the bus's tiny bathroom to do my make-up and hair.

Mom's making tea in the kitchenette when I come back out.

"Are you sure you want to wear that?" she asks.

"I'm going to be in front of tons of people tonight," I tell her. "I think I should look nice, don't you?"

She eyes my heels. "I'm just worried about your feet."

"Don't be. These are the most comfortable shoes I own."

"Really?" I can tell it's killing her not to order me to take them off. "I think you should bring some flip flops with you as a back-up. Just in case."

With Mom, there always comes a point where she decides to step in and dictate what's best. Shoes might seem minor, but we've had bigger arguments about smaller things.

"Flip flops?" I say. "With this dress?"

She leans against the counter, squinting at my feet. Like me, she's weighing whether this particular battle is worth fighting.

"Fine," she sighs. "Forget I said anything. Just make sure you're back well before the buses leave. I don't want you attempting to run after us in those ridiculous shoes."

WHILE I WAS INSIDE, the parking lot around our buses began to fill up. The fans fall into two groups. There are the ones with regular tickets who've gathered behind the back fences on the off chance that the guys will make a surprise pre-show appearance, and then there are the ones who bought VIP. Eisha stations me along a row of stanchions and tells me to have those people line up in front of the stage. From there, they'll go into the VIP tent, where the guys will shake hands and take photos. These fans are a lot quieter than the ones in back, probably because they know they're going to get close to True Meaning. The others can only hope the guys will take pity on them and come out to sign a few autographs.

"Excuse me, can you answer a question?"

A woman with a little girl waves, catching my eye.

"Um... yes," I stammer. "Can I help you?"

"My daughter brought a gift for Chase. He's her favorite." The little girl holds up what looks like a necklace with big glittery beads and a medallion featuring an incredibly realistic, hand-drawn picture of him. "Will she be able to give it to him when she gets her picture taken?"

The woman looks so hopeful it makes my heart melt. I can tell she doesn't want her daughter to be disappointed.

"I'll find out," I tell them.

At the front of the line I locate Eisha, who shakes her head.

"We have a table inside where people can leave things for the band," she says.

"But you should see what this little girl made. It's adorable, and she's so excited to give it to him."

"If they accepted gifts from everybody who came through it would take hours, right? The crew will take all of the gifts back to the green room and the guys can look at them there."

"But that doesn't seem fair. The girl won't ever know if Chase really got her necklace."

"I know you've never been to one of these, so you don't understand," Eisha says. "When you watch the meet and greet? You'll get a better appreciation of how it all works."

The line has started to move as people make their way inside the tent. She pulls back the flap and invites me along. It's cool inside, and dim. Chase, Karsten, Emilio and Landon are waiting near the back wall in front of a gray backdrop.

"The biggest watch-out here is be careful what you say to the fans," Eisha whispers. "Keep everything light and casual. Don't make any promises? Don't talk about the band? But do be super friendly. Got it?"

"So basically, don't have any personality at all."

"Your personality isn't the one these people paid $300 to experience."

The tent is filling with bodies as the line snakes up to a spot where people are being told to wait their turn. There are girls primped to perfection, little kids with their parents, a few grade school-aged boys trying to look cool. Each person or group gets an average of 30 seconds with the guys, certainly no more. The whole thing moves like a well-oiled machine, and even though it seems abrupt, I can see what Eisha was talking about. If they spent more time, they'd be at this for hours, and they still have a show to put on.

The girl I just met comes in and reluctantly leaves her necklace on the gift table. I mouth an *I'm sorry* to her mom, who nods to say she understands.

Even though there are tons of people, the guys give each one their full attention. They joke, flirt, play with the little kids, then lean in and smile the same exact smiles for every photo. Never once do they slump or sigh or give any indication they're getting tired or overwhelmed. They treat each person like they're genuinely happy to meet them.

Finally, the little girl gets her turn. She shakes each of the guys' hands, but before the handlers can herd her into the photo, she whispers in Chase's ear and points to the gift table. He breaks away and dashes over. I don't think I've ever seen a kid smile as big as that girl when Chase returns wearing her hand-made present. She throws her arms around his neck, and the other guys pile on for a bear hug. Meanwhile, people in line are "aw"-ing about how cute it is.

This, clearly, is why they call Chase "The Sweet One."

Eisha personally steps in to escort the little girl away. She smiles and nods, playing along, but her tight lips make clear she doesn't approve.

I, on the other hand, am starting to enjoy myself. Maybe this job will be fun after all.

10

This outfit? Total fail. Me at the merchandise table? Also a total fail, or I would be if I didn't have this show choir-trained fear of letting people down. Ms. Zebari always said, "*When the spotlight's on, you'd better bring it,*" and since I'm the only person working this station, I am definitely in the spotlight. But this isn't fun like show choir. This is hell.

People are loud. People are grabby. They try to haggle on prices, then get angry when I tell them I'm not allowed to bargain. Little kids cry. The grownups get impatient. I, meanwhile, am a huge hot mess. My hair has gone limp. My makeup feels like it's melting off my face. The worst part is that, after catching a bunch of boys snickering, I realized people can see right down the front of my sundress when I bend over, which is something I have to do a lot when getting stuff from boxes under the table.

And when I told Mom these were my most comfortable shoes, I totally lied. I've never worn them before, which, it turns out, was a huge mistake since they haven't been broken in. My feet have never hurt so much, and that's saying something since I'm used to dancing for hours on end at choir rehearsals.

Slowly, the crowd starts to thin as the show gets ready to start. When we're down to just a few stragglers, I glance across the concourse at the girl who's working the second table. She signals for me to join her. Together, we creep to the back row of seats, where we can keep an eye on our stuff but also see the show.

Sock Drama is first, but barely anybody pays attention. I feel sorry for them as they beg the crowd to clap along and then invite people to buy their album out on the concourse, which I can already predict nobody will do. I listen to some girls in the seats nearby trade stories about the last time they saw True Meaning in concert, showing each other their photos and gossiping about the latest band news. Dusk is falling, and as the warm-up band leaves the stage I race back to my table. Just as I predicted, nobody buys a Sock Drama CD or even uses the QR code for downloads. It's more craziness over True Meaning stuff. More grabbing. More haggling. But soon enough, the lights in the amphitheater dim again and people scurry back to their seats. Again, I creep to the back row.

There's a hush, punctuated by an "I love you, Emilio!" and a "Karsten! Marry me!" The lights framing the stage start to strobe, slowly and irregularly at first, like camera flashes. With each flash, I can see the silhouettes of Josh on drums, Yukon on bass, Hank on keyboard, and Griffin on guitar. Everyone in the crowd begins to scream. Josh starts to beat along with the strobes, picking up a rhythm while the lights play a synchronized show that gets faster and faster. The other instruments join in, building excitement until there's a burst of pyro, and Karsten, Chase, Landon and Emilio appear out of nowhere, walking through the smoke to the front of the stage as they sing about love at first sight.

"How you feeling, Salt Lake City?" Landon shouts.

He's answered by a near-deafening roar.

My first thought is what an awesome job Claire and June have done. The guys are dressed in different variations of black and red: leather jackets, crimson jeans, black fingerless gloves, combat boots and blood-colored sneakers. It's over-the-top rocker, but just tasteful enough to not be a cliché. The back-up band, on the other hand, dresses down. Griffin, I can't help but notice, wears ripped jeans and a plain black tee-shirt.

My second thought is that I can see now where the guys got their nicknames. Karsten, the "Serious One," seems shy and internal, like he's performing more for himself than the crowd. Landon, the "Funny One," cracks jokes. Chase acts like everybody's best friend, and Emilio smolders. He gets the most screams as he works the front of the stage, grabbing hands and kneeling down to sing to the girls hanging at the edge of the security barricade.

The four of them move from one catchy song to the next, breaking it up with a little banter. It's all super-choreographed and even a little cheesy. Not unlike show choir. But, as Ms. Z used to say, *"Everybody loves cheese!"*

About halfway in, stagehands bring out three stools and the guys slow things down. Karsten and Griffin sit on two of the stools, while Chase goes into the audience to choose a girl to pull up on stage.

While they wait, Landon asks the crowd, "Who here knows what a boom box is?" Emilio bounds off and comes back carrying a massive radio on his shoulder. Landon holds his phone up next to the thing, and everybody laughs.

"I bet some of the moms out there know what a boom

box is," Karsten says, strapping on a guitar. Next to me, a couple of women my mom's age wave their hands over their heads.

"So a boom box was how people listened to music in the old days," Landon explains. "It's also part of a scene from one of our guitar player's favorite movies." Landon reaches over to punch Griffin in the shoulder. "Everybody say hi to Griffin!"

By this time, Chase has returned with a girl who looks about 12 and can't stop shaking. When Emilio tries to lead her to the empty stool between Karsten and Griffin, she throws her arms around his neck. It takes a bit of work to untangle and get her seated. Griffin chuckles as he checks the tuning of the acoustic guitar that's replaced his electric one.

"Griffin wrote this song when we were getting ready to come on tour," Karsten explains. "We thought we'd sing it for you tonight, so you can all see how brilliant this guy is."

Griffin leans in to be heard over the mic in Karsten's headset.

"You flatter me."

"No flattery needed," Karsten replies. "You ready?"

They begin to play, Karsten singing to the shaking girl, Griffin hunched over his guitar. When the chorus comes, the others sing harmony.

> I'll stand outside your window, a boom box in
> my hands
> Girl you can say anything, you know I'll
> understand
> Say anything, baby, even if it's a lie
> Girl you can say anything, just don't say
> goodbye

It's a beautiful song—completely different from the stuff they've performed so far. When the crowd applauds at the end, they're almost reverent.

Then the lights strobe again. The stools are whisked offstage. Griffin is back on his riser, and the guys are down front, doing a number that involves backflips on the big trampoline. Forty-five minutes later, the show ends in a rain of streamers shot from two massive confetti cannons. Then I'm back at my table for a last whirlwind of selling, but not before I untie my shoes and pull them off. I finish the merch job barefoot.

Finishing up doesn't take long because the place clears out a lot quicker than I expected. Onstage, the crew is breaking down the set, and I can hear Mom's voice telling me to be back before the buses leave. As much as I hate her nagging, I hate the idea of getting left behind even more.

An odd quiet of concentration settles over everything as I make my way back, and that's how I become aware of the noise just beyond our little enclave. At least 30 girls and a few guys have gathered on the other side of the concrete barriers. A few of them are even climbing the fencing, demanding that True Meaning come out to see them.

I escape to our bus, but that isn't any more peaceful. A couple of fans, convinced they've found True Meaning's bus, have hoisted themselves onto the barricades and are pounding on the windows. Part of me wants to laugh because they have no idea that a girl just like them is on the other side of the tinted glass. The other part of me is freaked out and sort of scared. What if they tip us over?

"How'd it go tonight?" Eisha calls from the lounge, where she's working on her laptop. "Did you get to see any of the show?"

"Yes," I answer. "It was amazing."

A particularly loud crash sounds right behind my head, followed by more pounding and a girl's voice crying, "Karsten! Please come out! I love you, Karsten!"

Eisha sees me flinch and says, "Now you see why we have rules?"

More banging. More yelling. I think I actually hear someone sobbing. I sit across from Eisha with my knees tucked against my chest.

"Will they stop?" I ask.

"Security will go around and get them off the fencing. It's more a liability thing, though, so nobody gets hurt."

I picture Lenny and how pissed he got at me for breaking safety rules. What must he think about all of this craziness?

"But isn't there a law about climbing on the buses?" I ask. "Should we call the police?"

"Why would we do that? If it weren't for those people outside, none of us would be here right now."

"So the rules about dealing with fans... they're not that big a deal after all?"

Eisha closes her laptop and looks so intently at me that I can see gold flecks in her eyes.

"The rules are always a big deal, Avery. And it's not the fans' behavior I'm concerned about."

She keeps her gaze on me, one extra-long beat that tells me all I need to know about how she sees me and my role in all this.

"Don't worry," I tell her, grabbing my notebook and pen from a shelf that literally vibrates with the force of each bang on the side of our bus. "I am well-versed on the rules. In fact, I've been writing it all down."

11

S ick. So very sick. My first night attempting to sleep on a tour bus turns out to be utterly miserable. Every position I try just makes me more nauseous. And to make things worse, I seem to be the only person hating life right now. Mom is snoring away, chimes tinkle softly from inside June's double bunk, and there's no sound at all from Claire or Eisha.

We hit a bumpy patch of highway, making the bus sway. I roll out of my bunk and just manage to make it to the bathroom before puking up the apple and popcorn I ate before going to bed. I stumble into the lounge, sink into a chair and crack a window. I sit with my face pressed against the glass, gulping air, watching road signs and the lights from distant farms go by, getting my bearings before finally, blessedly, falling asleep.

~

WAKING up on a tour bus isn't much fun either, especially when it involves getting stared at by Eisha, who's perched in one of the seats across the lounge in a skirt and chiffon blouse.

"Are you OK?" She gives me a sympathetic look over her yogurt. "You look sort of green."

"I think I'm good."

I move my head and wince. Sleeping against the window has given me a major crick in the neck.

"Try some Dramamine tonight," Eisha says. "I'm surprised your mom didn't suggest it already."

Mom and Claire emerge from their bunks a few minutes later, followed by June, who has her own remedy for motion sickness. I raise a WTF eyebrow as she takes out a bag of crystals and starts placing them on my "chakras."

"June is one of the best stylists in the business," Claire murmurs a few minutes later when June heads for the bathroom. "That's why we're all indulgent of her."

Mom nods, winking at me, and maybe it's the crystals, or maybe I'm just getting used to the ride, but I do feel better—until the bus starts to slow and stop, slow and stop, indicating we're no longer on the highway. I look out the window to see strip malls and fast food restaurants creeping by. Mom closes the book she's reading. June flushes the toilet, and Eisha gets up from her laptop, stretching.

"We made it to day two!" Claire announces.

"Hello, Bismarck!" says Mom. "How long do we think it'll be before somebody needs an ice pack?"

Eventually the stop-and-start ends. We idle, letting the semis and other buses pull into their assigned slots. Finally, it's our turn. The engine shuts off and I rush out the door, desperate to be on a non-moving surface. Looking around, I see another big stage, another parking lot. It looks almost identical to where we were yesterday. I don't have much to do, and wandering around getting in peoples' way doesn't sound like a lot of fun, so I follow Mom to the office that's being set up behind the stage. She carries a standard-issue first-aid kit with her, plus a tackle box of supplies prescribed by Landon and Chase's doctors.

We hang around, watching Claire steam the band's outfits for tonight. Mom checks the news on her phone, looking up with anticipation every time footsteps go by outside. I wander the room and the space just outside it, singing softly—my go-to way of dealing with boredom.

After a while Mom gets out a clipboard and opens the tackle box.

"What are you doing?" I ask.

"Inventory. I figure I can keep better track of supplies if I record everything."

"Can I help?" Counting gauze pads sounds better than texting people at home, who are probably all at Choraliers rehearsal.

"Sure," Mom says as we set to work. "Having fun so far?"

"The concert was great last night," I tell her. "You should see it."

"I caught some of it from the sound tech's truck. Those guys are really talented."

"They are." I've been wondering where they were during all that post-show chaos. How do they let off steam after a concert? Do they go back to their buses and make sand-wiches, like it's just an ordinary night after an ordinary job?

"Have you talked to Daddy yet?" I ask. Last night, while trying to get my stomach to stop cartwheeling, I thought about how he used to go out and buy ginger ale when I was sick, no matter how late it was. And I realized I haven't heard from him since the morning we left Cincinnati.

"He hasn't called," Mom answers.

Now I have a vision of Dad alone in his apartment, missing us.

"Have *you* called?" I ask.

"You know, I've been so excited about the tour that I haven't had a chance. But I'm glad you're here. Between my work at school and you being so busy with choir and Hunter, I felt like we never got to spend time together."

"Well, now we're closer then you probably ever wanted to be. Did you know you snore?"

"I do?" She puts her face in her hands. "Oh God, how embarrassing."

"I don't mind. I wouldn't have heard it if I wasn't up all night puking."

"But what about Claire and Eisha?"

Ugh, Eisha. She spent the last half-hour of our bus ride obsessing over a typo in a press release and fretting that the gift bags for some upcoming event don't exactly match the True Meaning "brand equity" because they're the wrong shade of blue. Now, she's on Jack's bus in a call with Calliope. And she's wearing kitten heels, even though we're in a parking lot someplace in the middle of North Dakota.

Someone knocks on the office door. A head peeks in, and I jump to my feet, forgetting about Eisha, Dad, and Mom's noisy sleep habits.

It's Landon. *The* Landon, looking tasty in baggy shorts and a hoodie.

"Don't worry, I'm not having a reaction," he says when Mom reaches for an EpiPen. "Which is pretty amazing, actually, because I got stung by a hornet."

Mom springs to action, examining the wound. He nods at me over her head, and I say "hey," because that is what you do when you have a boy band singer you only met yesterday two feet away from you, right? You say "hey," like it's perfectly normal.

Mom squints as she uses a dull knife blade to remove the stinger.

"I'm probably going to sound like a total dummy, but I feel like I've seen you before," she says. "I mean someplace before all of this tour business."

"*Mob Dad? Rock-n-Roll High School? Scuttle Bug?*" Landon ticks off the names of some marginally popular shows.

"Yes!" she says. "That's it! Avery loved the Scuttle Bugs when she was little, didn't you, Avery?"

I shrug and roll my eyes. But the truth is that I did. I was obsessed with the main red bug. In fact, I still watch the show sometimes when I'm flipping channels, for old-time comfort.

"You were in *Scuttle Bug*?" I ask.

"I was the Wiggle Worm," he answers. "My character only lasted 4 episodes."

Another head pops in. It's Chase. After the past few days of seeing these guys from afar, I am suddenly experiencing an up-close boy band bonanza.

When he sees my mom tending to Landon's hand, he pulls out his phone.

"I have to get this for TikTok."

"What about the no social media rule?" I ask.

"Doesn't apply to us. We're actually required to do social media. The more the better."

"Chase loves it," Landon tells me. "He lives for the fans."

"I wouldn't be here without them," Chase says.

"We all have official accounts," Landon explains. "The stuff we do there is mostly messing around and promo. The personal stuff is private. Only close friends and family."

"C'mon and do something already," Chase says to Landon. "I don't have much battery left."

So Landon juggles his icepack while Chase narrates for the camera. Chase pretends the hornet that stung Landon was massive, and Landon acts like he's going to have to get his hand amputated. They pan over to Mom, who nods grimly, playing along.

Chase posts his video, then turns to me.

"Did you see the show yet, Avery?"

"I did last night," I reply, flattered he remembered my name.

"But from way in back, though, right?" says Landon. "You have to see it from backstage."

"I don't think I'm allowed."

I picture Lenny screaming at me and give an instinctive shiver of dread.

"I'll get you passes," says Chase.

"But I have to work." I'm growing flustered. How, exactly, does one turn down backstage passes from a guy like Chase?

"I like how dedicated you are," he replies. "I admire your commitment. But I'm on a mission now. There's no turning back."

Four hours later, I'm shuffling people through the VIP tent when Eisha hands me a badge on a lanyard.

"Chase was pretty insistent about you getting one of these," she says.

I take the badge and look it over. It says *Backstage Access* on the front.

"Are you sure you want me to have this? Aren't you afraid I'll do or say something I shouldn't?"

She considers this, visibly weighing the pros and cons of letting me run loose for the evening.

"I'm going to go ahead and trust you," she says. "Besides, what's the fun of being on tour if you can't get a really good seat every once in a while?"

12

Even with a pass, getting backstage ends up being tough. That's because right before the show, Jack realized we didn't have enough bottled water, so he sent me to one of the concession counters to get more for the band and crew. The errand requires three trips back and forth, so by the time I make it backstage water-free, True Meaning is well into the first part of the show. The security guard eyes me suspiciously as I start up the ramp, even when I show him my credentials. Once he's satisfied that I really am with the tour, he waves at a spot between two lighting rigs.

"Stand over there," he says. "And stay out of the way."

I slip into place, trying my best to be invisible. I can see Lenny across the way, talking into his headset, but there's so much going on that nobody else notices me. That includes True Meaning, who run offstage for a costume change just minutes after I get settled. They whoosh past me, shedding jackets and shirts, disappearing behind Claire's wardrobe rack. Minutes later, they're running back out to the lights and the crowd and the music.

As I'm watching, I feel something brush my arm.

"Hey, Avery."

It's Griffin, already jogging up to his riser, grabbing his guitar from a stagehand as he goes. He looks back as he puts the strap over his head and winks at me. I'd wave back, but they've already started the next song. Chase, Landon, Emilio and Karsten are crouched at the edge of the stage, grabbing the hands of fans in the front row as they sing about worshipping someone from afar. The first several rows roil with girls dancing, swaying and crawling over each other to brush fingers with the guys. But when I look out farther, I see a lot of empty seats. In fact, the amphitheater is probably only about half full.

Still, the guys perform like they're in front of a packed Madison Square Garden. I can see the sweat dripping from their chins and their soaked clothes as they go through the choreography. I also notice some lines from the night before. They tell the same jokes and do the same banter, changed up just enough that someone comparing videos of different shows wouldn't mind too much. They even bring a girl up again when Karsten and Griffin perform *Say Anything*.

The amazing thing is how much energy they have. They go and go until the confetti cannons erupt, and then they blow kisses to the crowd like they're truly grateful to have had the chance to entertain them. When the lights darken, the four of them run past me again, wild-eyed and deflating. They are ushered immediately to a green room at the back of the stage, while Griffin and the rest of the band wander off the risers, no less sweaty but looking a lot less exhausted.

Griffin catches my eye. He hands his guitar to one of the stagehands, then comes over.

"Want to hang out?"

"Sure," I say, trying to sound casual. "Let me just check if anybody needs anything."

Jack texts me back that everything's fine, I'm off for the rest of the night. So I follow Griffin through the bustle of crew breaking down sets and loading them up, wiping away all traces of tonight's show, getting ready to move on.

Griffin leads me to the band's bus, where he says, "Be right back" before disappearing inside. And I say, "Sure, no problem," because I definitely wasn't having a mini panic attack, wondering about the etiquette of boarding buses belonging to members of the band.

Fortunately, he doesn't make me wait long. Within minutes, he's hopping down wearing a clean shirt and carrying a beat-up acoustic.

"Didn't you just get done playing one of those?" I point at the guitar.

"I like to play real music after a show."

"What you just played wasn't real?"

"It was loud. It was catchy. It was loud." He strums the acoustic—a warm and gentle sound. "This I can hear without a piece in my ear. I've had this particular guitar since fifth grade."

"I like it," I say.

"Me, too."

We walk, he strums, until we're outside my bus and I'm back to wondering about etiquette. If I invite him in and the caravan has to get moving, he could be stuck there all night. Not that Mom would mind much since there'd be no way we could mess around in a space so crowded.

Wait. Why on Earth would Griffin and I want to mess around? Yes, he is attractive, and he's been sweet to me on a couple of occasions, but I barely know him. Either I'm really missing Hunter or I'm really homesick, or maybe it's a little of both. The fact that I'm even thinking about messing around tells me Griffin and I should probably stay out of each other's buses completely.

Plus, Eisha, Claire and June might not like having a random guy around. Especially not June, who gave Mom a speech at lunch about misogyny in the nursing profession. June would definitely have a problem with Griffin being on our bus.

So he and I lean up against the side where we can't be seen by the fans, who've gathered at the fence again, calling for the guys just like last night.

"I feel bad for them," I say over the racket. "They seem kind of desperate."

"Some people read or watch sports for their hobbies," he says. "Some people follow bands around."

"Do the guys ever go out to see them?"

"Depends on where we're playing. That sort of thing's easier if it's an indoor venue because it's more controlled. Out here it's too much in the open. Weird things can happen."

"Well, then, do the guys ever take fans back to their bus? Like in the movies?"

Griffin laughs.

"Most of the time they're too tired for that. I wouldn't be surprised if they were all in bed asleep right now."

"It's not very rock and roll is it?"

"There's nothing rock and roll about any of this. People are working their butts off. Nobody has time for trouble."

The way he talks reminds me of Eisha's teaching-the-intern tone. Or Mom, who felt like she had to remind me, yet again, to be back before the buses left tonight. I might be new to this boy band tour thing, but I'm not some idiot who needs to be talked down to.

"Well, what about Emilio?" I say. "Is it true he's in a secret relationship with Celia Nicholas?"

Griffin stops strumming. "Where did you hear that?"

I allow myself a small measure of satisfaction; I know more than he thinks.

"I saw it online. The whole Celia thing is big news with the fans, apparently."

Griffin sneers. "I'm sure it is."

"So is it true?"

He starts playing again, thoughtfully plucking the strings.

"Emilio really cares about Celia. It's not something he wants to put out there for people to pick apart. And she's having a hard time right now, so they're trying to respect her privacy."

"Oh." Now I feel like an ass. "Is that why he's on the phone all the time?"

"Right now, he's mostly talking to his agent." Griffin leans in and says, softly, "No one is supposed to be talking about this, but he's up for the *Dead at Dusk* movie."

"What do you mean up for it?" I whisper back. "Up for a part?"

"They're looking at him for the starring role—Noah, the shapeshifter."

"Wow." The *Dead at Dusk* books are huger than huge. I've only read one, but Hillary is obsessed. And Noah, the tormented shapeshifter who falls in love with the lead female character, is sort of a sex icon. *Dead at Dusk* has effectively ruined things for billions of teenaged guys who will never be able to live up to Noah's level of hotness.

Could Emilio play Noah? If he's as intense onscreen as I've seen him onstage, I can just imagine what he'd be like with the fate of all mortal souls resting on his shoulders.

"He's pretty nervous," Griffin tells me. "They're supposed to be coming out sometime soon to meet him. It's rare for a director to do that, so everybody's hoping it's a good sign." His fingers pick out a more cheerful melody. "But enough about that stuff, what do you do when you're not interning summer boy band tours? Let me guess: Cheerleading."

I laugh. "I am so not a cheerleader."

"Volleyball?"

"Not an athlete, either."

"OK, Drama."

"Close. Choir, actually."

"So you're a singer?"

"Yeah, and I dance and..." I feel my face go hot. "It's embarrassing. I'm in show choir."

"Why is that embarrassing?"

"It's just..." How do I explain? For years, choir was the most important thing in the world to me, but now here I am with a guy who actually performs for a living. He probably thinks high school show choir is incredibly amateur.

I put my hands up at either side of my face, spreading my palms wide and waggling my fingers.

"Some people think jazz hands are cheesy."

He shrugs. "We all have our guilty pleasures, right?"

My heart drops. He doesn't understand.

"It's more than that. People put a lot of time into it and there are these massive competitions, and the top choir at my school wins a lot. It's a big deal where I come from."

Clouds stretch across the sky, covering the stars. The crew is finishing up and people are getting onto their buses, getting ready to go. I put my jazz hands down and say, "The thing is, I don't know if I'm going to do it anymore. I was planning on getting into that top choir, but they didn't want me. So now I can either stay where I was last year, or I can quit."

"Do you *want* to quit?" Griffin asks.

I think about it, envisioning another year in Pops with the younger, new singers and the older ones who'll never have a chance at Choraliers. I used to feel sorry for the people who got to their senior year without realizing that dream. The idea that I could be one of them is almost more than I can bear. Part of me wants to forget I was ever a show choir girl to begin with.

Trouble is, if I'm not a show choir girl, then what am I?

"I gave show choir everything I had. Maybe it doesn't seem like a big deal to anybody else, but not making Choraliers makes me feel like nothing I've done for the last two years of my life meant anything."

"I get it," he says. "This business can really screw with your head."

The melody he's playing morphs into the tune from *Say Anything,* the song they perform during the slow part of every show. I listen, taking in the beauty of the melody without the background noise of a crowd.

"I love that song," I tell him. "It's amazing you wrote it."

"You know the words? Come on, you can do harmony."

"Nobody here wants to hear me sing."

"Nobody's paying attention. And this isn't an audition—I won't judge." He nudges me with his shoulder, smiling wickedly. "I thought you said this was what you do! I'm starting to think maybe you're really a lacrosse player instead."

If there's one thing I hate more than being overlooked and underappreciated, it's people who make others beg them to perform. I can either flat-out refuse, or I can force Griffin to ask me a few more times, neither of which is very attractive. The only response I'll be able to live with tomorrow is, "OK."

"But you have to do the verses," I tell him. "I don't know those yet."

"It's a deal."

He starts to sing in a voice less polished but much more endearing than Karsten's or any of the other True Meaning guys. When the chorus comes, I join in, tentative at first, but then louder when I get used to hearing myself with his guitar. In choir I'm always trying to be heard over Hillary, singing through the choreography, plastering on my big smile. Here it's just Griffin and me. Quiet and real.

"They were idiots not to take you," he says when the song ends.

"Thanks," I murmur back. "I think so, too."

Mom pokes her head out.

"Avery, it's late," she says, then notices Griffin, which is my cue to introduce them. Mercifully, she keeps the niceties short. "Say goodbye and come on in," she reminds me.

"See you tomorrow?" he says when she's retreated back into the bus.

"I'm easy to find. Just tell Jack you don't have enough water. Or better yet, steal Eisha's clipboard. She'll have me scrambling in no time."

"Or maybe I'll just ask for you."

"That'd work, too." A shiver ripples through me at the idea.

"Great," he says. "See you in the next town."

"Sleep tight," I tell him. "Don't let the fangirls bite."

13

Three days pass—three new venues in three different states. By now, I'm getting used to the routine and rhythm of the tour. At night, I'm better at sleeping on the bus; I actually like hearing the drone of the engine, feeling the bumps in the road as we whoosh along. During the day, I do odd jobs for Eisha, which include wrangling fans for VIP. And like everybody else, I've begun to lose track of where we are. Jack has started posting signs backstage with the name of the city we're in in big block letters so none of the guys trips up onstage and shouts, "HOW YOU DOIN', CASPAR?!" When we're really in "DELUTH!"

Contrary to Griffin's promise, I didn't see him in the next town, or the town after that. He's got a real job to do, while I spend my time putting together press packets for news outlets that have yet to join the digital age. I've tried not to think too much about his smile or his scar, and so far I've been reasonably successful. But the one thing I can't forget is how it felt to sing with him. Griffin didn't seem to care how I looked or sounded. And because of that, I sounded better than I probably ever have.

But a repeat performance doesn't seem to be on his agenda anytime soon. True Meaning are doing press events, switching up their set list, and trying out new choreography, so they're in meetings and rehearsals when they're not performing or on the road. Emilio brushes past me every now and then, always on the phone, and Karsten high-fived me once over the catering table at lunch. In general, though, everybody is just busy, busy, busy.

Even Mom has a fairly steady stream of patients as people strain shoulders, get blisters, and scrape themselves on equipment. The biggest injury happened when Yukon smashed his fingers in a freak accident involving a water cooler falling off a table. There was concern about whether he'd be able to play keyboard that night, but mom phoned the on-call physician, who phoned in a prescription for a steroid, and apparently all was OK because the show went on.

I, on the other hand, spend most of my considerable downtime reading and trying to keep up with home. I've had no news about Hunter and Zosia, so that part of my life feels like a gigantic black hole. Meanwhile, Hillary sent me a photo of Choraliers practice. **Wish you were here**! it said. And how do I respond to that? **Greetings from South Dakota, here's a photo of some buses**? I snuck a pic of True Meaning at sound check and texted it to her. She responded with a benignly cheerful **Looks like fun**!

So. The Choraliers are deep into rehearsals. Hunter's probably off doing all sorts of romantic summer things with his new girlfriend. And the last conversation I had with Violet consisted of her telling me about a shopping trip to get the right colored tights for Hillary's Choraliers costume

—as if she and Hillary are now BFFs who do random errands together. From out here on the road, Cincinnati might as well be another planet. And the message couldn't be any clearer: It turns just fine without me.

DAY seven of the tour brings something that perks me up a little. We're starting a stint of state and county fairs, which means from here on out, almost every show will be at a fairground with rides and fair food and other shows to see besides ours. As soon as the buses pull in and get settled at the first location, I sneak past the barricades to explore. It's something to do besides hang out in a parking lot.

The gates have only been open a couple of hours, but already it's super busy. Parents wander the fairway with children on their shoulders. Kids my age either hang out in packs or stroll along holding hands with their boyfriends or girlfriends. The sights, sounds and smells remind me of when Dad used to take me to the Ohio State Fair in Columbus. Mom went, too, and she'd check out the crafts and the baking exhibitions while Dad and I went on the rides. Then we'd meet up to watch fireworks, and I'd fall asleep on the drive back home.

Looking back now, I wonder if those trips really were as idyllic as I remember. I call Dad to check in, because I'm pretty sure Mom hasn't spoken with him since I asked her about it a few days ago. All I get is voicemail.

Pocketing my phone, I wander past 4-H stalls, following the familiar sound to an open-air pavilion packed with people. Show tunes, three-piece combo, glitter-encrusted party dresses: It can only be a show choir, and when I check the sign outside the pavilion I find that I'm right. I've stumbled on a performance by the West High Blue Notes. They're doing a Rodgers and Hammerstein medley, badly, but that doesn't stop me from finding a place in the back to watch. I don't know a thing about this group, and since I'm not competing against them, I can be 100 percent objective. The whole thing is a little ridiculous with the big smiles, the big hair, the big gestures. But the crowd loves them, and I can see that they take show choir every bit as seriously as we take it at home. Watching the Blue Notes from West High, I realize nearly every town has a choir like this one, filled with kids who think they're special.

Maybe Ms. Z did me a favor not putting me in Choraliers. Maybe now I can find something different from what every other spotlight-hungry high schooler in the country does.

Though what that is, I have no idea.

I vacate the pavilion, deciding to drown my sorrows in junk food. Back through the stalls I go, tempted by apple fritters, pizza, hotdogs, loaded potato skins.

And then, I smell it—the Holy Grail of fair food: Funnel cakes. Warm and sweet, the smell draws me to the back of a long line of other people who have been similarly tempted. And there, a few spots in front of me, is a familiar head. Or back of a head, to be precise. Dark spiked hair, pierced ears —I edge up a little, just to be sure.

"Griffin?"

He turns, recognition lighting up his face.

"Avery. What are you doing here?"

"Getting a change of scenery. What about you? Don't you have sound check or something?"

"Not for a while. I needed a break from buses and asphalt. Plus, you know, there's funnel cake."

He steps aside, inviting me to join him. When we get up

the counter, he pays before I can fish money out of my pocket.

"You don't have to do that," I tell him.

"I know," he says. "But I'm also pretty sure I know what they're paying you."

"Make that what they're not paying me. I actually have the word *Unpaid* in my job title."

"Then a funnel cake is the least I can do."

We take our cakes and sit on a bench to devour them. Neither of us talks as we concentrate on the crispy fried dough, our fingers getting sticky, powdered sugar dusting my black tank top and his Army shorts. When we're done, he takes our plates and tosses them into a trash bin.

"Funnel cakes are the kind of thing you crave once a year, then it's a whole year again before you want another one," he says.

"I've probably just had my entire summer quota of fat and sugar," I agree. "But it was so good!"

He pats more sugar off his shorts, then checks the time on his phone.

"We've got an hour to kill. Want to ride some rides?"

Before I can respond, he's at the ticket booth, paying yet again. Then he's off, striding up the fairway. We make our way through the carnival, doing the bumper cars and the Scrambler and the pirate ship swing. Next to the swing is an oversized Ferris wheel.

"I love these things," Griffin says, making a bee line toward it.

I laugh nervously, lagging behind.

"I always wonder what would happen if they didn't tighten all the bolts on these rides," I say. "Would we go rolling out into the crowd?"

"You just did the pirate ship that puts you 90-degrees to

the ground, but now you're suspicious of the Ferris wheel?" He snorts as he gives our tickets to the ride operator. "Come on!"

Pushing down panic, I slide into the seat next to him, triple checking the safety bar against our laps. The car gives a jolt. I hold my breath as we lift off.

Halfway up, we stop. I bring a hand to my throat, unable to keep from whimpering.

"You OK?" Griffin asks.

"Don't laugh, but I am deathly afraid of heights."

"Well, you picked a good time to mention it."

The car heaves up again and we rise a few more feet before coming to a stop at the very top of the ride.

"What's the matter?" I say. "Is it broken?"

"They're just loading more people." Griffin peers over the side of the car, and I clamp my hand over his thigh.

"Oh my God, don't rock it!"

He looks at me, amused. "You should see your face right now."

"Seriously, one of my biggest nightmares is about getting stuck on top of a roller coaster. Oh my God, my worst fear is coming true!"

"Then don't look down." His voice deepens, a soothing tone that I feel resonating somewhere within my own chest. "Look out. Isn't it a great view?"

With the ride finally full, we hit a groove and I am able to appreciate the scenery as we go around and around. From the top of the wheel, I can see the town nestled at the foot of some mountains. Very pretty. Closer in, I see our own little cluster of buses behind the grandstand, which is all set up, waiting for tonight's show. Even closer—right next to me, to be precise—is Griffin with his hands on the safety bar. They're long, strong-looking hands, the tips of his fingers covered in callouses that are indented from pressing guitar strings. He smells nice, too, like the dryer sheets Mom uses on our laundry at home. Breathing him in has the same effect as listening to his voice. My mind descends into a hypnotic haze while warm tingles spread across my shoulders.

"So," he says. "It's been a few days. How are you holding up?"

It's the first time anyone's asked, and the kindness in his voice makes me realize just how lonely I've been.

"This is embarrassing but I actually think I might cry." I clamp my lips to keep them from trembling and hold my fingers under my eyes to catch the tears before they can smudge my makeup.

He leans in, pressing the side of his arm against mine—a comforting little nudge that is both friendly and intimate.

"Tour can be hard," he says.

"I guess I didn't realize I'd be so homesick so soon."

"Are you leaving anybody behind? Like a boyfriend or something?"

"No," I say, finally admitting the truth. "I mean, I had a boyfriend, but we broke up before I came out here."

"Oh good. Not that you broke up, but that you don't have a boyfriend. That can make the whole thing harder."

I'm quiet, wondering what Hunter is doing, and why I even care since the last I heard from him was more than a week ago. So much for Violet's theory about absence making the heart grow fonder.

"I came out here with pretty much a clean slate," I say. "I thought that was a good thing, but..."

"But you still miss him?"

I focus on the horizon, searching for the right words.

"I don't know what I miss, exactly. I came with my mom

because it didn't seem like I had much of a reason to stay home. She and my dad are separated right now. On top of that, my boyfriend started going out with somebody else. Then there's the choir thing I told you about already. The farther away I get, the more I start to wonder if maybe I didn't really have anything back there all along. But I don't really have anything here, either. Everybody else is busy, while I'm doing meaningless jobs, not even getting paid. To be honest, I feel sort of useless."

I stop to let my brain catch up with my mouth. Hunter used to get annoyed when I blathered; I hope I haven't turned Griffin off now, too.

He bumps me with his shoulder again.

"Well, I'm glad you came," he says. "And you definitely aren't useless. You're a fresh face, which I know *I* need after spending every waking minute with the guys and the band."

"I thought they were like your brothers."

"Have you ever had a brother?"

"I'm an only child."

"Brothers can be your best friends, and then they can make you want to kill them, especially if you have to be with them all the time. That's why I snuck out to ride rides, and it's why I'm glad I ran into you."

The Ferris wheel is slowing down. To my relief we're one of the first cars let off, so I don't have to endure any more panic-inducing stops and starts.

"Was that so bad?" Griffin asks when we're safely back on the ground.

"It was terrifying. But now I'm sort of sorry it's over."

"Ah... I feel a song coming on." He hums, gazing up in thought. "*Ferris Wheel Girl.* Is that a lame title? I can change it later."

The tingles I felt on the ride become bona fide chills. I've never inspired a song before.

"So can I now add *muse* to my resume?"

"Technically, it's your phobias that are inspiring." He smiles.

"Well, my phobias would be honored to provide as much material as you want, as long as the result is as beautiful as *Say Anything*. That's one of my favorite old movies."

"Mine, too," he says. "I don't know if I did it justice, but the song just sort of wrote itself, you know?"

More chills. I can't believe I'm talking songwriting with a guy like Griffin. Hunter and I could never talk about music. Come to think of it, there was no one at home I could talk about music with at all—not even my choir friends. We were so busy talking about MUSIC, as in what numbers we were going to do and how they fit into a theme, and whether we could win competitions with that theme. Music was always a way of maintaining our domination. We never talked about music like it actually meant something. I barely took the time to *let* music mean something to me.

My phone buzzes. It's Eisha, wanting me at the VIP tent. I text her we're on our way, then shove the phone back into my pocket.

"So are all your songs based on movies?" I ask. "Are any of them inspired by real life?"

He takes so long to answer that I start to wonder whether he heard me.

"I haven't had much of a real life," he says. "I'm either on tour or rehearsing for a new tour, or trying to get a semester's worth of schoolwork crammed into a few weeks before the next tour starts. Movies are like vicarious living, especially with all the time I spend on buses."

"You'd never know it. I can't wait to hear what else you've written."

"They're not all winners. Inexplicably, nobody wants to perform my Monty Python-inspired ballad, *Just a Flesh Wound*."

We've arrived back at the grandstand and circle behind the barriers to avoid the fans who've already started lining up for photos.

"Wait here." Griffin ducks into the admin bus, then comes out and presses a pass into my hands. "Do you think you can come backstage again tonight?"

"Depends if something blows up out here with Eisha," I say. "If there's something only an Unpaid Intern can handle, then all bets are off."

"I'll spread the word. Nothing can blow up."

"You seem very determined to get me backstage."

He grins, and I watch the scar by his eye quirk up. It makes him look devilish and, I can't help noticing, devilishly hot.

"I *am* determined," he says. "I have a plan—it's a surprise."

14

"So what's up with this boy Griffin?"

Mom looks me over, taking in my turquoise capris and black trapeze top, my eyeliner and lip gloss, my freshly washed hair with the waves that took me an hour to do in the bus's tiny bathroom.

"Nothing is up," I tell her. "We're just friends."

"Long distance relationships aren't easy, you know."

Irritation ripples through me. Griffin said he had a surprise, and to me, surprises are something you try to look nice for. The fact that the surprise comes courtesy of a dark-haired guitar player with a wicked smile and an amazing talent for songwriting is just a bonus.

"It's not a relationship," I tell her. "And even if it was, we're not long distance."

"Not right now." Mom gets a bottle of water from the mini-fridge. She offers me one and I decline, not wanting tonight's surprise to be interrupted by a trip to the bathroom. "But what about when we go home, and he goes back to wherever he lives? I can't imagine he's from Ohio."

Ohio. This is the first time thinking about home hasn't made me homesick. In fact, at this moment home is one of the last places I want to be.

"It's way early to be talking about going home," I tell her. "Anyway, there's nothing to talk about since there's nothing between Griffin and me."

"I just don't want you to get hurt," she says.

As she settles back in with her water and crosswords, I notice she's not wearing her usual post-work outfit of shorts and a Reds tee-shirt. Instead, she has on a maxi dress and sandals.

"I don't know why you're obsessing over me," I say, "when I should be asking why you're so dressed up."

She runs a hand over her skirt, looking sheepish.

"I got tired of being a slob in scrubs all the time. I'm going to watch the show from the sound booth with some of the other crew again."

A simple answer instead of a lecture about my smart mouth? I'm not sure how to respond to that. Maybe I don't have to. Maybe, for one night, Mom and I can take a break from tiptoeing around each other.

"Sounds cool," I say. "Have fun."

"You, too," she says. "Don't stay out too late."

BACKSTAGE IS NO LESS hectic than the first time. The crew doesn't seem to mind as much, though, and I get a little bolder, coming closer to the action until Lenny sees me from across the stage. He says something into his headset and I panic, certain he's complaining to someone who will show up and haul me out of here.

I shrink back to my usual spot between the lighting rigs, but not before noticing that the grandstand is still only about two-thirds full. I also notice that they've changed up the show. There are more upbeat numbers at the beginning, more pyro, and more banter between the guys. The fans down front seem to be loving it, so I'm surprised, when it's time to slow down, that the guys don't bring one of them onstage. Instead, Karsten grabs a handheld and starts telling stories about what it's been like on the road so far.

"We're just starting the tour," he tells the crowd, "but we're already a family. We take care of each other. Like a couple of days ago when Yukon, our keyboardist, hurt his hand. We weren't sure if he was going to be able to go on, but our tour nurse made it good as new. She's got her daughter with her, and we've heard her singing to herself when she didn't think anybody was listening. Girl is *good*! So how about we get Avery out here to help with this next song?"

My body stiffens as all four of them turn and wave for me to join them. Griffin is walking over, holding out his hand.

"Are you kidding?" I squeak as he takes me by the arm. "I'm not going out there."

"Pretend it's just the two of us," he says. "Like the other night."

We start moving toward the lights. The first few rows of seats come into view. They're filled with upturned faces.

"I don't know what I'm doing!"

Griffin slides his hand down to mine, lacing my fingers with his own. He squeezes, warm and confident, sending a wave of tingles up my arm.

"Just play along," he says. "You got this."

We step out and the crowd cheers as, one by one, the

other guys give me a hug. I look out to see the hazy silhouettes of people waving their hands in the air. The stage lights are so bright I can't make out much beyond the first section, which is a good thing. Otherwise, I might pass out or puke all over the stage. I've never performed for a crowd this big.

Chase helps me onto the stool between Karsten and Griffin. Karsten gives me the handheld as Griffin strums the opening chords of *Say Anything*.

"Harmony," he says, softly, in my ear. "Just like the other night."

The song has started; it's too late to back out. While Karsten sings the first verse, I try to get used to having a thousand eyes on me. As he nears the chorus, I steady my breath. The first few words are tentative—I'm not used to singing with such a powerful mic. But the sound picks up beautifully, blending my voice with Karsten's.

At the next verse, the rest of the guys join in, and then it's all of us on the chorus to the end. The crowd remains silent when we're done, then the applause comes like a giant wave. It's better than any show choir performance, ever.

It could be addicting.

One by one, the guys hug me again, Griffin's arms staying around me an extra beat.

"See?" he says. "I told you you could do it."

Landon escorts me off and drops me backstage, where my high immediately vaporizes. Eisha is standing there with Lenny next to her.

"What just happened?" she demands. "Who told you you could go onstage?"

"I didn't know they were going to do that," I stammer. "They pulled me out there."

I search for someone who'll back me up, but the band is

performing again, and if any crew members felt the urge to vouch for me, I'm pretty sure they'd be stopped dead in their tracks by Lenny's glare of doom.

"It was a total surprise! I didn't plan it."

"Ladies," Lenny says politely, as if me getting in trouble wasn't exactly what he wanted, "we have a show to finish. Could I ask you to take this somewhere else now?"

"Absolutely," says Eisha. "Sorry, Lenny."

She stalks down the backstage ramp, and I trot after her like a frightened little dog.

"So am I in trouble?"

"Maybe," she snaps. "Possibly. I don't know."

"Awesome job, Avery!" one of the truck drivers shouts, giving a big thumbs up.

"Yeah," shouts another. "You crushed it!"

I continue to trail Eisha, afraid to acknowledge them. A million visions flash in my head: Mom losing another job, me going home in disgrace, never seeing Griffin again.

I push aside every urge to talk back and put on my most genuine, humble face.

"Eisha, I really am sorry. If I knew they were going to do that I wouldn't have been backstage at all. My mom needs this job. If I'm in trouble it will hurt her, too, and she doesn't deserve that."

Eisha sighs and stops walking.

"If it really was the guys' idea to pull you out there, then you're not in trouble. But I am going to have a talk with them about doing that in the future. And you need to stay out of sight until we figure out how to spin this."

"How about you just spin it that they wanted to do something nice? That's what happened. Why does everything need a spin?"

She shakes her head, looking more than a little fed up.

"If you don't get it, Avery, then I don't have the time or energy to explain it to you. How about from now on you just stick to doing your job, which involves doing what I say? If you really want to stay out of trouble, that's your best bet. Now do me a favor, go back to the bus, and keep to yourself."

15

My phone rings at 8 a.m., waking me up. It's Violet, shrieking.

"Oh my God, Avery, the fans HATE you!"

I lift the window shade by my bunk to look out at fields rolling by. We're headed to the next town, where we'll be staying in a hotel since tomorrow is a day off. The first thing I think of isn't being onstage with True Meaning last night, but how excited I am to share a bathroom with nobody but Mom.

"Why didn't you tell me about last night?" Violet demands. "That's huge!"

"It was late," I mumble. "And the whole thing was a surprise, and I was worried about getting in trouble, and—wait a minute, how did you know if I didn't tell you?"

"There are videos up everywhere. Check it out. I'll wait."

I grab my phone and Google True Meaning with the name of the city we just left. Almost every link that comes up has to do with me. The video quality varies, but it's definitely *Say Anything*. I hit play, reliving how Griffin's hand felt in mine, how it felt to sing with Karsten, the harmony from the other three guys filling my ears. Watching the video, I'm proud of how I look and sound.

Then I check out the comments.

It's like she thinks they're her BFFs. Dream on sis.

I wish my mommy worked for the tour, then I could get onstage with TM too

Those blue pants tho

"Oh my God," I gasp. "They do hate me."

"Stop reading comments," Violet orders. "Trust me, you don't want to know what they're saying."

But now I'm hooked. I check Instagram and find dozens of new follows. Then I get a text from Hillary: *WTF is up with our TikTok?!?* In addition to new followers, it appears I now have my own hashtag.

"They know everything about you," Violet says. "Where we go to school, the show choir stuff... My follows are way up, too."

I scroll, shaking my head at the sheer volume of comments to a cheesy *Glee* meme I posted two years ago. It's freaky and flattering at the same time.

"What do I do?" I ask Violet.

"Nothing," says Eisha, who has appeared out of nowhere. "Do you hear me?" she shouts over my shoulder into the phone. "You do NOTHING."

"I've got to go," I tell Violet. "I'll text you later."

Eisha glares at me as I climb out of my bunk.

"This is exactly what I was referring to last night," she says.

"I didn't know the fans were going to go crazy like that."

"You don't know anything." She grabs her morning yogurt from the fridge and rips off the lid. "That's your problem."

"Oh, I have a problem? They're the ones obsessing about the color of my pants."

"What's going on?" says Mom, coming into the kitchenette with Claire.

"It sounds like our Avery is suddenly famous," Claire says.

"Or infamous," Eisha mutters.

I shoot her a look. "It's just a bunch of online BS about last night, Mom. It's nothing."

"I'd hardly call it nothing," says Eisha. "Last night will blow over, but you're going to be a magnet now. They'll comb through anything you do and use it to get whatever information they can about the band."

Mom puts down the bagel she's started to butter.

"That sounds disturbing."

"The Internet is evil," June announces as she emerges from the bathroom. "With corporations and the government watching our every move, the World Wide Web has done more to jeopardize personal freedoms than any other movement in history."

I have to work really hard not to roll my eyes at that one. June, who thinks nothing of dictating what other people can eat, where they can sleep, and even when they can use the toilet, is concerned about personal freedoms?

"Why does it matter if they get information from me?" I ask Eisha. "Isn't it our job to get the word out about True Meaning? Wouldn't you be glad if I helped with that?"

"There's a difference between the controlled engagement we do and the stuff that comes through random channels," she explains. "For example, everybody on this tour is looking forward to relaxing at the hotel tonight. The band deserves a break, and they need one in order to keep doing great shows. How relaxing do you think it will be if someone figures out where we are, then a ton of screaming people show up, stalking the hallways and banging on doors? How fair is that to anyone?"

I have to admit she's got a point.

"I haven't posted. About last night or anything."

"Let's keep it that way."

But I feel like I need to do *something.* I get out my notebook and add to my list of things not to do on a boy band tour.

7 – Leave without good snacks
8 – Go #2 on the bus
9 – Let the VIP line back up
10 – Wear fancy shoes at the merch table
11 – Look down, look out instead
12 – Get onstage without permission

I close the notebook but still feel unsatisfied. All these new people are following me. What good is being an overnight celebrity if you can't bask in it just a little?

I glance around at Eisha eating her yogurt, Mom munching her bagel, Claire cutting a grapefruit, and June pouring soy milk over her organic granola. Food is safe and meaningless—sort of. The delicious-looking but utterly inedible sugar- and gluten-free cookies that June left out on the counter last night do sort of express the conflict I feel about what's happened over the past 12 hours.

I wait for Eisha to get on her laptop, then I surreptitiously snap a photo of the cookies. I give the photo a dramatic filter and post without a caption, gifting my new fans—or non-fans, as the case may be—with a cryptic symbol of my current state of mind.

BY THE TIME our bus arrives at the hotel, we are all yearning for a break from each other and a night in a bed that's not moving. Personally, I've been thinking about getting a massage at the hotel spa, dreaming of a nice meal in the restaurant, or maybe even room service.

But when the bus pulls in and I get a look at where we'll be staying, I realize my best chance at a decent meal is either delivery pizza or a burger at the sports bar across the street. This might be the nicest hotel around, but it's simple —just the basics.

At least Mom's and my room is bigger than eight feet across and has a nice big bathroom. We walk in to find two full-sized beds, a desk, and a life-sized cut-out of Chase standing in front of the TV. Someone's pasted a handwritten thought bubble above his head. It reads, *Hey, Avery! Meet us at the pool. We promise not to make you sing again.*

"That's cute," Mom says. "Do you think you'll go down with them?"

"Absolutely," I answer. The guys went out of their way to invite me! What's next, a recurring spot in their show? "But first I want to call Dad. I haven't talked with him since we left."

Mom lies down, and Dad picks up after the first ring.

"Hi, Avey! I saw you tried to call yesterday. Is everything OK?"

"It's fine." I go to the window and pull back the curtain on a view of a fast food-lined road stretching off into a sea of what look like corn fields. "I was just at a fair and it made me think about you. Remember Columbus every summer?"

"Of course I do. I would have called back, but work is picking up again and I couldn't get away until late. I didn't want your phone going off in the middle of a show if you were backstage or something."

"Actually, that was probably good thinking. Did you hear about me singing onstage with the band?"

He gasps. "No! Did you really?"

"It sort of happened out of the blue. They brought me out for a song. It was just one, but it was amazing!"

I almost offer to send him a link, but I'm not sure I want him reading the comments. I make a mental note to look for a couple that don't need censoring.

"I'm thrilled for you," he says. "Especially after all that disappointment about Choraliers. You deserve to have people know how talented you are."

"Thanks, Daddy." He always was the most enthusiastic supporter of my transformation from shy worm to butterfly. I wish he could have been there last night to see me fly.

I recap the details of my boy band debut and then try to fill him in on everything else. But it's hard to describe the homesick-one-minute, having-an-incredible-time-the-next roller coaster I've been on.

"How's your mom doing?" he asks.

"OK, I think." I glance over at her bed, where she lays with an arm over her eyes. She's been quieter than usual. At first I thought it was just irritation with our busmates, but I'm starting to get the impression there's more going on.

"I miss you," Dad says.

"I miss you, too." And then I tell him goodbye, because this conversation is starting to make me sad. Also, I want to get downstairs to the pool.

"Everything OK?" Mom asks after I've hung up.

"His work is busy. The AC went out at his apartment. He says he misses our house on Ramona."

She smiles from underneath her arm, and I wonder if maybe she misses him, too.

"Are you OK, Mom?"

"I'm fine." She rolls onto her side, snuggling into the hotel pillows. "I've just got a headache, and it's nice having some privacy. You go have fun at the pool. I'll probably sleep the whole time you're gone."

Sure enough, within seconds she's snoring. I search through my bags for one of my new swimsuits, pulling out a cute high-waisted bikini. I change quickly, throw on a cover-up, then hurry out into the hallway and book it for the elevator.

16

As soon as I step into the hotel lobby, I can hear the guys. From the propped-open door by the reception desk come the sounds of cannon-ball splashes and roars of laughter. I peek around the corner to see Chase, Karsten, Yukon and Josh in the water with a few of the younger guys from the crew. Landon and Emilio sit on the deck chairs, Landon with a book and Emilio with his ear glued to his phone. Griffin sits with his feet in the water, looking cute in red swim trunks.

I am the only girl.

I hesitate, adjusting my cover-up, seriously considering going back to my room when Chase spots me and lets out a whoop.

"It's Avery! Our new star!"

I plaster on a smile and step out from behind the door as the guys catcall and shout. I sit next to Griffin and dip my toes into the water.

"I wondered if you'd come," he says. "I thought you might be mad I drug you onstage last night."

He glances at me with an expression of genuine worry,

which zings me right in the heart. Even with Eisha and the fans mad at me, singing onstage with him felt like a dream.

"I loved it," I tell him. "I mean, it was freaky at first, but I had fun."

"Oh good." He looks relieved. "I told everybody you were a great singer, but they didn't need convincing. You are aware that you sing to yourself practically all the time, right?"

I'm blushing. "I didn't think anybody noticed."

"Too bad we got the smackdown from Jack, or we'd try to work you into the show every night."

"Ugh, that can't be good if Jack's mad."

"We made sure everybody knew it was our idea," Griffin says. "And since I was the one who actually came up with it, I've been officially delegated to apologize for putting you on the spot like that. So... sorry!"

"There's nothing to apologize for." I'm happy it was his idea. And I'm wondering what it meant that he brought me out for that particular song. Granted, *Say Anything* is the only TM song I know, but I'm sort of starting to see it as our song.

Does he see it that way, too?

The guys in the pool continue to horse around while Chase gets out of the water and starts filming.

"Dude, give it a rest," says Karsten. "Avery's going to think you have a social media problem."

"I'm just keeping my promise to the fans," Chase tells me. "When my parents were out of work, I said I'd do anything for anybody who'd help us. The fans put me here, so I try to give back as much as I can."

"Well, I'm going to put you in the ground if you keep sticking that phone in my face." Karsten pulls Josh in front of his body. "Video him, I'm done with cameras for a while."

Josh looks miserable, so Chase turns his phone on Landon, who shoves his middle finger into the screen. Watching the guys in private brings out a whole other side of their personalities. Chase is the Sweet One for sure, but part of me wonders what he would do if he didn't have the constant gratification of posting photo after video after update to thousands of adoring viewers. Karsten, on the other hand, is seen as serious, but under that shy exterior lies an extremely twisted sense of humor. Of the four of them, he's probably got the most genuine musical talent, but he doesn't seem as interested in playing the fame game.

Landon works probably the hardest of them all. He wants to be taken seriously, but that means overcoming the sidekick vibe that got him labeled the Funny One. Landon is definitely funny, but if you spend enough time with him you can hear bitterness lurking under most of his jokes.

And then there's Emilio, the Hot One, smoldering in a corner of the pool deck with his phone to his ear and what looks like a script in his lap.

"I have to go," I hear him say. "Just hang in there, and ask the doctors about switching your medication around, OK? I'll call you back as soon as I'm done."

"He's talking to Celia," Griffin confides. "And this can't be repeated anywhere else, but the *Dead at Dusk* people are coming."

"Today?" I look around for Hollywood types in suits and shades but all I see is a maintenance guy checking chlorine levels in the pool.

"They're flying in and right back out again. I guess they figured this was as good a place as any for a meeting."

Emilio stands, rolling the script in his fist.

"Just got a text that they've landed," he announces. "I'm gonna shower before they get here."

"You got this, bro," says Yukon.

"Yeah," says Chase. "You're gonna kill it."

One by one the guys wish Emilio well. Landon says a half-hearted "Good luck," then pulls the brim of his hat down over his eyes and lies back in his chair, a scowl on his face.

Now that I think about it, I'm not sure any of them seem genuinely happy.

"Is anything wrong?" I ask Griffin. "It seems like nobody can really relax."

"Isn't that what we're doing right now?" He uses his foot to shove Josh off the side of the pool. "Relaxing?"

I pull my legs to my chest to keep from getting drenched by Yukon and Karsten, who've started an alarmingly aggressive wrestling match just a few feet away.

"I don't want to offend anybody, but this isn't exactly what I'd call relaxation."

"I see your point," he says. "I guess some people don't know what to do with themselves if they're not going hard all the time."

"Are you one of them?"

"Probably." He jumps to his feet. "Speaking of which, I was planning on doing some laps. Want to join me?"

Getting in the water means possibly subjecting myself to getting dunked by Yukon or even put online by Chase, which would be a huge no-no. I can just imagine what the fans would say about footage of me romping in the water with Karsten and the True Meaning back-up band.

"That's OK. I'd rather just enjoy the sunshine."

"Whatever you want," Griffin says, and slips into the pool. I watch him go back and forth, wondering what the plans are for the rest of the day. Will he ask me to dinner? Could we sneak out to catch a movie, or just hang out with his guitar? And if we did those things, would it be considered a date?

One by one, the other guys exit the pool and head back inside. By the time Griffin gets out of the water, the only other people on the deck are Landon, still in the chair with his hat over his eyes, and a crew guy I don't know who's playing games on his phone.

"I really need to crash," Griffin tells me. "Would you be stranded if I went back to my room?"

So apparently the answer is no to dinner. No movie. No hanging out, making music. Did I mis-read things?

"Definitely, get some sleep," I say, trying to sound not-disappointed. "You need rest."

"Thanks for understanding." He flashes a smile. "You gonna be OK out here?"

I lean back on my elbows, catching rays, totally unphased.

"Yeah, I'm good."

"Great. I'll see you later."

Then, he's gone. My cheeks are burning, and not from the sun. Maybe I was wrong about the spark I felt between us. Maybe he and the guys really were just being nice when they brought me onstage last night. Maybe I need to get out of here before I literally die of embarrassment.

Mom's up from her nap when I get back to our room, checking email on her laptop, so I get mine out, too. I go back to see if more comments have been added to the videos from last night. There are a ton. A few actually stick up for me.

You're just jealous she's friends with the guys and you're not.

I re-read that one. *Am* I really friends with the guys? Or am I just something to help take their minds off the stress of the tour for a couple of hours?

It wouldn't be the first time I've completely misread a situation.

On X, Threads and Reddit, the Avery obsession continues. Some of it is sweet:

@averymiller You are a great singer

So jealous of @averymiller for getting onstage with TM last nite!

A lot of it is just abuse:

@averymiller get over yourself

Nepotism, thy name is @averymiller

I try not to let the mean comments add to the sense of uselessness that has started to creep back now that it's clear my few minutes onstage aren't going to translate to some grand discovery of my hidden star potential. But before I can close my browser, one message catches my eye. It's from an account called WorldofTM, and it appears to be an invitation.

@averymiller Would you like to guest on my podcast? Would be cool to hear about the TM tour from the inside. DM me if so.

I click through to WorldofTM's profile. It's a girl who runs a fansite called "In Search of True Meaning." It's really professional with tons of news about the band. The fans there seem enthusiastic but respectful. And the girl in charge, Nora, runs it like she really cares about keeping things civil.

Still, I don't answer. I don't even follow Nora back. Eisha would have a guaranteed stroke if I started communicating directly with podcasters.

"Oh, great," Mom says from across the room.

"What's wrong?"

"Calliope just sent an email about the tour. Ticket sales aren't as good as they were expecting. They're canceling nine shows."

As she's talking, the same email shows up in my inbox. This probably explains why the guys were so weird out by the pool.

"Did you know about this?" I ask.

"I'd heard rumblings, but I guess this makes it official." She shuts her laptop and lies back again. "I know you've been homesick. Looks like we might be going back sooner than we thought."

I don't tell her that what I'm really homesick for is a place where I had both my parents together. When I think about going home now, it feels like falling into a void.

Over on Instagram, I've gained more followers and the cookie photo I posted earlier has gotten a crazy number of likes. In my bag is a banana I took from the bus's mini-fridge on my way out to the fair, before I ended up eating funnel cake with Griffin. Today it is bruised and dejected-looking— a lot like me.

I get the banana out, take a photo, and then stare at it a while. In a minute, I'll throw the banana away. Maybe that's what will happen to me, too. The tour will end, and I'll get tossed back to Ohio, utterly forgotten.

I post, sending my sad, subliminal message into the world. Then I take out my notebook again. My list of things not to do on a boy band tour has been growing, but I don't want to add to it right now. Instead, I turn the page and start writing about Griffin, about Mom and Dad, about how lost I feel.

It's a real journal entry, the kind of thing I told Mom I didn't want to do. But the blank pages in this book are a space where I can say whatever I want and not have to worry about how it will sound. So I let myself write. I get it all out. And while it doesn't fix anything, it does help me feel better, if only for a little while.

17

Just as Eisha predicted, for the first couple of days after getting onstage with True Meaning, I can't do anything that might put me in view of the fans. If I work the VIP tent, people take my picture. If I work the merchandise table, they come up and try to ask questions. Even when I stay inside the circle of buses, if I go anyplace where I can be seen from the outside, the fans scream at me.

Eventually, though, the interest starts to wear off, both in person and online. The comments become fewer and farther between, until, finally, somebody posts that I am a *basic, boring bitch*. It stings, but at least it gets everybody to move on.

Just in time for a heat wave.

News calls the temperatures record-breaking, which isn't hard to believe. City after city, the sun beats down relentlessly, but the mugginess is worse. Stepping outside feels like walking through a steam bath, even though we haven't seen a drop of rain since the tour started. And when we do manage to catch a breeze, it's like having a hair drier blow in our faces.

During the day, we huddle in the air-conditioned buses and backstage offices, but there's no escaping the heat at show time. The guys have to give the same performance whether it's 70 or 107 degrees out. Within seconds of taking the stage, their clothes are soaked and they are dripping sweat, but they continue to sing and dance their hearts out. Backstage, they stand in front of cooling units, hunched over and gasping. Onstage, you would never know how tired they are.

The heat not only breeds exhaustion, it makes people accident prone. All of a sudden, Mom's seeing patients every 20 minutes. Dropping things, running into things, twisted ankles, cuts, scrapes, bumps, bruises... you name it, somebody's had it happen. And that's not even taking into account the hornets, which are everywhere no matter where we go, drawn to our sweat and the sweet drinks we guzzle to stay hydrated. Everybody's been stung. I got mine when I leaned against the stage ramp and accidentally sank my hand into a melting Jolly Rancher that had attracted a mini-swarm. Gross *and* painful.

The heat and the hornets contribute to a general air of desperation. There are rumors of more canceled concerts, lots of long meetings, and extra promo for the guys. I haven't talked with Griffin since the hotel; he's either in rehearsals or being shepherded around by Eisha, who's freaking out because the news outlets that matter aren't talking about True Meaning. Our press these days is mostly just small town papers, and it's never enough.

Worst of it all is the fact that we've got Cam Christian opening this leg of the tour. Cam is the latest winner of the talent competitions I used to love on TV, and his fans make

True Meaning's look like a tea party. At first, everybody was excited to have him onboard. Then we met him. Full of himself, a total dick to everybody—it's safe to say Cam Christian is a nightmare. When he performs, there isn't an empty seat in the house. The trouble is that when he exits the stage his fans exit, too, leaving TM humiliatingly small crowds.

"I've never seen anything like it," Claire says as I help her unpack fresh outfits for the guys. Jackets and jeans are a health hazard in this heat, so the wardrobe from here on out is tee-shirts and shorts in wicking, breathable fabric. "If it were anybody else, Jack would have told them where to step off."

"Why hasn't he?" I ask. The vision of our tour manager putting Cam Christian in his place is a truly beautiful thing.

"Have you seen the ticket sales?" says Claire. "He's selling out, so they're afraid to say anything."

"We only have two more shows to get through, though. Tomorrow's his last one."

"And I'm dreading what happens after that," June chimes in from the corner where she's setting up her styling tools. Usually I'd write a statement like that off as June being overly dramatic, but Claire nods in agreement.

Out on the stage, we can hear True Meaning going through sound check. One of Griffin's guitar riffs rises above the chatter, and I wonder for the millionth time what happened between us. Our only recent communication has been a couple of texts. Two days ago, a photo of his fingers on the frets of his guitar popped up on my screen along with three short words: "How you doing?" My stomach immediately dissolved into butterflies, and I sent back a little video of my fingers tapping on a stack of press packets. I also received a joke about funnel cake, to which I responded with what I thought was a devastatingly adorable comeback. But that was the day Jack pulled the whole band all into an hours-long meeting, so Griffin never texted back. Our guitar finger streak and witty funnel cake banter fizzled before they ever had a chance to get started.

Now I'm stuck trying not to obsess, keeping busy because that's all I can do. I've just started steaming a black tee with a British flag on the front when Chase, Landon, Karsten and Emilio walk in.

"Can I help you gentlemen with something?" Claire asks.

"Jack told us to come back here and try on the new stuff," Karsten says. He waves at me and so does Chase, but Landon stands stony faced while Emilio texts away on his phone.

"Oh!" Claire starts scrambling to pull things together. "I wasn't quite ready for a fitting, but if you'll give me a second..."

"I told you it was too early," Landon mutters. "We should have stayed at rehearsal."

"That stage is like an oven," says Chase. "No thanks."

"Oh, OK then," Landon snaps. "You can go on sucking, but at least you won't be hot."

Claire glances at me, a warning in her eyes.

"Seriously?" Chase says to Landon. "Did you just say I suck?"

"Somebody does, or we wouldn't be crashing and burning like we are."

"Come on, bro," Karsten says, trying to make peace. But Chase won't let it drop.

"I'm working my ass off, acting like I actually give a crap," he snarls. "I'm not the one buried in my phone all the freaking time."

All eyes turn to Emilio, who is still texting, oblivious. Landon swats his hand, sending the phone into the air. Emilio somehow manages to catch it before it smashes to the ground.

"Yeah, I just did that," Landon tells him. "Could you put that away for once? We're having a team meeting here."

"Really?" Emilio looks murderous. "Because all it sounds like to me is a bunch of bitching little kids."

"Kill me now," Karsten moans, and Chase looks like he'd like to.

"Boys," says June, who's fluttered in with her bangles tinkling. "Surely there's a more peaceful and constructive way to express yourselves to one another."

"If you call being worried about this tour bitching, then I guess I'm a bitch." Landon steps into Emilio's face. "Somebody's got to worry about it since you can't be bothered."

"What else am I supposed to do besides what we do every single night?" Emilio asks. "If they cancel more shows, then they cancel more shows."

"Easy for you to say. Some of us don't have directors flying out to meet us for movie parts."

"Some of us work to make sure we have something else to fall back on besides a tour put on by a kids' network."

"Are you saying I don't work?" Landon growls.

"No," says Emilio. "I'm saying don't blame someone else if the work you *are* doing isn't paying off."

Landon lunges for Emilio. June has managed to slip out and grab the security guards. They come rushing in now with Griffin and Yukon following close behind. Karsten grabs Emilio's punching arm, and Chase pushes Landon back into a chair, where Griffin holds him down so he can't go after Emilio again.

"Hey, calm down," Griffin says. "This isn't helping anything."

Across the room, Emilio looks deflated.

"Sorry, man," he says. "I just found out Celia's back in the hospital. Between that and all this Cam Christian bullshit, I'm barely holding it together."

"It's cool," Griffin tells him. "Everybody's edgy right now."

But Landon isn't ready to forgive. He pushes Griffin's hands away and heads for the door.

"See you onstage," he says before stalking out.

I realize I'm still holding the tee-shirt I was steaming when all of this started. Emilio takes it from me, holds it up to his chest, and says, "Looks like it fits. Thanks, Claire. I'm sure it'll be fine."

When he leaves, the security guards follow, probably to make sure he doesn't get into another fight.

"I also am going to have to vacate this room," June announces. "The energy is just too toxic right now."

The rest of us are left staring at one another. Karsten scrubs his fingers through his hair.

"Great," he says. "This is awesome. Thanks a lot, Chase."

"What?" Chase bellows. "How did this turn into my fault?"

Karsten sighs. "I don't know, man. I just think we all need some time alone or something."

"Yeah, well good luck getting it."

"I can clear the other guys out of the band bus if you want to hang out there for a little bit," Yukon offers.

"That'd be great," Karsten says. "Thanks, man."

After they've left, Chase looks at me, the corner of his mouth twitching up in a half-smile.

"Sorry, Avery. We have crap manners obviously."

"It's OK," I say.

"Totally OK," Claire adds, her voice motherly. "Everybody's under so much pressure. Frankly, I'm surprised you don't fight more."

Chase sinks into a folding chair by June's styling table.

"Is it OK if I hang out in here for a while?" he asks. "Emilio's probably on our bus, and God only knows where Landon is."

"Sure," says Claire. "As long as you don't mind us puttering around you."

"I like it," he replies. "Sort of reminds me of home."

He leans back, stretches his arms over his head, and within seconds he is snoring.

Griffin turns to me.

"I think it's probably safe to assume sound check is over," he says. "Want to go get some fair food?"

18

During the hour and a half before I'm due at the VIP tent, Griffin and I consume corn dogs, fried Snickers bars, a bag of popcorn, and pork tenderloin sandwiches.

"I think my arteries have stopped working," I moan as I wrap up the last couple bites of my sandwich. "I can't eat anymore."

"Then give it to me."

Griffin snatches the wrapper away and pops the rest of my tenderloin into his mouth. Watching him takes me back to the hotel pool and the hyperactive, almost manic way he kept himself in motion.

"Now you're starting to scare me. I don't think I've ever seen anybody cram down as much food as you can."

"I'm a stress eater," he replies. "If you hadn't come out with me, I'd probably be wandering the fairway stealing peoples' turkey legs and apple fritters. So thank you, Avery, for saving me from myself."

He gets up, tosses our wrappers into a trash bin, and

starts walking toward the carnival games. I scurry after him, determined not to let today fizzle out like the other morning at the hotel did. I catch up as he's selecting a ball for the milk bottle toss.

"You really can't sit still, can you?"

"I'm sorry." He leans against the game counter and appears to be willing himself to relax. "I guess all the crap with the tour is getting to me. I have days right now when I think I'm coming out of my skin."

I wince. "You do?"

A girl in Pops Choir used to have anxiety, and occasionally she'd panic before competitions. I remember how legitimately freaked out she seemed—far worse than the nerves all the rest of us were dealing with.

"I am definitely no doctor," I say. "And I know this is probably overly simplistic, but have you tried living in the moment? Don't worry about what's coming next. Just focus on what you're doing right now."

"I can do that when I'm onstage," he tells me. "Sometimes shows are the only place I can shut off the rest of my brain."

I pick up a ball, then hand the game operator $5 worth of tickets. I'm on a mission of distraction.

"Well, show time's not far off, but this right now is fun time. How about I play you for the fuchsia dolphin over there?"

He looks skeptical. "You think a pink dolphin is going to be enough to distract me from Cam the Douchebag Christian?"

"I don't have a pool where you can swim laps, and I'm not letting you put any more sugar and grease into your body," I answer. "Pink dolphins are the best I can do right now."

"Oh no, we can do much better," he says. "I want to see Jack's face when we try to cram that giant blue unicorn onto a bus."

"Alright." I eye the massive, electric blue prize, which hangs over the bottles like some kind of carny holy grail. "We're playing for the unicorn. Get your money out, 'cause we're going to need a lot more tickets."

JACK MANAGED to locate all four guys for the pre-show meet and greet, for which Griffin and I were late thanks to the fact that it's difficult to lug around a giant stuffed unicorn.

I won it, thank you very much.

But even though the guys are in the same space together, all is not forgotten. None of them speak as we wait for the VIP ticket holders to be let in. When the tent flaps open, they snap into performance mode. They smile. They chat with the fans. But they avoid talking with each other, and an extra physical distance remains between them. It's not enough that someone off the street would notice, but to those of us who know, those few added inches might as well be a mile.

I'm corralling an extra-big group for their photo when Eisha walks in, followed by a woman and a little girl. This normally wouldn't attract notice, except the girl has no hair. She's thin, with slightly sunken cheeks and shadowed eyes.

People step back as Eisha takes the girl to the front of the line. When her turn comes to meet the guys she bounds over, so full of energy that it's almost jarring considering how sick she looks. There's the slightest hint of a moment as the guys register what's happening.

Landon speaks first.

"Hi! What's your name?"

"Zoey," the girl responds, smiling huge.

"Zoey," says Chase. He bends down so he can look into her eyes. "How you feeling?"

The girl, now bouncing up and down, throws her arms into the air and shouts, "I feel awesome!"

The woman with her looks like she's trying not to cry.

"Zoey loves you guys so much!" she tells them. "These past few months have been rough, but she kept your posters on the wall at the hospital and she watches your show and listens to your music during her treatments."

"Really?" says Emilio. "That's a huge honor."

"I feel so special," Karsten chimes in. "Thank you, Zoey!"

"What's your favorite song?" Landon asks.

"Party Girl," she replies.

Emilio drops to his knees and starts to sing. *Party girl, you're my only girl, you're the one who gets me going, always in a whirl...*

The other three join him: *Party girl! Oh, oh party girl! Party all night with me!*

Zoey beams, her mother bursts into tears, and everybody else in the tent cheers. Zoey gets her picture taken and the guys give her and her mom extra big hugs before Eisha guides them back out of the tent. The line starts to move; it's back to the churn. But before the next fan approaches I see Karsten put a hand over his heart, Chase wipe his eyes, and Landon drape an arm around Emilio.

That evening, the heat breaks and the guys take extra time to joke with the audience, sharing cute anecdotes from the road. When it's time to slow things down, Chase tells the crowd, "We met a really special friend earlier today, and we haven't been able to stop thinking about her since."

Landon takes the handheld mic and peers into the audience. "Zoey, are you here?"

Someone from the venue shines a light into the audience as Zoey's mom pops up and waves.

"There's her mom!" says Karsten. "Can Zoey come up here?"

There's a squeal, then the crowd begins to part. While Zoey's making her way forward, Landon says, "We were having a not-so-great day earlier, but meeting Zoey reminded us why we do this."

"Yeah," says Emilio. "She's working so hard to get well, and we're just four dorks singing and dancing. But if we can do anything to help make it easier, then that's what we're here for."

Zoey appears onstage, even more bubbly than in the VIP tent. They settle her on the stool between Griffin and Karsten, and when they sing to her, the words, *Girl you can say anything, just don't say goodbye* have a whole new meaning.

No one in the audience or backstage—not even Lenny the perpetual grump—is dry-eyed. Especially at the end, when Griffin presents Zoey with a giant electric-blue unicorn.

AFTER THE SHOW, everybody sits on camp chairs outside the band bus, listening to Griffin play his acoustic. Even the guys join in—all but Emilio, who apologized for having to return a phone call from his agent. They sing old Beatles songs, 80s hair metal ballads, camp songs—it's probably the most relaxed I've seen anyone on the tour.

Eventually, people trickle away, back to their buses, but I don't want the evening to end. We've got a cool breeze and a sky hazy pink around the edges from the fair lights. And then there's Griffin, hunched thoughtfully over his guitar, toying with a new melody.

On the True Meaning bus, one of the windows goes dark. The others give off a wavering blue glow. I imagine the guys watching TV or surfing on their laptops, getting ready for sleep.

"It's not really fair," I say. "Emilio's up for that movie and some of the other guys are struggling. That's what they were fighting about today."

Griffin frowns but continues to play.

"That's how it is in this business," he says. "There's not a lot that's fair about any of it."

"But they're all really talented. And they work really hard. Emilio just has this certain *it* about him."

"They've all got *it*. If they didn't, they wouldn't be here. But you never know what's going to happen. Even if they last another year or two with the show, they'll have to do something after. Hard work doesn't guarantee you a career."

I try to imagine what it would be like to know that your entire life rests in the hands of strangers who can love you one minute, then forget you just as easily.

"That's a scary way to live."

"That's why I'm happy in the background. Playing in the band is enough pressure without everybody blaming you if an entire tour doesn't do as well as they wanted it to."

His words bring up the fear that's hung over all of us for the past week. It's something I've been trying not to think about, but it doesn't do any good to pretend we aren't all waiting for some giant axe to fall.

"What if the tour ends early?" I ask. "What will you do?"

"Probably get another gig," he says. "What about you?"

"I guess go back home."

"Would that be a bad thing?"

I look at the pink horizon and find it weirdly thrilling that I'm not really sure what city or state I'm in. Not long ago, that uprooted feeling would have made me miserable.

"Well, obviously, I'd be heartbroken to miss the Idaho state fair," I say. "And I hear Oklahoma is lovely this time of year."

I laugh, but Griffin doesn't.

"I hope they don't pull any more shows," he says. "I mean, obviously I hope they don't because then I'd be out of a job. But that would also mean I wouldn't get to see you."

We've grown closer as we've talked. I notice this when my shoulder touches his.

"Would that be a bad thing?" I ask.

Griffin shifts the guitar, and his arm brushes against mine, sending sparks up into my chest.

"When I'm in rehearsals or doing sound check or whatever else that isn't performing, all I really want is to be hanging out with you," he says. "If I couldn't do that anymore, I'd miss it."

I focus on my toes, scuffing my sandals against the parking lot asphalt, afraid to meet his gaze because this moment feels too delicate for the emotion swelling inside of me. If I look up, I might upset the balance and ruin everything.

"I guess what I'm trying to say," he continues, "is if all this ended early, I'd miss *you*."

I close my eyes. One of the sparks has ignited, starting a burn I don't think I can control. I'm no longer sure I want to.

"I'd miss you, too," I say.

It turns out I don't need to look up because Griffin

ducks, catching me from underneath, seeking me over the body of the guitar, which, instead of coming between us, seems to be pulling us together. We meet just as the buses start revving their engines, warning us it's time to get back on the road. When I kiss him back, I can feel the vibration of the motors on his lips.

19

It's amazing how fast things can go from "meh" to incredible. I feel like my entire world has shifted, all thanks to Griffin.

I want to spend every spare second with him, and I know he feels the same way because each morning for the next two days, he's waiting at the door to my bus when I come out to start work. He hangs out with me way longer than he should at lunch, wringing out every moment of togetherness until he has to go to sound check or a meeting with the band. And at night, he's there at my side as soon as he comes off stage until the second the busses pull away for the next town.

I've learned to sense him before I see him: the way he smells, the energy he puts off—an electric buzz that swirls my stomach into delicious little knots. When I see that spikey hair, those sleepy eyes, that scar, it's all I can do to keep from wrapping myself up in him, losing myself in that voice, those callused fingers, those lips.

The best part is that it's not purely physical. Some of my most incredible moments with Griffin are when we're making music together. He brings out his old acoustic and we find a quiet place—the edge of the stage if we can sneak onto it, the concrete barricades separating our busses from the rest of the parking lot, the shelter of a semi wheel when Lenny isn't looking. And then, he plays. I sing. He teaches me to strum out chords, his fingers on mine, his arms around my shoulders, and we build harmonies that are beautiful. Complex. Real.

I let Griffin hear how I sing when it's just me, not trying to blend in with a dozen other show choir performers. Sometimes I close my eyes and imagine the two of us on stage together, in front of a crowd like the ones who come to see TM every night. But it's us they want to see. Griffin and his guitar. Me and my voice. It feels like we have something special.

On day three, Griffin ventures onto our bus to meet Mom formally and hang out someplace a little cooler than the parking lot. Mom's washing dishes in the kitchenette sink, and when he steps into the room it's almost comical the way he towers over her.

"Hello, Mrs. Miller," he says. "It's nice to meet you. I'm Griffin."

Mom fumbles with the towel over her shoulder, drying off her dripping hands so she can shake Griffin's. Even though there are only the three of us, the kitchenette suddenly feels crowded.

"Hi, Griffin," she says. "I've heard a lot about you."

He blushes and says all the right things about hoping she's heard only good. She says all the right things to assure him the rumors are positive. Meanwhile I creep toward the hallway, ready to whisk him off to the lounge as soon as I can.

Mom asks Griffin about guitar. He tells her about his

past tours. She sounds impressed, and he sounds humble as he inches his way to my side. I tell Mom we're heading to the back, and as he starts to follow me through the bunks, he brushes my hand with his fingers.

Mom sees it. She looks at me, and I can almost read her thoughts. *Long distance relationships aren't easy... I don't want you to get hurt.*

I shoot her a look that says *mind your own business*, then push her voice out of my head, because Griffin and I are going to be different. How, I'm not sure, but right now I'm not thinking about the future. Right now, all I want to do is kiss this hot boy who is so temptingly close in this tiny tour bus lounge.

June and Claire and Eisha are all out doing show-prep stuff, so kissing is exactly what we do until I get nervous the silence will prompt Mom to check that we aren't doing anything more.

I pull away and tell him, "This is where the magic happens. And by magic, I mean Eisha obsessing over her email."

Griffin laughs. He wanders the small space, checking out the dream catchers June has hung in the windows and the stacks of papers Eisha has managed to accumulate even though nearly everything is digital.

"She calls those hard copies," I explain. "She's a big fan."

"Who isn't?" Griffin replies with a sly smile. "What's this?"

He's found my notebook, left on a shelf under one of June's aromatherapy candles.

"Oh that. I guess you could call it my journal."

He drops it like a hot potato. "I don't want to violate your privacy."

"No it's OK," I reassure him. "It's mostly just me angsting about stupid stuff."

The truth is I haven't written in the notebook in a few days, since things started going so well. I pick up the book and show him my list.

"*What not to do on a boy band tour*," he reads. "*Don't sing like a show choir girl.* Now that is something I'm going to have to disagree with. In fact, I think my next project should be a show choir song. What kind of dance moves would you do, I wonder?"

This makes me laugh. The sting of not making Choraliers feels so far in the past that joking about it doesn't bother me much at all.

"Any choreo would definitely have to involve jazz hands," I tell him as I spread my fingers wide and shake my palms at either side of my face.

He lifts his hands, mirroring me.

"They definitely bring a little something extra to the party," he says.

I step closer and press my open palms against his chest before leaning in for a good long kiss. When I come up for air, I tell him, "Everything's better with jazz hands."

20

I wake up to the sound of Eisha screaming, either like a fangirl or like an ax-murder victim, it's hard to tell from the sound alone. I poke my head through the curtain of my bunk and see Mom, Claire, and June poking out, too. Eisha is on her phone in the lounge, jumping up and down.

"You didn't find bedbugs, did you?" says June. "Infestations are a common travel hazard, and I'm afraid I'll have to bow out of the remainder of this tour if there's even the slightest hint of a problem."

"Emilio got the part!" Eisha shrieks. "He's Noah in *Dead at Dusk*! They announced it this morning!"

"I have no idea what you're talking about," Mom says. "But I assume it's good?"

"It's really good," I tell her. Violet is going to freak when she finds out. "That's amazing for Emilio."

"It's amazing for the rest of the band, too," Eisha says. "This is a huge story, and True Meaning is getting mentioned all over the place." Her phone chimes. She checks it and squeals. "Ticket sales are going through the roof. We just sold out Des Moines!"

Ducking back into my bunk, I text Griffin to see if he's heard the news. He has, and they're freaking out on his bus, as well. We still have two hours before we arrive at the next venue, so I get online for more details. All the entertainment sites are carrying the story, and since Emilio's on tour, they show a lot of our footage. I think there's even a blink-and-you'll-miss-it snippet of when I was onstage. The True Meaning fans have gone absolutely crazy with hearts and stars and banners featuring sparkling animations of Emilio's face. The *Dead at Dusk* fans are talking about him, too, debating his merits as Noah the shapeshifter. There's a fair amount of skepticism that a mere "boy band singer" can play a supernatural hero, but they all seem to agree that Emilio is hot enough.

When we've arrived and parked, I step outside and it's a completely different atmosphere from the past week or so. People are laughing and high-fiving. Just beyond the barricades, a fleet of news trucks lies in wait. The best part is that Cam Christian is pouting in his bus because his last performance of the tour is getting overshadowed by Emilio's big win.

I look for Griffin, eager for more inside scoop. But Eisha gets to the band before I do, prepping them on her plan to include all of the guys in the news coverage. As they follow her to a remote with Access Hollywood, Griffin brushes my arm.

"Wait for me at the bottom of the stage tonight," he says.

Immediately, my imagination starts spinning scenarios as to *why* he wants me to meet him, and an already electric day kicks into an anticipatory fever dream. Maybe he wants to take our relationship to the next level—maybe even say the L word. Am I ready to say it back? Right now I'd say anything if it meant getting to spend more time with him.

When show time comes, the energy onstage and in the audience is off the charts. Eisha worked with the studio filming *Dead at Dusk* to put together a sizzle video introducing Emilio as Noah, and people love it. I sneak out to the security pit in front of the stage and tape some of the performance to send to Violet, just so she can get an idea how intense things are.

Sending this to Hillary right now, Violet texts. ***She is going to FREAK OUT!!!***

I thought she didn't know who True Meaning is, I text back.

The fact that Violet and Hillary are hanging out yet again should be sending my mind into a paranoid spiral. Instead, I'm surprised to find that it doesn't bother me much. Maybe it's because I'm finally starting to feel like I belong here. The rhythms of each day, the people who make up this strange traveling team—they're familiar to me now. I might not have the world's most exciting job, but I understand better where I fit and how I contribute. Some of what I do—some of the people I've met, too—I truly like.

And Griffin wants me to meet him after the show! The timing of the invitation means he's not bringing me onstage again, so whatever he's planning must be just between the two of us. Thinking about the kinds of things that happen just between just Griffin and me makes it hard to concentrate on anything else, so getting my work done for the rest of the day is pretty much impossible.

When the confetti cannons go off at the end of the concert, I'm waiting at the backstage ramp. Seconds after the final pyro blast, all the guys come running down.

Griffin grabs my hand. "Come on!"

I stumble along, trying to figure out what's happening.

Up ahead, Emilio, Landon, Karsten and Chase are sneaking through the buses to a dark place wedged between the stage and a pile of concrete barriers. This tiny spot is so out of the way that nobody's thought to put security here. And there's a hole in the fence. One by one, the guys squeeze through. Griffin helps me, followed by Hank, Yukon and Josh. Then they're off and running toward the lights.

"I wanna ride the Tilt-a-Whirl!" Karsten shouts.

"Fried Twinkie!" Chase screams. "Must! Have! Fried Twinkie!"

"Seriously?" I say when Griffin and I catch up. "Does Jack know we're doing this? Does Eisha?"

"They'll get over it," says Landon. "How many fairs have we been to now, and we've never gotten on the rides without it being some stupid photo op?"

"It's not like they're going to leave us," Josh adds, and he's right. We're staying in a hotel again since tomorrow is another day off.

"But don't you need security?" A few people have already noticed us. I can see them whispering as we go by.

"Just keep moving," Emilio says. "Pretend we're nobody."

This strategy actually works. We ride the Tilt-a-Whirl and the swings, keeping as low-key as possible considering the guys are still in their concert gear. Only a few people seem to recognize us, and then only vaguely. It's a reminder that, even though Emilio is today's big entertainment news, there's still a huge universe outside of the TM and *Dead at Dusk* fandoms. The majority of people in the real world have yet to memorize Emilio Padilla's face.

Griffin takes my hand as we stroll down the fairway.

"Check it out," he says, pointing at the Ferris wheel. "It's our ride."

I squeeze his fingers, my entire body going warm. Griffin and I have a ride. Who knows what else we might have?

"You up for it?" he asks.

"If you're with me? Absolutely."

We get in line with the others and start creeping toward the front. An easy, just-a-bunch-of-friends-hanging-out vibe settles over our group. Landon and Karsten are laughing at something on Karsten's phone. Chase notices Griffin and me holding hands and gives a little thumbs-up.

Just as we're nearing the front of the line, Griffin gets a text.

"It's Lenny," he tells everyone. "They're looking for us."

"Quick, get on the ride!" Landon shouts.

The line surges forward, and Griffin drops my hand at the same time as he loses his grip on his phone. He stoops over to get it out of the dirt.

Just then, the next car opens up. Emilio slides into it. The ride operator looks at me. Emilio pats the seat next to him.

"Come on, Avery!"

I don't have a choice; Griffin is still digging around on the ground, and other people are waiting, getting impatient. So, I slide in next to Emilio. Griffin waves and laughs as the two of us lift off.

"Sorry," Emilio says once we're airborne. "I take it I'm not your first choice of ride partners."

"No, it's OK," I tell him, realizing how weird the situation is. Millions of girls would kill to be in my position right now, and here I am thinking about somebody else. "It's just that Griffin's used to my fear of heights. I'm probably going to drive you crazy acting like a terrified toddler."

"I like toddlers. And trust me, I'd rather ride with you

than Karsten. Dude was stinking up the Scrambler if you know what I mean."

I giggle at Karsten's trademark potty humor and then say, "At least I get a chance to finally tell you congratulations. That's amazing about *Dead at Dusk*."

"Thanks." Emilio blushes. "I don't think it's really sunk in yet."

We go around a couple of times, watching the fair below us. As we make our way up for another rotation, the gears on the ride start to make a grinding sound.

"Is it just me, or are we going slower?" I ask. My voice is drowned out by the sound of metal screeching against metal.

The car stops, almost at the top of the wheel.

"Oh no." I grip the safety bar.

"It's OK," Emilio says. "They're probably just starting to let people off."

But the wheel doesn't move again, and we start to hear the concerned voices of riders in the other cars.

Over that noise comes one that makes Emilio slouch like he's trying to disappear into himself. It's the manic chatter of fans. Even though I know I shouldn't, I look down. A crowd is swarming beneath the Ferris wheel. People point and shout. Phones jut out over heads. A local news crew pushes through to the base of the ride, camera trained right on us.

"Hope you're ready for your close-up," Emilio says.

The ride operator appears down below with a bullhorn.

"Ladies and gentlemen, we're having some mechanical difficulties. We've got our repair crew coming and it shouldn't take long. But right now we're asking you to be patient and sit still. Don't panic and don't rock the cars. Just wait, and we'll have you down as soon as we can."

"Great," I say, more scared than ever.

"Great," says Emilio, but for another reason. We are basically sitting ducks up here. He puts on a big smile, waves and gives a double thumbs-up. The fans scream in response. But he can only thumbs-up so many times. The ride just isn't moving.

Finally, he turns to me.

"So. Avery. Tell me about yourself."

I need to take my mind off the fact that I am sitting four stories off the ground in a swinging metal basket. So I talk. A lot. I tell Emilio about Cincinnati, about show choir, about how I'm enjoying the tour so far. He listens, laughing at my lame jokes.

Screech! The car jolts, then plummets about three feet before stopping again. Emilio's arm shoots around my shoulders. I cling to him, burying my face in his tee-shirt.

"Oh my God! Ohmygodohmygodohmygod..."

"Hey," he says, putting his other arm around me. "It's OK."

The car jolts again. Emilio swears. I scream, and the crowd on the ground screams right along.

"Are we going to die?" I whimper. "Tell me we're getting off this thing."

"We're getting off," he says. "This is my lucky day, so it'd be really effed-up if the Universe took me out now. See? We're going down."

Sure enough, the ride has started to lower, gently now. We stop twice, while they let the cars below us off, and then it's our turn to be back on the ground. Immediately, Emilio gets whisked away by security. Griffin, who's been waiting for me, reaches for my hand. Before I can grab it, a guy steps between us.

"Aren't you that girl who got up onstage in Omaha?" he asks.

A girl approaches. She's taking a video with her phone.

"So you're with Emilio now?"

I open my mouth, but I have no idea what to say except, "What? No!"

The girl smirks. "Then what was he doing with his arm around you?"

Emilio and the other True Meaning guys are long gone, along with Hank, Yukon and Josh. Griffin takes my arm.

"We have to go," he says.

A reporter shoves her microphone into my face.

"What was it like being stuck up there with Emilio Padilla?" she demands.

"I can't say anything," I tell her. "I'm sorry!"

Griffin hustles me away from the crowd. Instinctively, I cover my face, freaked out at having been recognized.

"You OK?" he asks as we make our way back to the buses. I look over my shoulder at the Ferris wheel, which is going around and around again like nothing ever happened.

"I think so," I say. Panic continues to spark throughout my body—little electric jolts that zap me with reminders of how it felt to be trapped, then ambushed by fans and cameras. I shudder as I give the ride one last backward glance. "But one thing is for absolute certain: I am never getting on one of those things again."

21

The next morning brings a knock on our hotel room door. It's Eisha.

"Can you come to a meeting?" she says, but this time it's not really a question.

"Is Avery in trouble?" Mom asks. "Do I need to come, too?"

"You can if you want," Eisha responds. "Nobody's in trouble, but there are some things we'd like to discuss."

"I'm coming," says Mom, and I'm glad. Last night really freaked me out. It doesn't help now that Eisha is taking us through the hotel lobby to a conference room, where Jack waits at a big long table.

I'm ready for a review of the rules, a scolding for sneaking out with the band—maybe even worse. Then I see Emilio sitting at the other end of the table with a speaker phone pod in front of him.

"Avery, Emilio's manager Gary is on the line from L.A.," Eisha tells me.

"Um..." I stammer. "OK..."

It has to be 5 a.m. in California. Why do we need Emilio's manager on the phone? Emilio gives a little half-smile, which doesn't explain anything other than the fact that he smolders early in the morning just as well as he does late at night.

Eisha invites Mom and me to join her at the table. After we've all sat down, she says, "Avery, last night was interesting on a lot of levels as I'm sure you're well aware."

"Yes," I say, quickly. "I'm sorry. I won't do it again."

"No one is here to blame you," Jack jumps in. "It wasn't your idea to go out to the fair."

"And it certainly wasn't your fault that the ride malfunctioned," Eisha adds. "But sometimes things have a certain serendipity."

"OK..." I repeat. Emilio is staring at his lap now, like he's embarrassed.

"You also know by now how fast news gets around," Eisha says. "And how fast rumors can escalate. It's a big reason why we try to control the online behavior of tour employees."

A groan creeps out of me.

"I'm sure there's a ton about last night. Right?"

Eisha purses her lips. "Probably the best way to get it across is just to let you see."

She slides her iPad across the table. There are photos of me and Emilio—photos of him looking fascinated as I talk, photos of him with his arm around me, photos of us chatting with our heads together, and photos of me with my head on his chest. It was all innocent, of course, but the photos don't look innocent at all.

Eisha swipes through headlines and captions and comments saying things like, *True Meaning Hottie Finds True*

Love with Mystery Girl and, *Emilio has a girlfriend…
nnnnnooooooo!* The fans who already know me are more
personal. *She's Baaaaaaack!* says one. *Avery the Intern Sinks
Her Claws into Emilio!* Says another. *Forget Celia, Here's Who
Emilio Really Loves.*

"Oh, Geez," sighs Mom.

I actually have to laugh.

"This is ridiculous! We get stuck on a ride together and
suddenly we're in love? Don't these people have lives?"

"I know, I know," Eisha says. "But again, serendipity.
What if people believed you and Emilio really were
together, just for a little while? What would you think about
that?"

Now Emilio is full-on blushing. If it's possible, this
conference room feels almost more invasive than last night
at the Ferris wheel.

"I don't get it," I say. "Why would you want people to
think we're together?"

The voice of Gary, Emilio's manager, crackles into the
room.

"Because Emilio has a connection with Celia Nicholas."

"I don't have a connection with her, Gary," Emilio warns
the speaker pod. "I am *with* her."

"I hear you, buddy, I hear you," Gary says. "But Celia has
a bit of an image problem right now. She's going before a
judge today for that DUI in Santa Barbara."

"Given the news about *Dead at Dusk*, and now that
Emilio is the focus of so much media interest, we feel he
shouldn't be associated with that kind of negativity, at least
for the time being," Eisha explains. "His personal life is
going to be under more scrutiny."

"We like the story that Emilio could be dating a nonceleb," Gary adds. "Someone who could be just a regular fan. And since you're with the tour, we can control the visuals."

"So what does that mean?" I ask. "Do we have to go on dates?"

I realize I'm making it sound like I think hanging out with Emilio Padilla would be a bad thing, and I hope he doesn't take it that way. I just want to make sure I understand what I'm getting into.

"You don't have to do anything much," says Eisha. "Just post every few days—I can help you craft them. We might have you two be seen together now and then, but we'd aim to keep it low key. We want people to catch glimpses of you, not put you out there for full-on scrutiny. Emilio is adamant he's with Celia, so we want to respect that as much as possible."

"But it could be good for the tour," Jack adds. "With all this news about Emilio, we're selling out shows."

OK, so no pressure. Several peoples' jobs could be riding on this, but it's cool. No big whoop. Actually, what keeps going around in my head is the idea that, if I do this, then *my* job could be safe, which would mean not having to go home early. Which would mean more time with Griffin.

I turn to Mom. "What do you think?"

"I think it's your decision," she says, then fixes Eisha with the kind of glare she usually reserves for me. "But I want to monitor this. If anything happens that I'm uncomfortable with, I want it stopped immediately."

She turns her gaze my direction, letting me know that this stipulation is non-negotiable, and even though it's embarrassing to have her go all Mama Bear in front of Emilio, for once it doesn't make me bristle.

Eisha nods.

"Absolutely, Mrs. Miller. We want you to know we respect your authority and only have Avery's best interests at heart."

"So it's settled?" Gary asks from his speaker pod. "Am I going to be seeing Miss Avery and Emilio on TMZ soon?"

"Not if I can help it," Eisha jokes. "My goal is to keep this as non-salacious as possible."

She shows me and Mom to the door. Emilio rushes to join us on our walk back to the elevator.

"Sorry about all this," he says when we're alone. "I know that was awkward."

"It's alright," I tell him. I was expecting to get kicked off the tour, so I can't really complain. "But what about Celia? Can I email or something and let her know this wasn't my idea? If I was her, I'd be mad."

"I already explained it to her," he says. "She's cool."

"Are *you* OK with it, though? Lying about something like this?"

He holds up his hands like there's not a lot he can do.

"It won't be for long, just until she gets things worked out and the tour's over. Celia and I will go public when there's a better time."

"I guess I never realized this kind of thing actually happens," Mom says. "Fake dating... I always just assumed it was something people made up for clickbait."

"This is tame compared to some of the stuff I've heard about," Emilio tells her.

"Well, I hope it helps," I say.

Our elevator arrives. Mom and I step in, and Emilio waves.

"Thanks for being a good sport," he calls as the door slides shut.

Back in our room, I put on makeup and pull my hair

back, embarrassed I went to the meeting without getting cleaned up first. I guess I didn't think I'd need to look good if I was just going to get yelled at.

I'm considering whether or not to paint my nails when I get a text from Griffin.

Can you meet me by the pool?

I throw on a sundress, tell Mom, "I'll text you in a little while," then fly back to the elevator, back down to the lobby and out to the pool, which isn't all that different from the pool at the last hotel we stayed at on our last day off.

Griffin lies sprawled on one of the beach chairs, wearing a rumpled tee-shirt and shorts.

"Hey you," he says as he moves over to make room. "What's going on? Everybody's talking about your super-secret meeting with Jack."

I sit beside him and snuggle in, savoring his scent of dryer sheets and sleep.

"It wasn't just Jack," I say. "Emilio was there, too."

"Oh no," Griffin groans. "Is he in trouble for last night? Are you?"

"No one is in trouble. But all the fan drama about us got Eisha thinking about *serendipity*." I make big air quotes with my fingers. "And now it looks like I might have a boyfriend."

His forehead wrinkles, his scar creeping adorably to the bridge of his nose. I hold his gaze until I see understanding register on his face.

"Do you want a boyfriend?" he asks.

On the surface, he's asking about the arrangement between me and Emilio. But there's a deeper, more meaningful question underneath.

"I guess that depends on if he wants me," I say.

Griffin pulls me closer, nuzzles his nose to my ear, and whispers, "He does."

I move closer still and bring my lips to his for a long, slow kiss.

"Then it looks like I *do* have a boyfriend," I tell him. "Just not who everybody thinks."

22

The whole "Emilio and Avery Are Dating!" thing turns out to be bigger than I ever imagined. The first day of our fake coupledom, Eisha had me post a photo of a True Meaning set list with the caption, in red Sharpie, *Been a surreal couple of days* and an ellipsis for extra cryptic-ness. It was almost frightening how fast it got reposted and shared. Comments ranged from heart emojis to diatribes about my looks, my family and my moral character. Keeping up with it all is like playing a game of emotional ping pong. One minute I'm basking in the thrill of fame, the next I'm in awe at how intrusive it can be. I try to remind myself that this is what happens in the spotlight: haters gonna hate, and all that. Still, talking my mom off a ledge over the latest nastygram isn't a whole lot of fun.

Not helping matters is the fact that Violet lost her mind when I told her about the arrangement with Emilio.

"Are you serious?" she yelped. "This is big-time stuff you're involved in now, Avery."

"That's why you can't tell anybody it's not real," I said. "OK? Not Hunter, not Hillary—God, especially not Hillary."

"Why not Hillary? She'd be cool about it."

"You don't know her like I do."

"I know her pretty well," Violet insisted, and I had to work hard not to let irritation creep into my voice.

"Just trust me on this. If anybody I know says anything or posts anything about this thing with Emilio not being 100-percent legit, it will screw everything up. I'm pretty sure I'm not even supposed to be telling you."

She looked irritated as well. I could see her deciding to drop the Hillary topic.

"What does Griffin think?" she asked.

"He gets it," I told her. "He's fine."

"Most guys wouldn't be."

"Yeah, but he has nothing to worry about. It's not like Emilio's even into me. We both have other people we want to be with."

"Just be careful," Violet warned. "TeenSoup.com is saying you gave Emilio Hep-B, which you contracted during sexy times in your hometown of Chillicothe."

"At least they got the first letter of the town right," I said, weakly.

If Eisha choreographed my days before, she's even more in charge now. She has me walk with Emilio to the VIP tent one afternoon, just to the entrance so the fans can see, then give him a hug and slip away. One evening she positions me backstage, within eyesight of the first couple of rows, and Emilio blows a kiss my direction after a song about secret love. After that, she has me post a photo of his hands holding a paper coffee cup. The same day, Emilio posts: *Coffee date on tour = Starbucks from catering.*

The fans pounce on it all. Every little tidbit gets deciphered, decoded and debated. They even find my posts with the cookies and the sad banana and interpret those, too. It doesn't take them long to decide that the cookies mean something sweet happened with Emilio. But they're puzzled by the banana. Since it's shaped like a guy's private parts, they're convinced it must have some sort of sexual connotation. I have fun with that one, posting a new, non-Eisha-sanctioned shot of a cucumber at the catering tent with the caption *Fressssshhhh! ;-)*

And then there are messages from @WorldOfTM. Nora has sent three more, asking if I'd like to do an interview and offering to meet up online or even in person since she travels to see concerts whenever she can. But I'm pretty sure Eisha wouldn't approve of me blabbing to a fan podcast, so, I continue to ignore Nora.

When I'm not making stealth appearances, I'm supposed to be lying low. I can only do jobs that don't require me to have contact with the public, which means no more merchandise table or wrangling the VIP line. Instead, Eisha has me monitoring True Meaning mentions online and posting on behalf of the band, which is hilarious, because if the fans knew it was really me gushing about how excited the guys are to be coming to Minneapolis or how much the concert in Lincoln rocked, their heads would probably explode.

If they were mean when I got onstage with TM for five minutes, then they are brutal now. Gary's idea that they'd like the thought of Emilio dating a non-celebrity doesn't seem to be holding up. For every fan who thinks we are *OMGSOCUTEEEEE!!!* there are ten who think I'm a try-hard and completely undeserving of someone as untouchably awesome as Emilio Padilla.

"Listen to this," I tell Eisha one afternoon while we're working side-by-side in the kitchenette. "*Avery Miller is a thirsty c--- *aw, man, I can't even say that word it's so nasty.

I'm going to substitute *cutie*. Let's try this again. *Avery Miller is a thirsty <u>cutie</u> who needs to be taken down once and for all. Who's up for it in Sioux City?*"

Eisha nods without taking her eyes off her screen.

"Now you know how seriously the fans take these things."

"But that was pretty much a death threat."

"Well, then it's a good thing you'll be helping Claire and June backstage in Sioux City, isn't it? Unless they're ninja assassins, nobody's getting back there if Lenny has anything to say about it."

"Wow. That's reassuring."

My phone vibrates and I glance over, expecting Griffin. A different name flashes on the screen.

Hunter.

It's like getting a message from the distant past, even though only a few weeks have passed since we last talked. I dash to the back of the bus for privacy.

"What's going on with you and that guy?" he demands before I can get out a proper "hello."

"What guy?" I say, genuinely confused. Does he mean Griffin or does he mean Emilio? Suddenly it dawns on me that keeping relationships with two different guys straight— at least publicly—is going to be a challenge.

But then I remember that there's no way Hunter could know about Griffin. He has to be talking about Emilio.

"The movie dude," Hunter clarifies. "The one in the band. Are you really with him?"

"Whoa, wait a minute." I peek out at Eisha, who's typing away on her laptop, then duck back into the lounge and lower my voice. "First of all, it's nice to hear from you, Hunter. Hi, and thanks for calling. Second of all, why do you care?"

"I'm not asking for me," he says. "Everybody is wondering what you're up to."

"I'm doing my job."

"And going out with some boy band singer is part of it?"

I sigh, thinking, *If you only knew.* And then I think, *How dare you?* Because he's the one who asked someone else to Prom. He's the one who's been happily dating that someone else while I've been roaming the country, lonely and homesick. And now that it looks like I've moved on and found my own someone else, he thinks he can call me up and start demanding answers.

"You sound angry, Hunter. Is there something about this that bothers you?"

"It just doesn't seem like something you'd do," he says.

"Maybe you don't know me as well as you thought."

"I've known you for a year, which is more than that guy Emilio can say. What does he want with you anyway? He could have anyone."

I suck in a gasp. For a split second I'm in grade school again. Back then, I thought I'd never be pretty or interesting enough to have anyone fall in love with me, let alone someone like Emilio. Now here is Hunter, telling me in so many words.

"I can't believe you just said that. Do you realize how insulting that was?"

"I'm sorry!" he says. "I didn't mean it like that. I just don't really believe you're with him. But there are pictures of you two everywhere, and people are saying all sorts of stuff."

I close my eyes, willing the stubborn part of myself to step back. I don't particularly enjoy keeping secrets, but none of this would have happened if Hunter hadn't told me to go on tour in the first place.

"I can't control what strangers say on the Internet," I tell him. "And for somebody who doesn't care, you sure are asking a lot of questions."

"I *don't* care," he insists.

"Then it won't bother you if I hang up, because there's nothing I can tell you or anybody else right now."

"Fine," he says.

"Fine."

Hands shaking, I turn off my phone.

Back in the kitchenette, I settle beside Eisha again and fish my black and silver notebook out of the bag I stashed it in.

"What are you doing?" Eisha asks when I reach for one of her fine-tipped Sharpies.

"Just writing something down so I won't forget," I tell her as I straighten my back and my lip, open the book, and put pen to paper.

WHAT NOT TO DO ON A BOY BAND TOUR

1. Talk about being on a boy band tour
2. Expect it to be glamorous
3. Be the only teenager in the room
4. Think too much about what you left behind
5. Expect people to get it
6. Lurk around back rooms and get kicked out in front of a cute boy
7. Have someone at home you can't forget
8. Leave without good snacks
9. Go #2 on the bus
10. Let the VIP line back up
11. Look down, look out instead
12. Wear fancy shoes at the merch table
13. Sing like a show choir girl
14. Get onstage without permission
15. Forget which boy you're actually dating
16. Let old romances bring you down

23

While Hunter and the fans are imagining all sorts of sordid things with Emilio, the real story is between me and Griffin.

In the safety of the buses, in the rooms backstage or the catering tent, we can steal a kiss or a couple or a hundred, and nobody thinks anything of it. We can hold hands and continue our post-concert jam sessions, making music just between the two of us.

Elsewhere, we can't stand too close. Can't brush up against each other. Definitely can't kiss or touch or do any of the other things I'm longing to do 24/7 with him now that we are officially together.

The secrecy may be exciting, but it is amazingly easy to slip up. Mostly because, even when I'm not officially out in public, there are dozens of tiny moments when I am likely to be visible. The bus lots are blocked off, but people can still see in—a fact I learned when a photo went up of me in cut-off shorts and a messy bun, a bottle of soda and a sand- wich in my hands. Someone had snapped it after I'd gone to catering for lunch.

Looks like someone let #PiggyAvery out to the trough again, read the caption—from an account with *anti-body shaming* and *Lover of Christ* in its bio.

Maybe the photo and caption were supposed to be ironic. Or maybe hypocrisy is a blind spot when you're blinded by love for Emilio Padilla. Whichever it is, Griffin and I have found it's easiest to stay out of each other's immediate vicinity during the day.

Nighttime is our time. And when we want our privacy guaranteed, Hank, Yukon and Josh have gotten used to having me on their bus. Griffin and I mostly hang out in his bunk, primarily because it's the one place no one will see us, but also—and obviously—because it's the best place to mess around.

The time always races by, though. We only have until it's time to leave, and then I have to head back to my own bus.

"Isn't it weird?" I say one evening as we're lying together. "I'm farther from home than I've ever been in my life, but I feel like the whole world is only the size of one of these buses. Or maybe it's as big as the parking lot and the stage, but that's it."

"I know," he says. "It's like being in one of those dioramas we used to make when we were kids. We're in this box, doing our thing, and every night people come and look at us. They go back to their lives, but we stay in the box, and it picks up and moves to the next place where we do it all over again."

I pick at a frayed corner of his comforter. "Maybe we really are in a diorama, and this is actually some creepy movie where we find out we've been in a first grade classroom the whole time. We just think we're in the real world."

"That's probably more realistic than any of us would like to admit," he says.

"Sometimes it scares me, though. I wonder if maybe all of this isn't real."

He traces my cheekbone with one of his callused fingertips.

"What we need is a break from the box," he says. "I could use one for sure."

I let out a groan of frustration.

"But how? Eisha's not going to let us go eat funnel cake again, unless we come up with a story about how you're my brother or something."

"We've got Fourth of July off. I've always had gigs then. Maybe we could find out what normal people do on the Fourth and then go do that."

The way he's talking makes me giggle. He sounds like a space alien trying to comprehend a strange new civilization. But I do know what normal people do on the Fourth of July, and it gives me an idea.

"Let me work on a couple of things," I tell him.

"Oh yeah?" I can hear the smile in his voice. "Are we going to a backyard barbeque behind the hotel?"

"Not if I can help it. Just let me see what I can do, and then be ready to go when I say."

ON JULY 3, we pull into a smallish city in Kansas, where we're staying the night and getting a day off for the holiday. It only takes a couple of minutes on my phone to find a fireworks festival scheduled for tomorrow. While making my way backstage to deliver the organic cough drops June ordered for her summer cold, I pass Griffin and press something into his hand.

It's a note. A real one like Violet and I used to pass in

grade school, written on paper ripped out of my black and silver notebook.

Meet at the lake tomorrow night. 8:00. Text me when you're there.

When we get to the hotel, everybody's in celebration mode. Chase's mom lives about an hour away, so the True Meaning guys are going to eat at her house. Most of the other tour people, Mom included, are doing fireworks together.

"Do you want to come along?" she asks as she finishes touching up her makeup. "Or I could stay behind. We could spend some time together."

"I'll be fine," I assure her. "I'll be with Griffin."

"At least ride with us. We're all cramming onto Jack's bus."

"If someone sees me getting off a tour bus, they might know who I am. I'm taking an Uber."

Mom frowns. "You need to be careful, Avery. This is a strange city."

"Yeah, it looks rough." I roll my eyes. "I might get run over by a tractor if I'm not careful."

"Bad things happen in small towns, too," she reminds me. "If I don't get a text by 9 p.m. telling me you're safe, I'm calling the police. And I want you back here by midnight."

For as cool as she's been about me fake-dating Emilio and real-dating Griffin, we always come back to that moment when the orders come down. Some things never change.

"Fine. Midnight," I say. "Can you let me get ready now? It sounds like they're leaving without you."

When she's gone, I straighten my hair so it looks different from the way I usually wear it and put on sunglasses. It's all very movie-star: Getting into the car, checking to make sure nobody's following. But the farther away we get from the hotel, the more I feel like just an ordinary girl again.

The lakeshore where the fireworks will happen is crawling with people when we arrive. I pull out the comforter I took from my bunk in the bus, find a shaved ice stand at the end of a row of festival games, and text Griffin where to find me. A few minutes later, he ambles over with a giant bag of Kettle Korn tucked under his arm.

"You look great," he says. "I like the hair and the shades. You look like a spy in a sundress."

"And you look like a guitar player from a boy band tour," I say, surveying his black tee-shirt, ripped jeans and Chucks. "No baseball hat and sports team jersey? Where are your Topsiders, young man?"

"I guess I don't really blend in with the locals," he admits. "But it'll be dark soon. If we can lie low until then, we should be golden."

Together we find a spot by the lake, where we lay out my blanket and share the sweet and salty Kettle Korn. Then we make out until the first test flares shoot into the sky.

"I love fireworks," I say, lying back in the crook of his arm. "In Cincinnati, the big fireworks are always on Labor Day over the river. When I was a kid my dad and mom would take me to his office building downtown, and they would let people up to the roof to watch."

"Sounds nice," he says.

"It's one of my best memories."

"So why do you sound so sad when you talk about it?"

I pause, surprised to feel tears stinging my eyes.

"Because it might not ever happen again. At least not with all three of us."

"You don't think your mom and dad will get back together?"

"If you'd asked me that a month ago, I would have said there was no way they'd stay apart. But the longer we're away, the more I don't know what's going to happen. The past just feels *really* past right now if that makes any sense."

Griffin nods thoughtfully, twisting a strand of my hair between his fingers.

"So if fireworks were on Labor Day, what did you do on Fourth of July?"

"Hang out with my friends."

I love that memory, too: Barbeques at Violet's, staying up late and listening to the neighborhood kids setting off Black Cats and bottle rockets. I wonder what everybody's doing tonight—especially Violet. She hasn't texted in a couple of days. I haven't exactly been blowing up her phone, either, but she usually checks in if too much time goes by without talking.

So what does it mean if she's silent? The last time we talked felt tense, especially when I brought up Hillary. If Violet is hanging out with her and the Choraliers now, what will happen when the summer's over? Will I find myself back to being on the outside?

"At least you have great memories with your mom and dad," Griffin says. "Mine weren't really the holiday type."

"What type were they?"

"The type that should have probably never had kids. My brother and I were in the way most of the time."

"Were your parents workaholics or something?"

"More like partyholics. And any other kind of *holic* you can think of. We were always getting kicked out of apartments, going places for jobs they'd inevitably end up losing. I don't know... There was a lot of drama."

"Is that how you got the scar above your eye?" I have a vision of a young Griffin, his father standing over him with a belt or some other instrument of punishment. I want to reach back in time and rescue that little boy.

He brings a hand up and fingers the space between his eyelid and the roof of his nose.

"Nah, it was my brother. He got stuck looking after me a lot, and I guess he was in a bad mood that day. He pushed me into the coffee table. All the grown-ups in the house were too drunk or high to drive me to the hospital for stitches. So they got the bleeding to stop, and my mom put on a Band-aid. It's been my beauty mark ever since."

"Well, it definitely makes you prettier. That and your guitar player fingers. Did I ever tell you how hot they are?"

He runs the rough part of his index finger across my open palm in the pattern of a heart. The callus against my skin sends enough heat throughout my body to make me dizzy.

"Guitar was my therapy," he says. "When I played, I didn't have to think about the fact that nobody wanted me at home. Music gave me things I didn't have in my regular life."

I remember when we rode the Ferris wheel that first time; he told me about movies giving glimpses into a world he's not a part of.

"So, living vicariously," I say.

"Right. As soon as I was old enough, my guitar teacher helped work out the legal details to let me take tour gigs. My parents didn't make it hard for me to go, since it meant one less kid to worry about."

"Do you miss them?"

"No."

I close my hand around his, lacing our fingers together.

"Then you're stronger than I am. I feel like all I ever do is miss people."

Griffin settles flat on his back, studying the sky with his free arm folded behind his head.

"I know I'm lucky," he says. "I've been places my mom and dad have never even dreamed about."

"But do you ever stop?" I ask. "Don't you want a normal life?"

"Being with you is the most normal I've ever felt."

The edge in his voice reminds me of another conversation: the first time we talked outside my bus. He sounded so much a part of a world *I* could never hope to belong to. Now I see the anxious boy underneath, trying to stay one gig ahead of his demons.

"You home sounds terrible. But ..."

I break off, worried what I want to say will sound insensitive.

He untwines our fingers and closes my hand inside his.

"You can say anything to me. You should know that."

"Like the song?" I ask.

"Just like that."

"OK. Well..." I let out a breath, deciding to be honest. "I guess I'm a little jealous. You get to perform every night. You know exactly where you belong and what you're meant to do."

"And I'm jealous you got to see fireworks every Fourth of July. I've never had someone to watch fireworks with."

"Seriously?" I say. "Not even a sort-of girlfriend?"

"I've been playing tours and trying to pass Calculus online. I've never been in one place long enough for a girlfriend."

"And now you are?"

"No, but you're not in one place long enough right along with me."

He sounds happy when he says that. Content. But now I have a vision of the next month and a half, stretching out ahead of us in one straight line with a big red X at the end.

"What happens when the tour's over?" I ask. "What do we do then?"

He frowns at the sky, starbursts reflected in his eyes.

"Remember what you said the other day? About living in the moment?"

I remember. It was something I said to take his mind off the stress he was feeling. At that particular moment, it didn't have anything to do with me.

"Living in the moment is great and all," I tell him. "But what if I want extra moments?"

Griffin rolls me underneath him, inviting my fingers to snake under his tee shirt, seeking the soft, warm skin of his back.

"I definitely am living in this moment," he says as his lips move across my neck. "And this one." He's reached my ear. "And this one." He bites down, making me gasp. Right now, Griffin and I are creating fireworks of our own.

"Less talk, more moments," I say before crushing my mouth into his.

24

The heat comes back again, worse than ever, just as we start a two-week leg of back-to-back shows with only one day off. The excitement everyone rode so high on just a week ago is fading fast. So is the public's fascination with Emilio, *Dead at Dusk*, and all things True Meaning. Eisha's back to fretting over media mentions, and the atmosphere everywhere has taken a turn for the tense.

When I'm away from Griffin, things aren't that great for me, either. Hiding from fans has officially lost its appeal, and the social media stuff is getting monotonous. I'm trying to figure out a new and exciting way to invite people to *Post your pics of last night's show!* when I hear Eisha swear under her breath. I glance over to see her hair in side poufs and her usually impeccable face makeup-free. She looks tired.

"What's the matter?" I ask.

She rubs her hands across her face and scowls.

"I was thisclose to getting Entertainment Weekly to do a feature on Emilio and it just fell through," she says. "They'll be doing press closer to the film opening, but that's not going to help True Meaning now. I tried pitching something about the tour, but they won't even respond to that."

"Isn't most of the tour sold out, though? I thought we weren't worried about ticket sales."

"Calliope's not thinking about the tour so much anymore. They want to see how the momentum from this summer affects the show next season. This could be the last one if ratings don't improve."

"They don't think Emilio being in *Dead at Dusk* will help?"

"Who knows? There's no guarantee fans of the movie will translate to fans of the show. The drop-off in interest right now isn't very reassuring."

She really does look depressed, and I find myself wanting to help—not just her, but the guys, too. Emilio will be fine without True Meaning, but what about the other three? A few months ago, I wouldn't have given a second thought about the careers of a few singers on a show for kids. But now that I know them, I genuinely like them. I don't want to see them lose their jobs.

Then it hits me. Maybe this fake romance could do more than just take peoples' minds off Emilio and Celia. I offer a suggestion, expecting Eisha to shoot it down.

"What if Emilio and I go out for real one of these nights? We could do the boyfriend/girlfriend thing for a couple of fair rides—just enough for a few pictures. We've never actually let people get that close before. Would that help?"

Eisha thinks for a minute.

"If the focus is going to continue to be on Emilio and not the entire group, I'd rather people be talking about his career versus his love life."

But I have a sense I'm onto something. Call it a gut

instinct, but I feel almost certain a new storyline—or a boost to an old one—could help re-ignite some interest.

"It's better than nothing," I say. "And maybe after a few pictures of Emilio and me get out, then I can 'accidentally' post something about the rest of the band. Or maybe we leverage the other guys and they come out with us, so they're part of the visuals, too."

I can't believe I'm using Eisha's PR-speak, but it perks her up.

"The entertainment outlets won't care, but it might keep the fans talking," she says. "And they're the ones who actually watch the show."

"Maybe I could post something about how no one loves True Meaning more than me. Then you get some random people—maybe if your neighbor at home has a kid and a few of her friends—to start a hashtag. Something like #true-TMfan or #IloveTMmorebecause. Then you could pitch a story like *Why an Ohio Girl <3s True Meaning, and You Should Too*."

Eisha pulls out her phone and starts taking notes.

"I like how you think," she says. "I was telling Jack the other day how impressed I've been. I was going to wait to mention this, but we both think you should continue to intern with me when the tour's over."

I raise an eyebrow. "Are you serious?"

"Sure. Calliope's always talking about bringing in younger people, and you definitely fit the demographic. Colleges love to see experience like that on applications. Doesn't your mom have a friend in L.A. you could stay with? You could finish high school online."

But it's not college that has me interested in the idea of working with Eisha. It's the inkling that maybe I wouldn't

have to have a long-distance relationship with Griffin if
I did.

"Do you think your mom would go for it?" Eisha asks.

I think, *Not in a million years.* But I don't say that. It's nice
to imagine, even just for a second, that there might actually
be a possibility that the magic of this summer doesn't have
to end.

"Maybe," I tell Eisha. "I'll ask."

Hours later when the show's over, I'm waiting at the
backstage ramp for Emilio and the rest of the band. The
plan Eisha and I worked out is for us to walk down the main
fairway, do the bumper cars, and then come back. There's a
spot by the front of the stage where a bunch of fans are
hanging out, so we've decided to make our entrance there,
close enough so they can see us but not too close. We don't
want it to be obvious we're trying to get their attention.

I hear the last song, hear the crowd scream, hear the
guys tell everybody good night, and then they're all coming
down the ramp. While Emilio and the other three veer off to
change shirts, Griffin gives me a long kiss hello.

"Ready for your close up?" he asks.

"I think so." I twirl, showing off the outfit I chose. "Do I
look innocent but on point? I'm sure my clothes are going to
get analyzed to shreds."

"You'd look great in anything. But for the record I think
you've hit on a nice combination of *cute* mixed with *don't
care.*"

"I'm just sorry you can't come. It's too risky. What if I
couldn't keep my hands off you? It would blow our cover."

"I'll take one for the team," he says. "As long as you're coming back to me, right?"

Taking his face in my hands, I plant a huge kiss right in the center of his forehead.

"Always."

Emilio, Landon, Karsten and Chase appear in fresh clothes, along with the bodyguard who is now mandatory whenever the guys venture away from the buses. After our escapade on the Ferris wheel, Jack's not taking any chances.

"Shall we?" Emilio asks.

His eyes are full of fun and conspiracy. What we're planning is daring and dishonest, but also 100 percent thrilling.

I take Emilio's hand and say, "Let's go."

One last kiss from Griffin, then we head out with the other three guys in tow, walking toward the fairground lights.

We barely make it to the main concourse before we're surrounded.

"Keep your head down and smile," Emilio coaches. "You want to look like you're OK with the attention, but you weren't expecting it."

I glance over for reference and see he's playing it humble —all sideways glances, mini-waves and low-key answers to the questions the fans keep throwing our way.

Meanwhile, Chase and Landon are mugging for the cameras. Next to them, Karsten hangs back, playing it cool.

The activity attracts more attention, just like we hoped. I try to envision how movie stars on a red carpet work the crowd. I stand straighter, trying to give a better angle, super-aware that everything will be out in the world within hours, if not minutes.

Someone from the crowd walks up as I'm pretending to

listen to Emilio telling a fan he hasn't met his *Dead at Dusk* co-stars yet.

"Hey, Avery," the girl says. "I'm Nora. From In Search of True Meaning?"

"Oh! Hi!" I gasp, surprised to see this girl who's been semi-stalking me. With her ponytail and blue tee-shirt, she looks like someone I'd see on any given day at school.

"I know you're probably really busy, and I'm not trying to be a pest or anything," she says. "You don't seem to be online much, so I wasn't sure if you were seeing my messages."

"I didn't see them," I lie. "Were you trying to get in touch with me?"

She presses a card into my hand with the name of her podcast and her contact info.

"I wondered if you might want to do an interview. You have a really cool inside look at the band and the tour, and I thought if we kept it low-key it would be kind of special."

"I'm not really sure if I'm allowed..."

"You don't have to answer right now," Nora says. "Let me know whenever, OK?"

And then she moves on, re-joining the crowd. I put her card in my pocket and go back to the mob scene. Even though I know at least 80 percent of what these people say about me will be less than flattering, it's still a rush being out of the diorama and free to enjoy the spotlight again.

I lean over to whisper in Emilio's ear, which makes the cameras go off even more furiously.

"Do you think we can still make it to the bumper cars?" I ask.

He squeezes my hand, like any good boyfriend would.

"I'll make sure of it," he says. "For you."

25

The next day, a decent number of sites post photos of Emilio and me together. They have headlines like, *Emilio Steps Out with His Backstage Bae* and *TM Mystery Girl Comes Out of the Shadows*. I look good in the photos. I look happy. And in most of the posts, True Meaning gets mentioned. All in all, Eisha is pleased—even more so when my *Why an Ohio Girl <3's True Meaning* article idea gets picked up by Teen Scene. I do the interview on our way to the next venue, refusing to answer questions about my relationship with Emilio but gushing about how awesome all four guys are.

And so, we go out again that night. This time, Eisha has Emilio and Chase post something cryptic about fried candy bars, and I put up a photo of a Milky Way, so that when we show up at the food tents there's a group already waiting. Someone asks Emilio if he gets bored being on the road, which creates the perfect entry for him to mention that the band is using the time to write songs for a new album, then ask Karsten to talk a little more about it. Since Karsten's shy, he gets teased by Landon, who then gets to elaborate on how these new songs showcase their true personalities and how much the band has grown as artists over the past year. Then Chase jumps in about how he can't wait for the fans to hear the new material, and everybody *awwww's* about how sweet he is.

When Teen Beat runs the fan-made video of that exchange under a headline trumpeting *New True Meaning Album in the Works*, Eisha practically tackles me with excitement.

"Tonight, try to work in something about how TM is writing a song for the *Dead at Dusk* soundtrack," she tells me as we travel to our next stop.

"Are they really?" I ask.

"Not at the moment. But mentioning it could put the idea into someone's head. These kinds of things can become self-fulfilling prophecies."

Later, over video chat, I try to warn Griffin.

"Eisha's getting a little extra over here. Be nervous: you're probably going to be asked to write post-apocalyptic vampire movie music."

He winces. "I'm actually more nervous about how close you and Emilio are standing in those photos from last night. Does he really need to hold your hand all the time?"

I can't help the flush that blooms across my face, because Emilio does hold my hand a lot, and I'd be lying if I said it was horrible. Any girl would enjoy having her hand held by Emilio Padilla. But it's purely a physical reaction. The guy whose hand I *really* want to be holding is talking to me right now on my phone screen.

"We have to be convincing," I say. "You know there's nothing between Emilio and me."

"But the rest of the world doesn't."

"It doesn't matter what anybody else thinks," I reassure

him. "You and I know the truth. What we have is more special because it's private."

Over at her computer, Eisha squeals.

"The head of marketing at Calliope just emailed! They're quite pleased with the recent coverage. Those are her exact words: *quite pleased*. Of course, I told her it was all the idea of my amazing future intern!"

"Wait. What?" Griffin says. "You're Eisha's *future* intern?"

I look around for Mom. Luckily, she's at the front of the bus with Claire, well out of earshot; I am so not ready to have this conversation with her yet.

"I'll explain when I see you later."

"Ooh, something to look forward to," he says.

"I'll make sure it is," I promise, and now it's his turn to blush.

"I can't wait," he says.

"Neither can I. See you at the next stop."

We sign off and I get up to choose just the right outfit for tonight. I'm deciding between a flowered skirt and cropped jeans when Mom comes in with her laptop.

"Guess what I found on Netflix," she crows. "*The Innocents* _and_ *The Other*!"

"Wow," I say. "I didn't think anybody knew about *The Other* anymore." It's this movie from the 70s about twin boys with a truly creepy bond, and even though it's considered one of the best horror films ever, finding it even for rent can be next to impossible.

"I couldn't believe it either," Mom says. "How about we have a scary movie night? It'll be like old times."

I hold the skirt up, squinting into the tiny mirror on the bathroom door.

"I can't," I tell her. "I have to go out with Emilio."

She looks disappointed but still hopeful.

"We've got an hour before we get to the next place. We could watch a little now."

"I actually need Avery to help monitor the band's hashtags," Eisha cuts in. "Once she's decided what to wear for this evening, that is. For the record, Avery, I like the skirt. It's stylish but wholesome."

Eisha's words are a reminder that I need to stay on Mom's good side if I'm serious about getting her to let me go to L.A. this fall.

"We'll watch the movies soon," I tell her. "Get started, and I'll catch up when things calm down."

Then, I put in my earbuds so I won't be tempted by the sounds of old horror flicks as I go back to trolling the internet. The #trueTMfan hashtag is trending, and one photo of me in semi-profile, looking willowy and glamorous, seems to be everywhere.

Looking at that photo triggers a flush of pride that has nothing to do with my appearance. It's a feeling of accomplishment. No one from home can say they helped score publicity for a major network's summer concert tour. None of my friends has been invited to intern with that network when the summer's over. I've found something bigger than show choir. And for the first time since leaving Cincinnati, I can honestly say I don't care anymore about Choraliers.

I'm moving on.

26

Something feels off from the minute we arrive at the next fairgrounds. The buses idle forever while we wait to pull into our spots because whoever's in charge didn't block off enough space behind the stage. Then, it's the kind of overcast day where you think it might rain, but instead the clouds just hang around, too low and close, making everyone feel trapped and gloomy.

This is by far the sketchiest place we've ever played. The stage has rickety scaffolding and an almost non-existent back-of-house. Most of the equipment and help the crew usually gets from a venue either isn't right or isn't there at all, which means our team has to scramble for a plan-B. When I venture off our bus, I pass Lenny shouting at Jack.

"If that scaffolding goes down and kills a hundred people it's going to be all our asses on the line," he says. "You better hope Calliope has good insurance, because I wouldn't trust the rocket scientists running this place to be covered for diddly squat."

Over in the food tent, a sad-looking catering company is unloading some sad-looking sandwiches, along with tubs of potato salad that look like they might have been fresh a week ago. This is where I find Griffin, braving a ham on wheat with the rest of the guys.

I pick out a veggie wrap, figuring it's the safest bet, then go join them. And it doesn't take long to figure out that all is not well here, either. The guys aren't really hanging together so much as doing their own thing in the general vicinity of one another. I can hear Emilio on the phone, using words like *probation* and *therapist*, which means he's talking to Celia. So I understand why he's not as cheerful as usual. But the others?

"Why is everybody so down?" I ask.

Griffin grimaces at his sandwich, tossing it back into the wrapper.

"Karsten wants to record with his other band during the week they're supposed to be shooting the first episode of the new season," he says. "Calliope said they'd work with him, but it messes up the other guys' schedules, plus they're not thrilled about him having a side project. And Landon just found out he didn't get an audition for that new cop show everybody's talking about."

"What's wrong with Chase?"

"His sister's turning seven today, and he hates missing family birthdays."

I'm starting to get a much better appreciation for how complicated these guys' relationships must be. I don't think they're faking being friends because I've seen them away from the cameras, and they seem to genuinely like each other. But they never get a break. As much as I love and miss Violet, I would probably want to kill her after spending every waking minute together on a tour bus.

"I hope they can work it out," I say. "Jack's got enough to worry about without having to break up another fight."

"They'll be fine," says Griffin. "Let's focus on us. I actually just got some good news."

"Good news is great! What is it?"

"I'm doing the Ariana Grande tour! I found out right after I got off chat with you this morning. The tour manager asked for me specifically."

The smile on his face is so big and proud. My be-glad-for-others instinct tells me I should be gushing about how happy I am for him. But the something's-not-right-here switch in my brain has been tripped.

"How long is the tour?" I ask.

"Four months. We start rehearsals two weeks after this tour wraps, then we're on the road October to January."

I should be congratulating him. But I can't match the smile on his face, no matter how hard I try. Because the same Universe that screwed up my plans to have an amazing summer in Cincinnati with Hunter is now, it seems, deciding to screw up my plans to have an amazing fall in L.A. with Griffin.

"What about us?" I ask. "We're never going to see each other."

"That's what video chat is for," he says. "And I know for a fact that the tour stops in Ohio. I checked."

"But I'm not going to be in Ohio. I was going to intern with Eisha. In L.A. So we wouldn't have to do video chat."

His eyes go wide as he processes what I've just said.

"That would be amazing!" he says.

"Not if you're on tour."

I can see him trying to regroup, to convince himself nothing is wrong.

"Even with you in L.A. I was going to be touring at some point," he says. "It's just happening sooner, that's all."

I put down my wrap and scoot away, unnerved by the casual tone of his voice.

"So you're effectively dooming us to a long-distance relationship."

"We were going to be long distance no matter what. What happened to living in the moment?"

Tears have started, despite my attempts at keeping them in. I swipe my arm across my face, trying not to sniffle and attract attention.

"I can only live in the moment so much before I start to wonder if there are going to be other moments. I want more. I thought you did, too."

"I do!" He pulls me to him, using his free hand to dry my cheek with the tail of his shirt. "I guess I just thought we'd figure something out."

"Figuring it out would mean talking to each other before making big decisions."

He runs his fingertips along my cheek, tipping my chin to look into my eyes.

"Avery, I get that we have things to work out here, but can we talk about this when we're not in the middle of a crap-ass food tent surrounded by pissed-off people?"

"When?" I say. "When else are we going to talk?"

"Tonight, after the show."

"I'm going out with Emilio then."

"You can skip it, right? This is more important."

"Not according to Eisha. It's part of my job."

He pulls back, eyes narrowing.

"So you can yell at me for doing my job, but I'm not supposed to have any say in how you do yours?"

"This is different," I protest.

"You're right," he says. "My job doesn't entail telling the

world I'm with one person when I'm really with someone else."

It's the first time we've ever had real tension between us. I know he's right: We need to work this out, and I need to help make that happen. I already promised Eisha I'd go with Emilio—I can't just cancel. But Emilio and I don't have to stay out as late as usual. I can make both things work.

"I'll be back in plenty of time," I tell Griffin. "We'll just go out long enough to get seen, then I'll come right back here. I promise. You won't even realize I'm gone."

Griffin stands up, clearly not appeased. Before I can say any more, he's heading for the stage

"Just be there," he says. "I have to get to sound check now. See you tonight."

27

I spend the rest of the day alternating between being mad at Griffin and feeling mad at myself for being mad. The practical part of me has known all along that he'd go on another tour at some point, but I thought we'd at least get some time together in L.A. before he rushed off again.

I tell myself we'll figure this out. Maybe he doesn't have to do the whole Ariana Grande tour. Or maybe I could go on some of it with him—assuming I actually get to do the internship, and assuming my parents let me travel the country for weeks on end with a group of people none of us has ever met.

Which is assuming a lot.

I really want to talk about all of this with Violet, but she's at tennis. Then, when I finally get her on video chat, she's sleeping over at Hillary's, and there's no way I'm letting Hillary know that my life is anything less than fabulous. Instead, Violet and I talk about whether it's a good idea for her to cut her hair short, and what she and Hillary should get on their next Starbucks run. Hillary hangs around in the background, giving opinions nobody asked for, until I can't stand it anymore and have to hang up.

The entire afternoon turns out to be a slog of heat and boredom and people being cranky under overcast skies. It's only when night falls that color and light start to return. The rides twinkle on, the day's almost done, and I'm looking forward to getting dressed up. Instead of Avery the Unpaid Intern, who's in a big awkward mess with her boyfriend and whose friends are having sleepovers without her, I'm a mystery girl who's won the love of a smoldering boy band singer. Right now, the Emilio and Avery Show is pure escape.

That's why I'm backstage a good 10 minutes before the show ends. It's not the best concert, I can tell just by listening. The guys don't sound as great and the crowd isn't as into it as usual, but none of that really concerns me. I'm busy figuring out how to work in a ride on the Spider, which I can see twirling in the distance.

So I guess I wasn't paying attention when the guys came offstage all loping and surly, not bouncing from a post-show high like usual. I might have been tipped off when Emilio took my hand mechanically instead of playfully like he has the past two nights. And I might have gotten a clue when Griffin slinked off to his bus without so much as a *Hi* or a peck on the cheek.

It's not until I hear Karsten and Chase that I know this evening might end up worse than the day.

"This is BS," Karsten says as we make our way toward the fair. "Nobody cares about this fake girlfriend crap anymore."

"Yeah, this is just where I wanted to be with my career," Chase agrees. "Following Emilio around like some lame-ass wingman. Sure makes you feel respected as an artist, doesn't it?"

I look behind me, and their faces are stony. They don't even try to disguise the fact that they were talking about me. I glance over at Emilio, who seems lost in his own thoughts. Landon, meanwhile, trudges behind everyone like he'd rather be on his way to a root canal.

At least a decent crowd has gathered when we make it to the fairway. I put on my shy-flattered-somewhat-over-whelmed smile for the cameras, only to find myself pushed aside.

"Nobody wants a picture of you," one of the fans informs me.

I want to shoot back that she's wrong, that Emilio's and my love story is big news, and that this girl is clearly just jealous. Except the truth is six feet away from me: Emilio surrounded by requests for hugs and autographs. Next to him, Chase, Karsten and Landon have their own crowds to manage. Nobody is paying attention to me, and why should they? Is it me writing the songs the guys perform every night? Is it me onstage, singing and dancing my guts out? What have I done to deserve any part of the spotlight, besides get stuck on a Ferris wheel?

Realizing all of this would be humiliating enough if I weren't standing in a group of people on high alert for something juicy to post. I want to hide. Instead, I have to smile and pretend to be happy on the sidelines.

OK. I can do that. Except time is running out. I promised Griffin we'd keep this short. If we don't get out of here soon, I'll be late meeting him.

I wait another 10 minutes, hoping the crowds will break up. When they don't, I push through and whisper in Emilio's ear. "I need to get back. Can we go now?"

"In a minute," he says.

Nearby, a funnel cake stand belches out a sickeningly sweet smell. It's not at all tempting like before, but maybe Griffin will be more forgiving if I bring a gift to let him know I was thinking about him—a token of the first time we really got to know each other. Also, getting a funnel cake will give me something to do besides stand around. So I buy one, hoping everyone will be ready to leave by the time I'm done.

Except when I return, they're still going strong.

"I really need to go," I tell Emilio.

"So go," he says. It's not mean, but it is definitely dismissive—another reminder that I'm an accessory, not the main attraction.

Well, fine. Except now I've got a dilemma: Do I walk back alone and open myself up to getting accosted by fans? Will it look bad if I leave, and will Eisha give me crap about it tomorrow? As I'm considering the options, our security guard gets on his phone, then motions to the guys that the busses are getting ready to leave.

Now beyond late, I sprint ahead, balancing my funnel cake in one hand and my phone in the other as I text Griffin that I'm coming.

When we get back to the buses, they're all dark and idling. No one's outside.

I run to the band bus and knock on the door. The driver slides it open, looking down at me from behind the wheel.

"I need to talk with Griffin," I say. "Guitar player. Is he here?"

"They're all in the back," the man tells me.

Yukon's face peers around the corner.

"Hey, Avery," he says. "Griffin got tired. Said he was going to bed."

A sinking feeling threatens to pull me into a panic spiral.

I try to ignore it, telling myself Griffin will understand if he'll just let me tell him what happened.

"Can you get him?" I plead. "I know he's mad at me for being late and I want to explain."

"I'm pretty sure he's asleep," Yukon says. "And we're all sort of needing to rest now, so maybe try him tomorrow?"

I crane my neck, trying to see into the bowels of the bus. I make out what I think is Josh's leg on the couch and a pair of hands playing games on an iPad.

"We gotta leave now," the driver tells Yukon. "Is she getting on or off?"

Yukon looks apologetic, but he doesn't invite me on. The message is clear: Griffin doesn't want to see me.

"Would you tell him to text or call me?" I ask. "Oh, and I got him this."

I hand up the stale funnel cake, then step down and trudge back to my own bus, feeling dejected, disappointed, deserted. All I want is to get into some sweatpants and curl up with Mom, watch those creepy old movies and forget today ever happened. Maybe I'll even tell her about what happened with Griffin. I've been so stuck in a loop of shutting her out that we haven't talked—really talked—in a long time.

I miss it.

Our bus driver is deep into a *Dead at Dusk* book when I tap for him to open the door. I tell him *Hi*, step up into the kitchenette, and run straight into my mom making out with the sound engineer.

28

For a horrifying minute, I am frozen. Not so much because of shock, though I definitely am beyond freaked out, but because I literally have no place to go. I can't run to my room and slam the door. I would have to push past Mom and her—what is he, her boyfriend? Then I'd have to climb into my bunk and pull the curtain, which would have nowhere close to the same impact. And it's not like I can take off somewhere else because the buses are leaving, and I don't want to get left in the butt crack of the lower Midwest or wherever it is that we are.

So I back up, step down, and stand just outside the bus door, trembling in the shadows as Mom's guy comes out and heads to his own bus. Then I slink back inside and make a beeline for my bunk.

"Avery," Mom says.

"I can't talk," I tell her, pulling my curtain as tight as possible. I burrow under my comforter, still in my clothes, as everything floods to the surface. Griffin. Violet and Hillary. My humiliating attempt at being a celebrity girlfriend. My family disappearing, first slowly, and now, tonight, all at once before my eyes.

Turns out crying is one more thing you shouldn't do on a boy band tour—not if you don't want everyone else on your bus to hear.

I STAY in bed all morning, long after we've arrived at the next venue. I called and texted Violet until midnight but she never answered. Griffin isn't texting back either. I don't want to leave the bus because I have no desire to see Emilio or the other guys. Going out in public together was my idea, and while I got caught up in it, thinking it was super-cool, they clearly thought it was super-lame.

So I lie in my bunk, dozing off and on, having weird dreams about show choir try-outs and old movies where boys hold boom boxes outside their girlfriends' windows. In the weirdest one, I'm auditioning girls to play me in a reality show-style version of my life, except everybody is a little kid like the ones who come to the VIP tent every night. I wake from that one covered in sweat.

Glancing at my phone, I see a new text waiting.

It's Hunter, of all people.

Hey. Just wanted to check in. I'll be around

I pull up video chat to see if he really is there. He gets on immediately.

"Hey," he says. "What's the matter?"

"Nothing." I yank my hair out of the tangled bun I slept in, trying to look less stark and depressing. "Nothing is wrong."

"Your nose is red. You always get red when you've been

crying. Is something wrong with you and Movie Star Dude?"

I cover my nose with my hand, knowing he's right. When I cry, my face turns into a splotchy scarlet mess.

"Don't even ask," I say.

"Uh oh. Are there pics of you guys fighting or something? Am I going to see you on a bunch of magazines when I go buy milk at the store?"

"No. We're not fighting. It's just..." I search for a way to express what I'm feeling without letting him know every detail. "Let's just say dating a celebrity isn't as much fun as it seems."

Hunter's question brings up something else I hadn't considered before. What exactly is Eisha's exit strategy here? When Emilio and I do officially "break up," am I going to become a villain? I probably should have thought about that before agreeing to this stupid plan.

"Avery?" Hunter says. "What's going on?"

"Nothing with Emilio. It's something else. Last night..." I stop because I don't know if I can bring myself to say it. I swallow, then try again. "Last night I walked in on my mom kissing one of the guys from the crew."

"Oh," Hunter says, quietly. "Ouch."

"Yeah."

"Are you OK?"

"Not really. When Dad left, I thought it would be temporary while they figured out whatever was wrong between them. I didn't think she'd actually go off with somebody else. It was awful. I just want to disappear."

I pull the covers up over myself, creating a little fort for me and my phone.

"So what do I do? Do I tell my dad?"

Hunter runs a hand through his hair, thinking. "Do you think he already knows?"

"No!" It comes out louder than I'd intended. I lower my voice and add, "Are you kidding?"

Hunter scrunches up his face, like he knows what he's about to say will hurt.

"Maybe he's seeing somebody else, too."

"Ugh, no." The idea of that is incomprehensible. "I would know if he was."

Hunter looks at me with a level gaze that says he knows me better I know myself.

"No offense, Avery, but you think you know a lot."

And now my stubborn side takes over, because it's hard not to be defensive when someone you haven't seen in months starts dropping truth bombs all over you.

"What is that supposed to mean?"

"You create these scenarios in your head," he says. "Then when they don't work out the way you planned, it really screws you up."

I consider this, running my tongue over teeth that are in desperate need of brushing. Hunter is right that I'm no good with change. But Hunter's parents have been divorced since he was four. Most of my friends have homes that are broken in some way, including Violet, whose mom died of breast cancer before she moved to Cincinnati. Having my family together and happy was something I always felt I could call uniquely mine.

"I don't think I could be much more screwed up than I am right now," I say.

His expression softens, and his voice turns helpful.

"Well, see if you can hold it together until next week. We're coming to see you in Columbus." He squints into the camera. "You're supposed to look happy about that. Why don't you look happy?"

"This is the Violet and Hillary road trip," I say, flatly. "Right?"

"It's a trip to see you."

I roll my eyes, trying to look annoyed instead of close to crying again.

"It might have started out that way, but I'm sure it's their big BFF bonding thing now. They're attached at the hip, if you didn't notice."

He frowns. "They're probably just working out the details."

"How many details can there be? I go days without hearing from Violet, and when I do, she's always got Hillary in the background." Despite my best efforts, a tear escapes and gets halfway down my cheek before I can brush it away. "Sorry, but it's a little hard not to feel like I've been replaced."

"Why do you care if they want to be friends?" he says. "Your summer is ten times more amazing than theirs is."

Ugh. That punched in the stomach feeling hits again as I realize everything I've done these past couple of weeks is backfiring. Of course Hunter thinks that. They probably all think that. It's what I wanted them to think.

"You don't understand," I tell him.

"I never did." he says. "That's probably why we used to argue so much."

Hunter is right about that, too. Even though I told myself we were perfect for each other, he and I clashed more than I ever wanted to admit. Still, talking with him feels good. I needed to hear a friendly voice.

"Thanks for calling," I tell him. "I was starting to feel like everybody had forgotten about me."

"You're impossible to forget." His chipped tooth shows when he grins.

"And you're sweet for saying that. Goodbye, Hunter."

I hang up, roll over and try to go back to sleep. It's lunchtime but I don't have any appetite. Outside the bus, I can hear people getting ready for tonight's show. I wonder if Griffin has noticed my absence. I start a new text then delete it, not wanting to look desperate.

"Avery?" Mom's voice startles me. "Eisha's asking if you're going to be helping her at all today."

I toss off the covers, emerging from the safety of my hiding place.

"Tell her I'm taking a mental health day."

"She says she really needs you."

"Nobody really needs me."

"OK, now. This is getting ridiculous."

A hand reaches up and pulls back the curtain. Mom's head pokes in.

"Come on. I let you mope in here all morning, and now that's enough."

"Go away," I mumble. "I don't want to talk to you."

"Fine, then I'll come talk to you."

Next thing I know, she's climbing into my bunk, sitting cross legged at the foot of the mattress.

"Really, Mom?" I pull my feet up, trying to scoot away. Out in the real world she's a small-ish person, but here in this tiny space, she seems way bigger. "You drag me out here on this crappy tour, and then you won't even let me have a bed to myself."

"Now that's not fair," she says. "I didn't drag you out here. It was your choice to come."

"What was my other choice?" I lift my hands, looking

left and right in an exaggerated search for non-existent options. "Oh yeah, staying in a tiny apartment with Dad while some nursing student lives in our house. Those choices were really appealing."

"So what else was I supposed to do? Give up a great opportunity?"

"I don't know. Maybe you could have worked at a clinic. Maybe you could have made an actual effort to work things out with Dad. All I know is that everything was fine in Cincinnati. Then it all went to crap."

She rubs her temples, slumping as her expression goes from defensive to weary.

"I took this job because the money was good and it sounded like fun," she says. "But I also thought it would help your dad and me get some perspective on where to go from here."

"And it didn't?" I can barely look at her; what she's trying to say is too painful.

"It did, but not the kind I know you've been hoping for. I did think getting away from all those disappointments at home would help you deal better what whatever we decided."

"Yeah," I mutter. "Remember all that Mom-Daughter time we were supposed to have? That really turned out great."

"Well, whose fault is that? I never see you, and I've tried. You're always with Griffin or Eisha. And then Aaron and I started talking in the sound booth and, frankly, it was nice not feeling lonely for a change. I would have told you sooner, but I was afraid you'd react exactly like you are now."

I can't deny it's my fault we haven't spent time together. I was so busy with my fake Emilio romance and my real Griffin relationship that I didn't leave any space for her. Still, that doesn't mean what she's done is OK. It's like she's giving up instead of fighting for the way things used to be—the way they could be again.

"Maybe bringing you along on the tour wasn't the best idea," she says. "When we get to Columbus, I'll have your dad come and take you home."

And... here we are again. She's nodding to herself, deciding what's best for me, like always. But I'm done being told what to do. What, exactly, is in Cincinnati if I go back? Tagging along after Violet and Hillary like a fifth wheel? Watching my dad deal with the fact that his marriage is falling apart? Going back to being a nobody?

No.

"I'm not going home." I open the curtain and swing my legs over the edge of my bunk. "Eisha wants me to intern with her at Calliope when the tour ends."

"What? Ow!" She straightens, bumping her head on the low ceiling. "In Los Angeles? That's ridiculous. Where will you live? What about school?"

I hop down, liking the look of surprise on her face. Suddenly she's not in control anymore.

"I can stay with Brynn," I say. "And I can finish school online. That's what Griffin is doing."

"Is that what this is all about? You're not moving to Los Angeles for some boy."

"Why not? Unlike you, my relationships mean enough for me to actually try and make them work."

She looks more hurt than I've ever seen before. Part of me wants to take back what I've said; the other wants to let it sink in.

Before I can decide which instinct will win out, someone calls out from the door of our bus. I step over to see who it is, finding an anxious-looking Jack on the stairs.

"Get your mom," he says. "Landon's having an allergic reaction."

29

The next hour is a whirlwind of ambulance lights, people running around, and confusion about tonight's show. The guys all followed Landon to the hospital, so that leaves the rest of us back here, trying to piece together what happened.

For a while, the rumors run wild: That Landon almost died, that he didn't have his epi-pen, that they had to cut a hole in his throat to help him breathe. But then Jack sends Eisha out with an update. It turns out Landon did use his epi-pen. Mom helped him, without the need for cutting of any kind, until they could get to the hospital. He's going to be OK, but tonight's show, and possibly tomorrow's, are canceled.

Since another act is coming in to perform after us, we can't keep the buses at the fairground, so the tour books us into another hotel. I go to our room, then wait for Mom to come back from talking to Calliope headquarters and whatever else a situation like this requires. When she does, she slams her bag to the floor.

"You and I aren't done talking," she informs me. "What

you're thinking about doing, moving to Los Angeles, is serious. Your father and I need to discuss it before you make any more promises to Eisha or anybody else, do you understand?"

The soft spot that had been growing as I thought about her helping Landon hardens as this morning's conversation comes back in all its painful detail.

"How convenient," I say. "I do something you can't control for once, and *then* you decide to be a family again."

"I know this is hard for you, Avery, but it's hard for me, too."

She looks pleadingly at me, and it's the first real emotion I've seen since she and Dad told me they were splitting up. All it does is remind me how different our lives are now.

"Yeah," I answer. "It looked really hard last night when you were sucking face with the sound guy."

She whirls around, heading back toward the door.

"You know what? I'm going to the restaurant to meet *Aaron* for a drink," she tells me. "It's been a rough day, and I don't want to look at you right now."

She walks out, leaving me to stare at the hotel room walls and the TV, which offers my only chance at company now that I am alone again. I still haven't heard from Griffin, and one part of me says I shouldn't expect to since he and the guys might still be with Landon. The other part is getting freaked out by the silent treatment.

The only person to reach out to is Violet, who doesn't respond the first two times I text. The third time, I get **Will call in 20.**

And then, it takes an hour for her to show up on video chat.

"Hey, sorry, tennis went long," she tells me. "Even after I told Coach I had to go."

"Are you alone?" I ask.

"What?" Violet's hair is in a wet ponytail and her face shines with sweat. She takes a swig from a sports drink. "Yes, I'm alone. What kind of question is that?"

I shrug, checking email on my laptop in an effort to look like I don't care as much as I really do. I know I can't continue pretending nothing is wrong; there's so much I haven't told Violet, but my pride doesn't want to let her know I'm upset, not if she's going to turn around and tell Hillary. This summer was supposed to be my chance to do something better. The last thing I need is my biggest rival knowing what a mess things are.

"It's just that stuff is happening over here," I say. "And I can't talk about it with other people constantly around."

She squints into the camera, finally catching on.

"By other people you mean Hillary?"

"Primarily. But it's cool. I'm used to you never being around."

"I have tennis every day," she says. "How is that possibly a problem now?"

It's no good, this attempt at keeping it all inside. I can't unload on my Mom or Griffin, but Violet is right here. Before I can get control of my mouth, I'm letting everything out.

"It's not the tennis that bothers me. It's the fact that half the time when I can't reach you, it's during times when I know you're *not* at tennis. You don't have tennis at 11 o'clock at night, do you? Did you have it on the Fourth of July?"

"No," she answers. "I didn't have tennis on the Fourth of July."

"And yet you didn't call."

"You didn't call me, either."

"That's because I assumed you were with Hillary."

She glares into the screen now.

"You didn't call because you were busy with your guitar player boyfriend—or was it the movie star? You seem to forget I can see all the pictures online."

"And you seem to forget it's not as fabulous as it looks."

"Well, boohoo." She lets out a bitter laugh. "If it sucked so bad, you could have made time to talk to me more. And as for me spending time with Hillary, we've been planning a trip to see *you*."

No. I can't accept that. Because it's obvious to anyone with a brain that Violet isn't just hanging out with Hillary so they can coordinate a carpool to Columbus.

"Planning a road trip doesn't involve going to the mall to buy tights for Hillary's Choraliers costume," I say. "Planning a road trip doesn't require sleepovers and endless runs to Starbucks."

"Oh my God, can you even hear yourself right now?" Violet says. "Do you have any idea how selfish you sound?"

"So I'm selfish because I don't like getting ditched for someone who's been on a personal campaign to steal from me since the 9th grade?"

She grits her teeth. For a moment it looks like she might be close to tears.

"You're not being *ditched*, Avery. Up until two minutes ago, you were being *missed*. Did you ever stop to notice that your ratio of friends to mine has always been off the charts? You have show choir, which comes with a million built-in people to hang out with. Tennis is a lot lonelier. Especially in the summer. I know I told you to go on that stupid tour, but when you left it really sucked. So excuse me for trying to make other friends so I don't have to spend my entire summer alone."

She's definitely about to cry, which is something Violet

rarely does. I've never thought about tennis being lonely before.

"I don't care if you make other friends," I say. "But why does it have to be Hillary of all people?"

"Because she needed someone, too. Choraliers is a lot harder than she thought it would be. We started planning the trip, and it turns out she's nothing like you always made her out to be. She's actually really cool. And to be honest, it seems like you're determined to be pissed at her no matter what she does."

She glares into the webcam, daring me to deny it.

"OK, great," I say. "Well now that you've psychoanalyzed a relationship you know nothing about, can we get back to the fact that *I* could use a friend, too?"

"No," she says. "We can't get back to that, because I'm done. You're mad that I haven't called, but half the time I can't get hold of you, either. And when I do, it's nothing but listening to your problems. I'm sorry I wasn't sitting around waiting to help you deal with your latest drama. And I'm sorry you can't handle the fact that the world doesn't revolve around you."

I pull back, stunned.

"I am well aware that the world doesn't revolve around me. I've done nothing but be reminded of that for the past two months."

"And you're completely unable to deal with it, obviously."

As I'm attempting to summon an appropriately stinging response, an email pops up from Eisha with the subject line *Mandatory Dinner Meeting.* I open it and skim quickly. Eisha wants me to meet her at the hotel restaurant to talk about my newest job, which will involve wrangling media for our new opening act.

Good. No matter how screwed up things are everywhere else, I do still have a job, which is more than my so-called friends can say.

"I can deal just fine," I tell Violet. "In fact, I just got an email that I have to *deal with* right now. It's about work. You know, important stuff, as opposed to Hillary's show choir issues."

Violet sighs, before fixing me with a stare that isn't just cold, it's Arctic-level frozen.

"Fine, go," she says. "I would say I'll see you next week, except now I'm not sure I want to do this road trip anymore."

I pick up my notebook and pen and tuck them into my bag, trying to cover how hurt I am with a façade of professionalism.

"Do whatever you think you need to do. If I see you, I see you."

"Fine," she says. "Whatever. Thanks a lot, Avery."

"No problem."

"Oh, and Avery? I was going to tell you this before you started being a complete and utter bitch: Hunter and Zosia broke up."

30

I sit longer than I should after Violet signs off, trying to sort out what I just heard. Is this why Hunter called this morning? If it was, then why didn't he mention breaking up with Zosia? Do I even care that Hunter is single now that I'm with Griffin?

Am I still with Griffin?

And did Violet really just call me a bitch? So much about that conversation makes me cringe when I play it back in my head. I didn't mean to be hateful, but she didn't have to be so harsh, either. And I have no idea where she got this whole, *Avery can't deal* crap. I can deal just fine.

As soon as I figure out what in the hell I'm dealing with.

My phone rings. It's Eisha.

"Avery?" she barks. "Are you planning on joining us?"

"Yes. Absolutely. I'll be right down."

I wash my face and put on a skirt, blouse and ballet flats. Then I head down to the restaurant, which turns out to be a pseudo-Italian bistro with ultra-dim lighting.

It doesn't take long to spot Mom with Aaron, the sound engineer. I take the long way around her table so she can appreciate how businesslike I am, going to a dinner meeting instead of sulking in my room. I also scan the restaurant for Griffin. He's nowhere to be found, and because of that I feel myself wilt a little. But I can't dwell on drama when I am supposed to be dealing.

Eisha pops her head up from a booth at the other side of the bar. I scurry over and slide in across from a girl with long black hair. I get a good look at her and realize this isn't your standard opening act. This is Serena Sato. She has her own show on Calliope, about a girl who lives a double life as a warrior in a video game. I recognize her because she had a song that was all over TikTok last year, and because Violet used to be obsessed with her Lolita-style dresses.

Today, Serena's in a pair of jeans and a peasant top. She squeals when she sees me.

"Avery Miller!" she cries. "Did you really try to kill Landon Baker with a funnel cake?"

"Excuse me… what? Funnel cake?" I stammer. "What does that even mean?"

Serena laughs. She has an enormous smile and a voice to match.

"There are new pics of you and the True Meaning guys. In about half of them you are holding a funnel cake. In a few of them, you also are standing close to Landon. Everybody knows he has food allergies. People are saying you either gave him some of your cake, or you bumped into him with it and got gluten on him or something. According to the fans, him going to the hospital is all your fault."

Eisha swings into action while I try to hinge my jaw back to my face.

"That's not what happened at all," she tells Serena. "We had an inexcusably irresponsible catering company at our last venue, and Landon took one of their wraps back to his bus to eat later. They'd made it on the same counter as the peanut butter sandwiches, so it was a reaction to nuts, not gluten or eggs or whatever could possibly cause an allergic reaction in a funnel cake."

"Also hello!" I add. "He had the reaction today, not last night. If I'd given him some funnel cake, we'd still be at whatever fair that was because he would have gotten sick then."

Serena nods as she dumps sweetener into her tea.

"For people who spend so much time dissecting photos and things for hidden meanings, the hard-core fans aren't very good at logic sometimes," she says. "I wouldn't worry about it, though. The legit media didn't even mention that it happened."

Eisha deflates at the revelation that not even a medical emergency can drum up press for True Meaning. She only perks up when her salad arrives. A few bites into it she says, "So, Serena? Avery is ready for more responsibility with her internship, and I'd like her to start having a more hands-on role in publicity. Avery? Serena will be with the tour for the next two weeks, and these appearances are important because her new album just came out."

"Oh!" I say. "Congratulations."

Serena smiles, and I can't help noticing her deep brown eyes and the freckles dusting her nose. She is ten times more beautiful in person.

"Avery, Serena has her own publicist to set up press coverage," Eisha continues. "But we are handling the on-site details. It's our job to make sure whoever interviews her sticks to their allotted time. We need to make sure they enter and exit in an orderly fashion. We need to make sure Serena has water and whatever else she needs…"

From across the room, I see Mom looking at me. I sit up straighter, nod, and tell Eisha, "I can do that."

I want Mom to see I'm taking my job seriously. I want her to know I'm not just talking about going to L.A. because of Griffin or because I'm angry with her or because I think the world revolves around me.

Because I don't think that. At all. Right now, my world revolves around making sure Serena Sato gets through her interviews so word gets out about her album and it is successful. Because I absolutely, 100% can deal with whatever needs dealing with.

So there, Violet.

"So, Avery?" Eisha says. "Tomorrow's concert is on as scheduled. We're getting back on the road first thing in the morning for the next stop, which is less than four hours away. Once we're there, you'll meet Serena in the green room. Come see me before that for the final media list and any last-minute details. The first set of interviews start at 2 p.m. and they're scheduled to run until around 4, at which time we'll re-set for the True Meaning meet and greet. Serena's having her own, small meet and greet at the merchandise table out on the concourse, so you'll go with her to handle things there, too. OK?"

"OK," I say. "No problem."

"Great. Cool," says Serena. She grabs the sleeve of a passing waiter. "I think we're ready for entrees now, aren't we?"

"Oh, not me," Eisha says. "But you two can order if you're hungry."

Serena leans across the table.

"What do you want, Avery? I'm sure you're sick of mini-fridge snacks by now."

What I am really dying for is a home-cooked meal—Mom's tuna and noodles or Dad's pot roast. I open the menu and study my options. Serena's right, I am officially out of patience with the health food June insists on keeping in our bus fridge. And, as recent events have proven, the stuff from catering isn't always the freshest. At least here I should be able to get something hot off the grill.

Serena orders pasta. I order the biggest burger they've got.

"Good choice," Serena says when the food comes. "You gotta love a girl who likes red meat."

I dig in, trying to drown out the day, but all I can hear in my head is Violet telling me she's lonely, Violet telling me I'm wrong about Hillary, Violet calling me a bitch. Underneath all that is a little voice saying she's right. I've been obsessing over my own problems, not thinking about anybody else. And now, I guess I'm getting what I deserve.

I used to worry about being invisible. Turns out being alone is a hundred times worse.

31

We roll into our next venue around noon, and I head to lunch so I'll have plenty of time to get ready for Serena's interviews. On my way to our unofficial green room slash media spot, I run into her chatting with a couple of guys from the crew. Most opening acts don't socialize with the rest of the tour—either they're not in the same league as True Meaning and feel more comfortable keeping to themselves, or they're like Cam Christian with a massive superiority complex. I assumed Serena would be the latter.

Apparently not.

"Did you sleep well?" she asks me while the crew guys go back to work.

"Yes," I tell her. "Thank God for beds that don't move."

I don't mention that my mom is still mad at me, which made last evening and this morning pretty painful. Mom banged around the bus, talking to June and Claire like I wasn't there. By the time we got here, everybody was tiptoeing around like I was some kind of rabid dog.

"Living on a bus is harder than people think," Serena

sympathizes. "The first time I went on tour, I barfed every night for a week."

"Been there, done that," I say.

Someone goes by with a cooler full of water bottles. Just as I'm grabbing one, Griffin comes up the backstage ramp with Hank and Josh.

"Hello! Cute boys ahead!" Serena nudges my shoulder. "I know *they* aren't True Meaning."

"They're the back-up band."

Seeing Griffin with his hair spiked up and that scar above his eye zings me extra hard. We haven't spoken in two whole days, and everything inside me is vibrating with yearning. I want to tell him it's OK if he takes the Ariana Grande tour, that I'm sorry for staying out too late with Emilio. I want to tell him about Mom and Dad, about the fight with Violet, and I want to talk about the internship with Calliope. If I could figure out some way to get my parents to let me take it, Griffin might be on the road 80 percent of the year, but 20 percent together is more than I would ever see him if I lived in Cincinnati.

That, of course, assumes he still wants to be together.

I know this isn't the place to hash out our relationship, but at least now that we're in the same spot, he'll have to acknowledge me.

Hank and Josh say hi. Griffin mumbles something, his eyes glued to the ground.

"Come in the green room with us," Serena tells them. "There's this fabulous 70s leather couch in there I'm dying to try out."

And so, I find myself in a tiny room on a plastic folding chair while Serena, Yukon and Hank pile onto a mustard yellow couch that must have been sitting in this exact same spot for the past 50 years.

Griffin sits on the coffee table. He looks up, just for a second.

"Hey, Avery," he says.

"Hey." I strip the label from my water bottle, trying to hide how triggered I am that he's still so closed off. Finally, Hank starts a conversation.

"So, Serena," he says. "Where's your band?"

"I don't have a band, I have a DJ," she answers. "He's around here somewhere."

"I think I saw him," says Josh. "Grouchy-looking Euro-hipster?"

"That would be Christophe," Serena laughs. "My stuff isn't exactly his style, let's put it that way. But the label didn't want to pay for live musicians, so we're stuck together. At least he pretends to be into it when we're onstage."

I check my phone, because it's something I can do to fill the space, and because I'm desperate for an excuse to get out of here.

"We should probably go," I tell Serena. "Your interviews are starting soon."

"Oh," she says. "Right. My favorite part of the day."

As the guys get up to leave, Griffin manages little more than a grunt of a goodbye. I say, "Mmhmm," which allows me to keep my lips clamped shut, saving me from a) unloading on him and b) crying.

As soon as they're gone, Serena turns to me.

"What's going on between you and the guy with the little scar right here?" she asks, waving a hand at her eyelid.

I shuffle the papers I'm carrying, playing it cool.

"Nothing's going on. At least not anymore. I think."

"Hmm..." She purses her lips. "Why does it seem like there's a story here I need to know?"

"I can tell you about it, but later. In 10 minutes, you've

got a meeting with Karen from the North Hills News-Record."

"So come to my bus after the show tonight," she says. "You can give me the details then."

"You really want to hear about it?"

She pulls a mirror out of her bag, applies a light shade of lip gloss, loosens her ponytail, shakes out her hair, and she's camera ready.

"I've done nothing for the past two months but promote this album," she says. "And now I'm here for the next two weeks. My best friends so far are my bus driver and my publicist, who I only ever see on Zoom. I could use some real-life girl talk, and it looks like you could, too."

By the time Serena's interviews are over, I feel almost as exhausted as she must. She still has to do a show, but I am ready for some down time—until Eisha catches me playing games on my phone.

"Don't you want to watch Serena?" she asks.

Before I can protest, she's getting me a seat. And that's how I end up sandwiched between an arguing couple with three kids and a group of college girls who, from the smell of things, have been overserved at the beer pavilion. I'm steeling myself to try and hear over their drunken chatter when Serena struts onstage and everyone goes quiet.

Unlike most opening acts, Serena commands attention. In her black and purple crinolined skirt, corset top, and boots, she looks like an anime badass. And her voice! Big and bluesy with just the right amount of pop polish—Serena Sato draws people to her. I'm no exception, but for me, the attraction is bittersweet. Because watching her up there, I realize: Everything this amazingly talented girl is doing is everything I miss.

I don't miss having my picture taken by strangers, I don't miss having my name plastered all over the Internet as someone's girlfriend. What I miss is performing. Connecting with an audience. Riding a buzz earned entirely through my own efforts.

When Serena leaves the stage, I leave the stands, unable to stomach the idea of watching Griffin perform. I'm not sure I can hang out with Serena, either; my feelings are too raw.

Except my only other option is hanging out in my bunk, hiding from Mom.

Serena's buses are parked at the edge of the caravan. She has two, one just for her and the second for her small crew, which includes Christophe the cranky DJ. They aren't hard to find, since, unlike True Meaning's bus, Serena's has her face plastered on both sides.

The driver lets me into a kitchenette similar to the one on our bus, except on Serena's, the sleeping area is in back.

"Avery?" she comes to the door wearing yoga pants and a powder blue tank top. She's taken off her makeup and looks ready for bed.

"I'm sorry if it's too late," I say. "I can go and just see you tomorrow."

"No, stay! I was getting ready to make lattes." She pats an espresso machine on the counter. "My mom gave me this for good luck and now I make better fancy coffee drinks than Starbucks. We'll split a shot so there's less caffeine."

She's so excited that I feel like it would be rude to turn her down. I watch while she brews the espresso, steams the milk, and creates two lattes that really do look and smell better than any coffee shop's.

"Some days I think I'd be happiest being a barista," she says as she hands me a mug. "Nothing to do all day but just get peoples' drinks right sounds heavenly."

"I'd rather do what you're doing," I tell her. "Singing for thousands of people every night looks amazing."

"So have Jack put you on." She says this like it's the simplest thing as she sprinkles cinnamon into her cup. "I saw those videos of you from a few weeks ago. You have a good voice. Tell him you want to warm up the crowds in the VIP line or something."

"I'd love that, but the last thing Jack wants is me anywhere near the stage."

"He does keep things pretty tight, doesn't he?"

She invites me to take a seat on one of the couches in her lounge, then sits across from me in a leather swivel chair.

"This is nice," I say. "It must be great not having to share your bus with anybody else."

She tilts her head as she takes a sip of latte.

"You don't like traveling with your mom?"

I use my free hand to try and wave the topic away. "That's something else you probably don't want to hear about."

"I do, actually," she says. "But first I want to hear about Griffin the guitar player. I met him alone backstage tonight. What a sweetheart."

I cringe over my coffee cup.

"He didn't say anything about me, did he?"

"No, and I didn't ask because I was planning on asking you. What's wrong there?"

The fact that she is sitting right in front of me, not on a screen chatting from hundreds of miles away unlocks the floodgate. I tell her the story in all its awful messiness, including the fake romance with Emilio.

That part makes her roll her eyes.

"I hate it when publicity does crap like that," she says. "A few months ago, I got asked if I wanted to pair up with Cam Christian."

"Oh my God you are so glad you didn't." I laugh, allowing myself to relax. She laughs too, and it's clear Cam's reputation has reached far beyond the bubble of our tour.

When Serena's done laughing, she gets serious.

"So... What are you going to do about Griffin?"

"I don't know." I tuck my hair behind my ears and stare up at the ceiling. "I know about dancing on risers and smiling huge while singing four-part harmony in show choir. Dealing with a guy who can't stop moving around is definitely not my area of expertise."

"Well, professional musicians are *my* area of expertise," she tells me. "And if he's a touring guitarist—a touring *anything*—then moving around is sort of all he knows."

But it's more than that. I'm positive it is. These past couple of days, thinking back on everything Griffin and I have shared this summer, I've realized that his constant touring isn't just about his career. He's running from his past, from a family that let him down. When the real world got too hard to bear, he escaped to a world of bouncing from city to city and concerts every night. The distance between us might be painful, but it's given me perspective.

Now, he's running from me.

"It's not like I'm expecting to get married," I tell Serena. "I just want to know we're not going to be over when the tour ends."

She folds her legs under herself and gives me a hard look. "Did he say he wanted it to be over?"

"He hasn't said anything to me at all in three days."

"So why even bother? If you guys can't work things out, then what is there to even end?"

I search inside myself for a way to describe how Griffin makes me feel. And I keep coming back to singing—the two of us after a concert, my voice and his, real and raw, with nothing underneath but the sound of his old acoustic.

"He writes beautiful songs," I say. "And he knows my real voice. Before any of the other stuff that's come between us, there was just me, Griffin and music."

"Have you tried talking with him?"

"I've sent texts."

Serena flashes a *come on* look.

"Why don't you talk to him in person?"

"Because the last time I talked in person with a guy about the future of our relationship, he told me I should leave town and then asked another girl to Prom behind my back."

My phone vibrates. It's Mom. The buses are ready to move, and she wants to know where I am.

"Tell her you're spending the night with me," Serena says.

The phone rings seconds after I text back.

"Where are you really?" Mom demands. "Are you on Griffin's bus?"

Serena grabs the phone before I can respond.

"Mrs. Miller? Avery really is here on my bus. We're having lattes and I have an extra bed. I asked her to sleep over, is that OK? It is? Great. Awesome. Thank you!"

She hands the phone back to me with a triumphant grin.

"OK," she says. "So we've got boyfriend silent treatment

and not-in-a-good-place with Mom… is there anything else? Because something tells me that isn't all of it."

I sink back into the couch, deflated.

"I'm also in a fight with my best friend at home. God, I must seem like a complete loser to you."

She lets out a low whistle at the sheer amount of drama. But then she says, "You're not a loser. You're lucky."

This causes me to almost spit latte all over the bus's white carpet.

"Excuse me?"

"You have a best friend to fight with. You have a *back home*. I never went to a regular school. My mom's my manager, which means I basically pay her salary, so you can imagine how awkward that makes our relationship sometimes. I have people watching to make sure I do what they need me to do and people watching, hoping I'll screw up. But what I don't have is someone who just wants me to be safe and happy, you know?"

What she's describing does sound less-than-great. I understand what she's telling me—I do. And yet…

"But isn't it worth all that to be able to get onstage every night?" I ask. "I only sang out there once, and now all I can think about is doing it again. Don't you love it?"

Her phone chimes. She checks it, quickly responds, then says, "I think I loved it when I was little. I definitely liked the attention, and I enjoy the music, which sometimes feels like the smallest part of this job. I don't know. The more I do this, the more I wonder if it's what I really want, especially if it looks like I'm not ever going to go any farther than this."

"Emilio got *Dead at Dusk*," I say. "Something like that could happen to you."

"Or it could not. And if it did, what happens then? More

taking care of other people? More being tired and lonely all the time?"

"What would happen if you quit?"

She takes our empty mugs to the kitchenette and gazes out the tinted window over the sink.

"Honestly, I don't know," she says. "I wouldn't know how to act at school if I tried going to college. I'm pretty sure I'd constantly be worried about becoming one of those *whatever happened to?* former child stars. Ugh, now I'm the one who sounds like a loser."

"This?" I gesture around her bus. "This is definitely not what anyone would even remotely call being a loser. And I'm sure you'd be great at whatever you wanted to do next."

Her smile says she appreciates the encouragement, even if she doesn't exactly believe it.

"What's the name of the friend you're fighting with?" she asks.

"Violet. And Hillary. They're both my friends, I just haven't been treating them like it." The bus starts to move. I look out the window, wondering what the two of them are doing tonight. "We're headed to Ohio in four days. That's where I'm from. They were supposed to come see me, but after the way I acted, I'm not sure if they still are."

Serena gets up and goes into the back room. She returns with a tee shirt and shorts, which she hands me to sleep in.

"I'm not an expert," she says, "but it seems like real friendships can stand it if somebody's a jerk sometimes— especially if that person is really sorry. Violet and Hillary... if they're really your friends, then they'll come."

32

I drift awake on Serena's bus feeling peaceful and refreshed. No June demanding to get into the bathroom. No Eisha dictating what she needs for the day. Just the quiet sound of the road whooshing underneath us. Serena is asleep in the bunk across from me, so I get up and pad into the lounge, where I watch the scenery go by and think.

I remember how Hillary flew to my side the first day of Pops Choir Freshman year, hell-bent on standing next to me. I thought it was because she was being competitive, but maybe she was just as scared as I was. When Hillary started getting solos and praise from Ms. Zebari, I saw her attempts to downplay it as humblebragging. Maybe she really was trying to save my feelings. I used to think Hillary wanted to be friends because it gave her someone to feel superior to. Maybe it was me who decided to feel inferior.

And then there was Violet, looking in from the outside. With tennis, it's just her and her coach a lot of the time. Not like show choir, where I'm surrounded by people who might sometimes drive me nuts but who, at the end of the day, are always there for me.

I pull out my phone and send Violet a photo of Serena from last night's concert.

Check out who's on the tour right now. Thought you'd like her dress. Sorry for being a jerk. Tell Hillary I'm sorry too

Serena walks in as I'm hitting send. She takes two bottles of orange juice from her fridge, hands over one, then sits next to me. We check our phones until the bus pulls into the parking lot of the next venue. She pops out of the room to change clothes, but I stay in the tee shirt she loaned me for bed. When we've made our final stop, I'll sneak back to my own bus to clean up.

Serena's just returning when a knock sounds on the door.

"I'll get that!" she says, flying down the steps. I hear her saying, "You're a life saver. Can you carry it up to the lounge?"

And then Griffin appears, toting a guitar case.

He freezes when he sees me, sleepy eyes going wide. I can see a crease along the side of his cheek left by his pillow, and it fills me with an almost overwhelming urge to hug him.

"Avery." His expression matches the shock that I'm sure is written all over my face. He holds up the guitar. "Hank told me Serena wanted to borrow this for practice. I didn't know you were here."

I wait for Serena to pop back up behind him, but it doesn't happen. Griffin and I rush to the window, and there she is with Hank, walking away toward the grandstand. I crack the window as far as I can, press my face against the screen and shout, "Hey! Where are you going?"

They both look over their shoulders and grin.

"Don't mind us," Serena calls. "We'll be back in an hour or so!"

I flop onto Serena's couch, my face and neck on fire. Apparently, sometime between last night and this morning, she and Hank hatched a plot to get Griffin and me together. Nice. She couldn't at least have let me brush my teeth and borrow some deodorant first?

Griffin looks at me. I look at him. When our eyes meet, I get zapped by that old electricity but look away, in case I'm the only one who still feels it.

"Did you get my texts?" I ask.

"Yes," he says. "And I'm sorry I was such an ass."

"You weren't! I should have come back early like I promised I would." The whole sentence comes out like one connected word, I'm so relieved we're talking again.

He runs a hand through his hair, which looks about as sleep-matted as mine must.

"But I was still an ass," he says. "Leaving you outside the bus like that and turning off my phone. Especially after you brought me funnel cake."

"It was a peace offering."

"I know. And unlike the fans online, I know you didn't use it to send Landon into anaphylactic shock."

I can chuckle now that some time and distance have passed between that night and this morning.

"Remember how we said funnel cakes should only be eaten once a year? Well, now we know what happens when you break that rule."

"It's the funnel cake curse," he says. "Maybe we should stay away from each other until we're certain it's run its course."

I reach for his free hand, desperate for an end to this fear that what we had was too weak to survive our first fight.

"I don't want to stay away," I tell him. It doesn't matter anymore that I'm wearing borrowed clothes and haven't shaved my legs in days; I'm just glad to be with Griffin again. "I miss you."

He puts the guitar case down and sits beside me, filling my senses with his familiar sleepy smell. It almost makes me dizzy.

"I miss you, too," he says. "I've been a wreck. I wouldn't be surprised if Hank teamed up with Serena just to get me to quit moping around the bus."

"If you were that miserable, then why didn't you answer when I was trying to reach you?"

He lets his head fall back, frowning.

"I've met a lot of people I care about on tours," he says. "People I've stayed friends with—people I even miss. But you're the only one who, if I let you in too much and then lost you, it could really mess me up. I guess I thought it would be easier if I stayed away."

"And was it?"

"No, it was worse."

"But maybe it doesn't have to be." I take his other hand, trying to pour hope into both of us at once. "This internship with Eisha—at least I'd be in L.A. all the time, versus in Ohio, where you'd probably just be stopping for one night. I haven't figured out all the details obviously, and my Mom's probably going to try and shoot the whole thing down. But if I did go to L.A...."

He sits forward, the spark I've lit catching fire in his eyes.

"Then we could see each other between tours," he says. "And if I do another one for Calliope, you could come."

"That's what I'm hoping." Now that we're talking, the whole thing seems more real. I would be doing something I'm good at, something I enjoy. And I'd be with Griffin.

It's more than just an idea now, it's becoming a plan.

I excuse myself to duck into Serena's bathroom and smear toothpaste on my teeth, then climb into Griffin's lap so I can kiss him properly. He responds by reaching into my shirt, running his calloused fingertips across the skin on my back. He smiles when he feels me shiver.

"I couldn't have gone without this much longer," he tells me. "Even if Serena hadn't gotten involved."

"Thank goodness she did," I say into the spot just behind his ear—the place I've come to know always leads to the next level. "I was starting to wonder if I was going to have to stand outside your bus with Karsten's massive boom box. And I wasn't sure how that was going to go because I doubt it has batteries, or even that it still works."

"It doesn't work," he says. "It's just a prop."

Then he rolls me under him, and I'm so happy I feel like crying. We kiss until Serena returns and it's time for us all to get moving to our various jobs, and I've never been more grateful for a normal day on tour now that it looks like those days might not have to end.

33

I am home! Or at least, I am an hour and a half away and in the same state. Yesterday's concert was in Indianapolis, and as we drove toward the city, the scenery started to look familiar. When I stepped off the bus in Columbus this morning, it was odd and comforting at the same time knowing I wouldn't have to wander far to find something I recognized, like a United Dairy Farmers instead of the Quick Trips and Git & Go's in other states.

And just down the highway is Cincinnati, right where I left it.

I'd be able to enjoy this better, though, if Violet would say more than two words at a time. She responded to my apology from Serena's bus with a terse **OK Thanks**. And when I tried ever-so-gently to ask whether she was still planning on coming to Columbus, I got, **Maybe**.

Instead, it's Hunter who's keeping me updated.

We're on the way! he texts as I'm helping Griffin with his online English course. He follows that up with a selfie in front of his mom's van. *Avery or Bust* is written on the windows in soap.

"Who's that?" Griffin leans over, trying to get a look at my screen. I switch it off so he won't see Hunter's name. There's no reason Hunter shouldn't be coming, of course. But still. In all of the lead-up to today, I hadn't yet processed the fact that my current boyfriend and my ex-boyfriend will very soon be in the same space. Right now, that's anxiety I don't need.

"It's just my friends," I say. "They're about to get on the road."

Griffin looks excited. "So I finally get to meet them?"

"Ye-e-esss," I croak as additional problems start popping up in my mind. Not only am I facing potential Hunter/Griffin awkwardness, but there's the fact that everybody who's coming still thinks I'm with Emilio. As if to put a cherry on the sundae of my deception, just this morning Eisha showed me paparazzi shots of Celia Nicholas doing lines of coke at some Hollywood club.

"Normally the press would be mentioning Emilio in their coverage, but so far his name hasn't come up once," she said. "Thank goodness we have our Avery to spin things in a different direction."

Because of all this, introducing my friends to Griffin would only invite questions I won't be able to answer. I'm playing a real-life game of Jenga, every piece I move threatening to topple the other pieces if I don't keep them balanced just-so.

My best bet is to throw myself on the mercy of the clock. If everything works out, then Griffin will be doing pre-show stuff when everyone arrives, and it won't be possible for any of them to have any meaningful interaction.

"I don't know if you'll see us that much," I tell him. "You might be at sound check."

"I can find you after," he says. "I can't not meet your best friend."

"I'm not even 100 percent sure Violet's coming. I'm pretty sure she's still mad at me."

"If she's a real friend, she'll come."

"That's what Serena said."

"Serena is wise."

Griffin finishes the essay he's been working on, then opens the next one. He's trying to finish this course in the next couple of weeks so he can spend more of his downtime before the Ariana Grande tour with me instead of on schoolwork.

While I'm helping him, my phone buzzes again. It's Hunter.

We have surprises!

Great! I text back, even though I'm not sure I can handle any new developments. Right now, the rules I need to follow are simple: Keep things moving along, and keep everything that needs to stay secret secret.

WHEN I FINALLY GET A TEXT THAT my friends are within city limits, I walk Griffin back to his bus, then go wait in the parking lot. Sitting on one of the concrete barriers, I tilt my face toward the sky, letting the sun kiss my skin and calm my nerves.

From somewhere in the distance, I hear a car honking rhythmically. Hunter's mom's van rounds the corner, the windows emblazoned with my name. The van pulls up, the doors open, and people start jumping out.

Hillary launches herself at me, sweeping me up in a bear hug.

"Oh my God I missed you," she squeals.

I hug her back, feeling undeserving of such a greeting.

"I missed you too," I tell her. "Thanks for putting all this together."

Hillary lets me go and I turn to see who else is here. There's Hillary's girlfriend Mimi, plus three other show choir kids and Hunter, of course, sporting his baseball cap and that chipped-tooth smile. Violet emerges behind him. She's wearing the True Meaning tour shirt I sent her, the one that sold out after the first four shows, and an expression I can't decipher.

"Hillary doesn't know what you said about her," she whispers when it's her turn for a hug. "She's super excited, so I'm putting you on notice to be nice."

"I will," I say. "I mean it, Violet, I'm really sorry."

"Then prove it and be cool."

She gives me an extra hard squeeze, then passes me on to the next person. I'm still giving out hugs when a second car pulls up and more of my friends spill out.

Dad steps out of the driver's seat.

"Daddy!" I run to him and leap into his arms. "Nobody told me you were coming."

"A few of these guys wanted to spill the beans," he laughs. "But we figured it'd be more fun to keep it a secret."

"I told you we had surprises," says Hunter.

I am beyond happy to see Dad, and he is obviously thrilled to see me, so I feel bad about the small part of me that wishes he'd stayed home. Because now there's an even bigger potential for awkwardness. I'd planned to have everyone tour my bus until the band went to sound check, which Jack has arranged for us to watch. We were going to get together with the guys afterward for a very quick, very controlled meet and greet. The idea was less time for people to ogle me and Emilio, and less time for Hunter and Griffin to be in close proximity.

But now, if we tour the bus, it will put Mom and Dad together. Does he know she's been cheating? Did she know he was coming? It would be the first time in months that they've been around each other.

"So, Avery," Hillary says. "Are we going to meet Emilio? I still can't believe you're going out with the guy who plays Noah!"

I make a split-second decision: Avoiding an awkward fake-boyfriend encounter trumps avoiding an awkward run-in between Mom and Dad.

"Emilio's busy with the band right now," I explain as I lead everyone to my bus. "Why don't I show you where I live?"

Just like I feared, Mom's in the kitchenette when we arrive. I'm not sure how to set her up for Dad's appearance, so I settle for, "Look who came to see me!"

She smiles as, one by one, my friends file up the stairs. The smile wobbles when she sees Dad. He offers a tentative "Hello." She stands, almost spilling her iced tea. He reaches over our heads, attempting a hug, but with so many people in such a small space, all they can manage is an air kiss before Mom springs into hostess mode.

"Who wants to see our home sweet home?" she says.

I let her lead the tour, showing off our bunks and then taking everybody back to the lounge.

"It's bigger than it looks from the outside," Hillary observes.

"That's because our other bus mates aren't around," I tell her. "If June and Claire were here, the tour manager would probably have to bring in the jaws of life to get us all back out again."

"Well before anybody else shows up," says Hillary, "we have something we need to tell you."

Everyone goes quiet. Violet steps to the front of the group.

"So. We have news. Believe me, Avery, it was really hard not telling you this on the phone, but we thought it would be better if you heard it in person."

"Lauren Asher is moving," Hillary blurts out.

"Her dad's work is sending him to Italy," Violet adds. "And of course she's not going to turn down a chance to go along."

"That means there's an opening for an alto," Hillary continues. "We told Ms. Z we thought you deserved the spot. She said you were the first runner up at auditions anyway, so you were next in line. You're going to be in Choraliers!"

I gasp. "No way are you serious?"

"Yes!" Everybody screams at once, then they're throwing their arms around me, and for a good long minute we all jump, scream and celebrate.

"We asked if we could tell you first since we were already coming to see you," Hillary says. "Ms. Z is sending an email to make it official."

I untangle myself and take a step backward, trying to gather my thoughts.

"Wow, Avery," says Mom. "It's what you've always wanted!"

"I know," I say, still trying to process the news. "Wow."

My dream of joining Choraliers as a junior is coming true after all. So why am I not happier? Six weeks ago, I would have been strapping on my character shoes, ready to start the new school year in glee club paradise. But that was before Griffin. Before I knew there was a possibility of going to L.A.

I'd buried my old high school dream. I was making other plans.

The bus is starting to get claustrophobic with so many people in such a small space. Plus it's time for sound check. As we're filing out of the lounge, I look back to see Mom and Dad on the couch, deep in conversation.

"I'll catch up with you guys later," Dad tells me, while Mom gives one of the first real smiles I've seen from her in days. "Don't worry about us, we'll be fine."

34

True Meaning's not on stage yet, so we shuffle into the empty grandstand to wait. I look for Violet and find her a few rows away with her arms crossed over her limited-edition tee-shirt.

I climb over the backs of seats, landing ungracefully in the one next to her.

"Hey," I say.

"Hey," she answers.

She's still so closed off, and now that we're alone I have to take a minute to figure out what to say.

"I'm really sorry," I start. "For everything. I was wrong, and I don't blame you for being pissed at me."

She keeps her eyes on the stage, the muscles in her jaw twitching.

"I was serious about not coming today," she says. "I wasn't going to, but Hillary insisted because she wanted to be here for you. You were really awful about her, Avery."

"I know." I rest my feet on the seatback in front of me, wrapping my arms around my knees. "Remember when we were freshmen and I got into Pops Choir? At first, we were both excited, and then, when rehearsals started you were in a bad mood—for months, it felt like. I didn't even think to ask you what was really wrong, and now I know. I was always off doing choir stuff, and you were left behind. When tennis started it got better, but still—you were lonely and that's my fault."

She pulls in a deep breath, and I realize she's been clenching her jaw to keep her lip from trembling.

"When you and Hillary are off in Choraliers, I'll probably be right back there again."

"No!" I've been trying to respect the distance between us, but it's impossible now that I know how she really feels. I put my arms around her even as she stiffens. "I'll make sure that doesn't happen. Hillary and me, *we* will make sure. And if you ever do feel like that again, just say something, OK? This time will be different."

"OK," she says. I feel her starting to relax.

"I mean it, Violet. You're my best friend."

"OK, fine," she says again. Then she leans over and bumps me with an elbow. "You have to admit that was a pretty epic surprise, you getting into Choraliers. Are you happy now? You're finally getting what you wanted."

I try to smile, but now it's my lip that's wobbling.

"You *are* happy, aren't you?" Violet says.

Thank goodness for the guys walking onstage at this very moment, saving me from having to answer something I don't have an answer for yet.

Griffin comes out first in his black tee and spiky hair. People applaud politely for the band and the rest of True Meaning. It's not until Emilio appears that everyone, Hillary especially, loses their minds.

Normally sound check is just snippets of different numbers, but for us the guys perform a couple of full songs.

It's been a while since I've seen them from the audience, and I'm reminded all over again what great performers they are. I can tell my friends are starting to appreciate just how cool this summer tour has been. But I can't focus on any of that right now.

All I can think of is Griffin, totally unaware of the news I just received. The last thing he knew, we had a plan for how to be together when the tour ends. Now, the plan might be changing.

Serena joins the group after their third song, and now it's Violet's turn to go crazy. Afterward, they all come to the edge of the stage to chat. Chase, Karsten, Emilio and Landon are their usual selves, telling gross jokes one minute, polite the next. Serena talks about the evening the two of us spent drinking lattes on her bus, and she gives Violet the contact for the designer who creates her dresses.

Griffin, hanging out in the back with the band, catches my eye and flashes a private smile that almost breaks my heart. Luckily my friends don't notice. They're busy watching Emilio and me for a spark of romance.

Hillary leans over and whispers, "What are you and Emilio going to do when all this is over? Will you get to go to the *Dead and Dusk* shoot?"

"I don't know," I say. "We'll have to figure something out."

This answer seems to satisfy Hillary, but it only adds to my anxiety, because the guy I actually need to be figuring things out with doesn't know yet that there's anything to figure out. It looks like it'll be hours still before Griffin and I will be able to talk about it.

And when we do talk? I have no idea what I'm going to say. Because if I go back to Cincinnati for Choraliers, then the end of my boy band summer might just be the end of us.

35

"That was amazing!!" Violet shrieks as we file out of our Jack-provided front-row seats. The concert just ended, and confetti is still flying. We've got it in our hair, our mouths—I can even feel it down the front of my tank top.

"Oh my God, they were incredible," Hillary says. "I cannot believe we got onstage!"

During the slow part of the show, instead of pulling one girl up like usual, the guys invited every girl in our group to join them. There were too many of us to each get paired with a True Meaning member, so the band got in on the fun, too. Hank took Violet. Yukon took Essence McHenry.

Griffin, of course, took me.

We stood together, in front of more than a thousand people, doing our best to look like strangers, even as he leaned in to murmur, "Your friends are great."

He looked so happy, so in-the-dark, and I couldn't do anything except play along. Even though I knew it was against the rules, I inched in close enough to brush his shoulder with mine.

"I hope you know how much you mean to me," I said, and he responded with a lopsided grin before launching into *Say Anything*. Those opening chords almost undid me. And when it was time to sing along, I just couldn't.

Now, as I lead my friends back through into the post-show bustle, I reach for Violet again, pulling her close.

"I don't want you to go," I tell her.

"I'm not leaving yet," she says. "Hunter promised Skyline, and we are going to honor that, even though I hate the stuff and it might kill me to watch you eat it."

The thought of a meal at my favorite restaurant brings up a million more emotions I thought I'd put in the past: Homesickness, nostalgia, yearning for all things familiar. I'm dying to go with them, but I'm not sure it's possible.

"I don't have a lot of time. The buses are leaving soon."

"Your tour manager said if we're back by 11 it'd be OK," Violet tells me. "There's a Skyline just up the road, and I've already prepped myself not to throw up at the smell. We're going, if only so you can appreciate the gastronomic sacrifices I make on your behalf."

And so, I climb into Hunter's mom's van, sprawling out across peoples' laps because there aren't enough seats. We follow Dad's car until we see the familiar yellow and blue sign with a silhouette of the Cincinnati skyline on it. Inside, the restaurant is full of people our age out on dates and a few families on their way home from the fair. We grab booths and I order my favorite: a three-way with hot sauce. When the steaming plate of spaghetti topped with meaty chili and shredded cheese comes, Violet makes a face.

"Don't be a foodie snob," I tell her. "This is the taste of my childhood."

"That's why you love it," she says. "Where I come from,

chili is red with lots of beans, not brown and runny like something that came out of your..."

"Oh my God, shut up," Hillary moans, putting down her coney. "If you really hate it that much then go wait outside."

"I'm enduring for Avery's sake since I haven't seen her all summer," Violet says. "We need to talk!"

But then, we don't talk—at least not the kind of talking I want to do, about Griffin and L.A. and how conflicted I feel about finally getting into Choraliers. The tone is too light for serious conversation, and it would be weird for the two of us to go off by ourselves since so many are here just to see me. I watch them all, plus the people in the other booths. They're all going home to their own houses and their own beds. Tomorrow they can go to the pool, to a baseball game, to the store or their favorite restaurant, where they can talk face-to-face with their best friend all day if they want.

Right now, I envy them.

Dad washes the last of his meal down with the rest of his root beer, then slides out of his booth.

"As much as I hate to cut this short, I have to be at work in the morning," he says. "And some of these guys have jobs and other stuff tomorrow, too. I'm going to hit the road, Avery, and take a few people with me."

"I'll come say goodbye," I say, and follow him into the parking lot.

He links his arm with mine as we walk to his car.

"Your mom told me things have been rough between the two of you," he says. "She tells me you've been arguing."

I draw a breath against the butterflies in my stomach. "Did she tell you why?"

"Yes."

"So you know she's been seeing somebody else?"

He sighs. "It's not like I didn't expect it. Avey, your mom and I are getting a divorce."

The butterflies erupt into a swarm, causing my heart to knock painfully against my ribcage. I stop in my tracks, words coming out in machine gun rounds of panic.

"I knew it. I knew we shouldn't have left Cincinnati. I knew this whole tour thing was a bad idea! I should have made Mom call you more. *I* should have called more. I got caught up in my own drama and I didn't pay attention, and now..."

"Avery!" Dad grabs my shoulders, stooping to peer into my eyes. "You are not responsible for holding this family together."

"But Mom..."

"I don't want you blaming yourself, and I don't want you blaming her." He gives my shoulders a shake, forcing me to look at him. "We're all trying to find our way here. But there's one thing I want you to understand loud and clear. You are still the most important thing in the world to both of us. Especially your mom. She loves you more than you'll ever know. She worries about you."

"She nags me."

"To you it seems like nagging, but to her it's trying to keep you safe—and even help you be happy, as much as that's possible. Give her a chance, Avery. You two are more alike than you know."

I search his face, looking for an indication he's not really handling the situation as well as he wants me to believe. But all I see is concern. And love. I guess I've known for a while that one or both of my parents would eventually say the D word to me; Mom as much did the other day in my bunk.

That doesn't make it any easier to hear.

"Is it final?" I ask.

"Legally, not yet. But it's decided, and we're both OK with that. My main concern is you. Your mom also tells me you're talking about moving to Los Angeles in the fall. Are you serious about that?"

When I thought about having this conversation, the last place I envisioned it happening was a Skyline Chili parking lot minutes after hearing my parents' marriage is over.

But here we are, ready or not.

"I thought I was serious about L.A.," I say. "But then the Choraliers thing happened. And even if I still wanted to do the internship, I don't think Mom would let me."

We've reached his car, where Mimi, Essence, and Drew Brinkmeyer are comparing concert videos while they wait for Dad. He takes me in his arms.

"If California is something you really want to do, then we'll discuss it," he says. "But we need to make decisions like this as a family. Your mom and I might be divorcing, but when it comes to you, we're still a team. OK?"

"OK." It feels so good to be close to him again. I wrap my arms around his neck and let him lift me off my feet one last time. "I love you, Daddy."

"I love you, too, Avey. And I'm proud of you. It was wonderful seeing you onstage tonight with your friends. I felt like you were back where you belong."

He gets into the car and waves as he pulls out of the parking space. I watch him drive off, already missing him.

When I turn back around, Hunter is standing two feet away.

36

"Oh my God, Hunter!" I feel myself stumbling backward in shock. "You scared the crap out of me!"

He lunges to keep me from falling on my butt.

"I thought you'd want someone to walk you back through the parking lot," he says.

"That's really valiant of you, considering it's maybe 30 steps."

I start back and make it halfway before realizing he's going about half my speed. I slow down and search for a conversation topic to get us from point A to point B, finally settling on a lame, "So... what did you think of the show?"

"It was good," he says. "Better than I was expecting from a group of guys who make music for nine-year-olds."

"They're not actually singing for nine-year-olds," I inform him. "If you asked them, they'd probably say they were going for an older audience."

"That's sort of sad, then. Can you imagine being trapped in a kiddie band no matter how hard you tried to *not* be in one?"

I swallow the urge to be defensive for the guys, reminding myself that Hunter doesn't understand their life like I do.

"Sometimes you have to make trade-offs to do what you love," I say. "Nothing is as easy as it looks from the outside."

We've arrived at his mom's van. He stops and leans against the bumper.

"So did you hear about me and Zosia?"

"Violet told me. What happened?"

He lifts his baseball hat, runs his fingers through his hair, then puts the cap back on—something he always does when he's uneasy.

"Zosia was nice, but—I know this is going to sound weird—she was sort of too nice."

"Oh," I say. Because what else can you say to that? *I'm sorry your girlfriend wasn't more awful to be around?*

"Can I be honest?" he asks.

"Sure," I say.

"I sort of missed all the drama with you."

I raise an eyebrow, considering whether to be offended or not.

"So you're saying I'm *not* nice?"

"That's not what I meant. It's just that you had ideas and actual thoughts and feelings about stuff. When we went out, you knew what movie you wanted to see. You knew where you wanted to eat. If you didn't agree with me about the movie, we'd fight about it over pizza."

"I didn't agree with you very often," I say, smiling.

"Well, Zosia always does. But you... you were kind of restless. That's why I told you to go on this tour. It seemed like the kind of thing you'd be sorry if you didn't do."

He's right. I remember how freaked out I was when Hunter said I should spend my summer on the road instead of with him. But I've had such an incredible time on tour, and not just because of Griffin. I've seen things I never would have seen, done things I never would have done. Looking back, I know Hunter was right.

He moves closer, the sleeve of his tee-shirt brushing my bare arm.

"The problem is that I missed you a lot."

One half of my brain has started to flash a big neon *uh oh*. Another part of me has gone warm and a little mushy. Hunter and I might not be together anymore, but that doesn't erase everything we used to have. It doesn't mean I don't like hearing him say he notices when I'm not around.

It also doesn't mean he can expect me to drop everything and go running back. Two months ago, I would have given anything to hear him say he misses me. Now I see things more objectively.

"Getting away from each other was probably a good thing," I tell him. "You and I weren't getting along, and I can sort of see why now. You have to admit we don't have a lot in common."

"We have everything in common," he says. "We have home. That's where you belong, Avery."

I manage a solitary "But..." before he steps forward and kisses me. And I can't help it—I kiss him back. I do it because he feels familiar and safe. Under the lights of this Skyline Chili parking lot just up the highway from where we both grew up, he is the Hunter I knew before my world got turned upside down, before I went on this crazy cross-country road trip.

But.

All the things I didn't say before his lips met mine are clamoring in my head. I have to be honest; things have changed since Hunter sent me on the tour. *I've* changed.

I push away.

"I can't do this. I'm with someone else now."

"Who, that Emilio guy?" Hunter laughs. "I don't think you're really serious about him. He's such a douchebag, Avery."

Now I *am* offended, because Hunter has no idea what he's talking about.

"Emilio absolutely, 100 percent is *not* a douchebag."

"I'm sorry," Hunter backtracks. "Maybe he's not, but I still can't see why you're with him. Even after meeting him tonight—especially after meeting him tonight, I don't get it. You and this Emilio guy just don't add up."

I feel my cheeks redden as every insecurity I've ever had comes flooding back.

"You really think I couldn't be with someone like him?"

"It's not that I think you couldn't. It's just... You're too real, Avery."

I can tell he's trying to take away the sting, but I hear what he's *not* saying.

"By *real*, you mean *boring*. Right? According to you, I'm not special enough for a celebrity boyfriend."

"That's not what I meant," he insists. "You have an amazing voice. You're smart. You're passionate. You don't need all that other crap. You're special to the people who really matter. Isn't that enough?"

It should be. But Hunter doesn't know the full picture of who that group includes.

"It's more complicated than that," I say.

"It doesn't have to be. You're in Choraliers, just like you always wanted. You could come back to Cincinnati right now. Then we could have the whole rest of the summer together."

In spite of everything, I have to admit the idea of grabbing my stuff, driving two hours down the highway with my friends, and picking up where we left off is tempting. It would almost be like the tour, and everything that went along with it, never really happened—like it was all just a dream.

But it's not a dream, it's real. Griffin is real. I can't just disappear on him like that.

I check the time on my phone; I've got to get back if I'm going to the next tour stop. As if to remind me, Violet and the others start spilling out of the restaurant.

Hunter takes my hands. He looks into my eyes.

"Think about it, OK?" he says.

"I will," I tell him. "But now I have to go."

As we ride back to the fairgrounds, I work hard to hide how I'm feeling. I must be doing a great job because not even Violet senses anything wrong. When we pull in behind the grandstand, the trucks are loaded, the buses idling. I hug everyone one last time and promise her and Hillary I'll text as soon as I'm someplace semi-private.

People hang out the windows, waving as the van rolls out of the parking lot. I watch until they turn a corner, then step onto our bus. Everybody's quiet in their bunks, and a note waits for me on the table in the lounge.

Hope you had fun tonight. I love you. Mom

The bus starts to move as I'm washing my face. I get into my bunk and try to let the sound of the wheels against the road soothe me to sleep. It doesn't work. I can still feel Hunter's lips on mine. I can hear Violet telling me I'm going to be in Choraliers. And I can see Griffin, smiling next to me onstage. I text him, but he doesn't answer. He's probably sleeping. I should be sleeping, too. Instead I'm lying here, awake, trying to figure out what to do.

37

The curtain to my bunk rips open, revealing daylight and Eisha's furious face.

"We have a problem," she says.

She thrusts her phone in front of my nose. A photo fills the screen that, despite being dark and grainy, it is unmistakably me kissing Hunter in the parking lot of Skyline Chili.

My sleeping brain had managed to forget about last night. Now it all comes rushing back.

"Oh no," I moan. "Seriously?"

"My thoughts exactly! What in the hell is this, Avery? What about Emilio?"

I sit up, my stomach lurching with nerves and the 3-way that I now thoroughly regret eating.

"I was with my friends," I tell her. "Hunter and I were talking, and I wasn't thinking—at least I wasn't thinking somebody would be taking my picture..."

Eisha throws her hands up.

"People are always taking your picture!"

"Well, maybe I don't like having my picture taken all the time!"

This shuts her up momentarily, but I know we can't leave it like this. I have to explain.

"I was doing stuff I'd normally do in the summer with people I haven't seen in months. And for once I wasn't thinking about being some pop star's girlfriend."

"Does your normal summer activity include making out with guys in public?"

I glance into the corridor, trying to calculate the quickest route to the bathroom. The bus isn't moving, so the queasiness I'm feeling can't be motion sickness.

A burp escapes. I cover my mouth and clear my throat.

"Look, Eisha, a lot happened yesterday that you know nothing about and probably wouldn't understand anyway. I'm sorry someone got a picture of it, but it's just the fans pulling their usual crap. It'll blow over tomorrow probably."

"Actually, it's gone mainstream." She holds up her phone again to scroll through the headlines. "It's all over the place that you're cheating on Emilio!"

I squint at the screen. These are legit, big-name entertainment sites she's showing me. And I am, indeed, all over them.

Emilio Padilla Cheating Scandal!

Heartbroken Emilio Ditched

Dead at Dusk Star's Relationship Dead in the Water

"But why now?" I croak. "They went weeks without caring what any of us did. Why do they all of a sudden want to make a bunch of drama?"

"Who knows? Maybe it's a slow news cycle. Maybe the moon is in the seventh house. If I could predict this stuff, I'd have my own PR agency. One thing I do know is that

Emilio's manager won't be happy, and neither will Jack if this reflects poorly on the tour in any way."

The curtain to the bunk below mine opens and Mom's head emerges.

"What's going on?" she asks, sleepily.

"I've got a bit of a problem with Avery," Eisha tells her.

"Can I help?" says Mom.

"I'm dealing with it."

Mom's on her feet within seconds. "If there's a problem, it's my call whether it needs dealing with or not."

"Fine," Eisha says. "You should probably know about this anyway."

She hands over her phone. Mom scrolls through, then looks at me.

"Avery, you and Hunter are back together? What about Griffin?"

Oh my God, Griffin! My stomach does a triple back flip as I hop to my feet. I grope for the other bunks to hold myself steady while my gut, my spinning head, and my weak knees sort themselves out. Then I push through, grabbing a pair of shorts on my way to the door.

"Mom, I'll tell you about it later. Eisha, I'm sorry, I'll try to fix this, but right now I need to go!"

I rush off the bus, scanning the parking lot for Griffin's lanky form, his dark hair. It's early so everyone's still waking up and having breakfast. But I do hear the zip of ATVs coming from behind one of the semis. I dash over to find Emilio and Karsten circling each other in a tight figure 8. Emilio sees me, turns off his ATV and walks over.

"Hey, Avery," he says.

I brace myself to get yelled at, but he doesn't look angry, just tired.

"Did you see?" I ask.

"Yeah." He quirks the corner of his mouth in a half-smile. "I gotta say, you caused some heartburn for Gary back in L.A."

I hug myself, rubbing my forearms for warmth. I am suddenly freezing.

"I'm sorry, Emilio. I'm really sorry!"

"Hey, calm down," he says. "It'll be OK."

"How? Everybody's going to hate me. Not the fans—they hate me already. But Jack, the other guys. I've ruined everything."

Emilio goes to the barrier where he's stashed a hoodie. He brings it over and drapes it around my shoulders.

"This whole arrangement was a crap idea to start with. It's not your job to make me look good or help my career. That was too much to ask, and I shouldn't have said yes to it in the first place."

He's being so nice, which almost makes me feel worse.

"How are we going to fix it?" I ask.

"I'm not sure. But I'm probably not the person you should be fixing things with right now anyway."

"I know." I crane my neck to see over Emilio's shoulder. "Do you know where Griffin is?"

Emilio shakes his head.

"Maybe on the band bus? You want me to walk you over there? You don't look so good."

"I'll do it."

The voice belongs to Serena, who has materialized behind me in a sports bra and biker shorts with a home-made espresso in her hands.

"I think I know where he is," she tells me. "I saw him a little bit ago."

I hand Emilio back his sweatshirt, now feeling hotter than hot.

"Thank you, Emilio. And in case I didn't say it enough already, I'm so, so sorry. For everything!"

Serena turns to me as we head toward the stage. "Rough morning, huh?"

"You have no idea," I say. Then I fill her in on everything that's happened, not just with Hunter but with Choraliers, too.

"OK the Hunter-Griffin thing sucks, but the choir thing is good right? That's the group you wanted to be in, and now you are."

"Yes..." I hesitate. "I mean no... It's not that simple. Right now I just need to talk to Griffin."

We've reached the stage, which is still quiet since the crews haven't started setting up for tonight's show. A solitary form sits at the edge. It's Griffin, hunched over his old acoustic.

Serena sets down her espresso cup and gives me a hand as I climb the scaffolding. Once I'm up, I lower myself beside him.

"Griffin."

He doesn't answer, only strums out three angry, staccato chords.

"I know it looks bad, those pictures," I say. "But it didn't mean anything. Hunter is just a friend."

Griffin smacks his hand against the body of the guitar. The sound makes me jump.

"I'm not stupid, Avery. He's your old boyfriend, isn't he? The one you broke up with—or at least that's what you said."

"We did break up," I insist. "And I should have told you he was coming, but I didn't want to make a big deal out of it because I wasn't looking to get back together with him. I'm with you."

"Really? Because it sure doesn't feel like it."

"Griffin..."

"No. This is why I was afraid to get too close. I knew it would screw me up, and I let myself love you anyway."

His words hang between us, the words I've waited so long to hear. It's not the beautiful moment I've dreamed of. Still, I cling to the idea that I can turn this around—make it the moment that will help me decide everything.

Sweat trickles down the back of my neck. Every one of my nerves feels like it's attached to a lighted sparkler. I put my hand on top of his. "I love you, too."

I hold my breath. If those four words bring us closer together and stronger, then I'll go to L.A. I'll stick with the plan. I won't even tell him about making Choraliers.

He lets my hand linger before moving his out from under it.

"I can't do this," he says. "You need to figure out what you want."

"I know what I want."

I reach out and he moves away—a short inch that might as well be a mile.

"I need to be alone right now."

"OK."

I get up and climb back down the scaffolding. As I do, my stomach lurches—a sickening combination of stress and something else that seems determined to claw its way out. I rush for the fence at the edge of the parking lot and heave what's left of last night's dinner into the scrubby grass on the other side.

38

Food poisoning or some kind of flu? Mom is leaning toward the latter given my symptoms, which include a fever and chills. It has to be the flu, because the other explanation—that something might have been off with my beloved Skyline Chili—is just unthinkable. No, this thing that is making me wish I was dead is a stomach virus. But knowing that doesn't make it any less craptastic.

As soon as I can move without puking, I video chat Violet and Hillary. They've been trying to reach me since seeing the photos with Hunter. Explaining that is easier than explaining why I'm not sure I'll be taking the open Choraliers spot.

"I thought you didn't act as happy as you should have when we told you you got in," says Hillary, who by now has been filled in on the whole Secret-Dating-Emilio-Real-Dating-Griffin situation.

"Yeah," Violet agrees. "You're finally getting what you want, and you're maybe going to turn it down?"

I suck on the ice Mom gave me to stay hydrated until I

can keep down juice or soup, and finally realize what's bothering me. The truth is I'm still angry about being the second choice after working my butt off for so many years. And that Ms. Zebari just assumed I'd drop everything once she decided to finally let me in.

"I'd gotten used to the idea of *not* being in Choraliers," I tell my friends. "I was making other plans."

"But are they plans you seriously think you're going to like?" Hillary asks.

I put another piece of ice on my tongue, sucking hard against a fresh wave of nausea.

"Believe it or not, I'm good at marketing, and it would look good to colleges. It's not all for Griffin."

"But you worked your ass off to get into Choraliers," says Hillary. "You've dreamed of this since forever."

"And they didn't want me, even after I did more than probably anybody else to prove I was good enough. Eisha at least appreciates me."

Violet gives me her best *come on* face.

"Eisha appreciates when you make her look good."

"Well now Ms. Z wants me to make *her* look good too and…" I spit the ice out, feeling fed up. "No. You know what? I don't want to think about this right now. Give me a couple of days. Let things calm down with Griffin, and then I'll see how I feel."

Hillary winces.

"What?" I say.

"Have you checked your email?"

"Ugh what now?" I pull over my laptop and find the very first thing in the queue is from Ms. Z.

Dear Avery,

I hope you've had a wonderful summer! By now, Hillary

should have told you about the alto opening in Choraliers. I'm thrilled to offer that place to you. Congratulations!

While we're excited to have you, we do have a lot of work to get you caught up. Because this year's show is especially challenging, I've called a mandatory choreography boot camp, which starts Monday. Regionals take place two weeks after school starts, so we don't have time to lose. Please plan to be at choreography camp at 8 a.m. August 10, and if you provide me the best address to mail you at, I will overnight a packet of music for you to begin learning on your own, immediately.

All my Best,

Jo Anne Zebari

I read the email twice to make sure I didn't misunderstand. Monday is three days from now! That leaves just tonight and tomorrow, with Sunday to travel home in order to make it to choreography camp the next morning. My boy band summer would be over, just like that.

I pick up the phone again to find both Violet and Hillary waiting.

"So I don't have a couple of days. Great. What do I do?"

"Well, I miss you like crazy," Violet says. "So the selfish part of me says you should ditch the tour and come home."

"What does the unselfish part say?"

Violet looks at Hillary, who shrugs.

"There is no unselfish part," Violet says. "I have no idea what the right thing to do is."

"What does your heart tell you to do?" Hillary asks.

"If I knew that, I wouldn't be asking other people for advice. Gah!" I smash a pillow against my face, stifling a howl of frustration.

"Well, what about Hunter?" she presses. "Isn't there a little bit of you that wants him back?"

"Ooh, right," Violet chimes in. "You've been worrying about Griffin, but maybe it's really Hunter you want."

I close my eyes, remembering all the times when I would have given anything to have him back, the way things used to be.

"This would all be easier if I didn't wonder about Hunter," I admit.

"A relationship with him would not be long distance," Hillary reminds me.

"Griffin would still be going on tours," Violet adds. "How are you really going to feel if he's all over the country while you're by yourself in L.A.? You're no good when things are up in the air."

"That used to be true," I tell her. "But nothing this summer ended up like I expected, and I've had an amazing time. Going to L.A. just seemed so much more *important* than show choir. I feel like I could learn a lot at Calliope."

"You'd get to perform if you went there?" Hillary asks.

"Probably not. It's a marketing job."

"So you'd be sending emails and setting up interviews for other people, but you wouldn't get to do any singing."

I'm getting frustrated as the vision I had of myself as Eisha's intern blurs under the weight of these questions.

"It's still something nobody else gets to do."

"That's if Eisha still wants you after all the scandal you made," says Violet.

"And we need you," Hillary adds. "I can't think of anybody else who can learn all the music and choreography and kick butt the way you could. Ms. Z made a mistake not letting you in to start with, but now she needs you. All of us do."

I glance over at Violet, and her expression says it all: *It's not all about you, Avery.* As if to underline that thought, Eisha's voice comes from outside my bunk.

"Avery? If you're feeling better, is there a chance you could help out with a few things?"

I make a mental inventory of my symptoms. The chills have stopped, and a weary ache has settled in my bones. I'm nowhere near *better,* but I'm a lot better than I was.

"Yes, I'm coming," I say, then turn back to my friends. "I have to go. No matter what I decide about Choraliers, life's still going on here."

"Well don't wait too long," says Violet. "You only have a couple of days to get plane tickets and pack..."

"And learn music!" Hillary adds. "I mean, assuming you decide you're coming home."

"No pressure," Violet jumps in. "L.A. sounds good too."

"I get it," I tell them. "I'll keep you posted, just please, whatever you do, do NOT tell Hunter we talked."

Now it's Hillary's turn to flash the *come on* look.

"Please," I repeat. "One guy at a time."

"Avery's right," says Violet. "Hunter needs to chill. I'll tell him that myself. Avery, you just focus on figuring this out. You're running out of time."

"Right. Fine. Thank you, I love you, goodbye."

I sign off, then toss my phone to the foot of my bunk and kick it under the covers. The last thing a girl needs when she's trying to figure out her love life is a deadline.

39

I climb out of bed and go to the kitchenette, where Eisha and Mom sit, each deep in their laptop screens. Before anything else, I pull Mom into the lounge and fill her in on what I've just found out about choreography camp Monday morning. She gets to work looking for flights if I decide to go home.

Back at the front of the bus, I search the mini-fridge for something I might be able to keep down, deciding on a nectarine and some plain white sandwich bread. I settle at the table to peel the fruit and pull off the bread crusts. Through the open window I can hear the pre-show warmup, and I feel every second that passes like the beat of Josh's drums. I'm going to have to talk with Griffin—really talk, sooner rather than later.

And if he won't talk, what then? I could take it as my sign to go back to Cincinnati. Maybe even back to Hunter. But that feels too easy, like I'd be giving up hope for what Griffin and I could be if we just gave it a chance.

Eisha's stopped clacking on her keyboard. I can feel her staring from across the table.

"Do you have to glare at me?" I ask. "I know I screwed up. I don't need the evil eye."

"I'm not giving you the evil eye," she says. "I'm trying to figure out what our plan is going forward."

"Well." I suck on a slice of nectarine. "Damage control is probably objective number one, right? I'm sure you've already started the spin cycle."

"We've released a statement."

"Really?" I pull out my phone to see it.

"We simply said that Emilio wants to concentrate on his career. And while he does believe in love, he's putting it on the backburner for now. Questions about his personal life are a distraction so he's asking for privacy." She looks pleased with herself. "It's simple and elegant without giving too much away."

"I hate it."

"What?" Eisha draws back, shocked. "Why?"

With every bite I'm able to swallow, I feel strength returning, along with a new determination to stand up for myself. I've followed the rules these past couple of months, done a great job with my internship, even let Eisha create a story about me dating someone I'm not.

Now, I'm done.

"Because you gave Emilio an elegant out, but you left me dangling," I say. "Everybody thinks I was cheating on him. How would you like having strangers harassing you and making assumptions when you couldn't stand up for yourself?"

Eisha looks at Mom, who's come into the kitchenette and flashes me a smile of solidarity.

"I didn't realize you'd feel that way, Avery," she says.

"Well, I do."

She folds her hands on top of the table, regrouping.

"I certainly don't want you feeling like you're left alone in all of this. What can we do to help make it better?"

Outside I can hear the opening beats of *Party Girl* and the muffled, but unmistakable, sound of Griffin's guitar. They'll be breaking soon so the guys can get ready for the VIP meet and greet. If I don't take this window, it won't open again until late tonight.

"It's not what you can do," I tell Eisha, "it's what I need to do."

"And what is that?" she asks.

"I have no idea. I'll figure it out by tomorrow night. I promise. Right now there's someone I need to talk with. I know I said I'd help, but can it wait for later?"

"Sure..." I can tell Eisha's confused. Mom, behind her, is only slightly less puzzled, but I don't have time to explain. I shower quickly, throw on a tee-shirt and shorts, and head back to the front of the bus. I stride past our driver, making the sharp turn down the steps, feeling stronger every second.

The door slides open.

Crack!

"Ow!"

Pain shoots from my eye to the back of my head. For a second, I can't see. Then Griffin comes into focus, holding his nose. He's on the bottom step, clearly on his way up at the same time I was coming down. Considering recent events, it doesn't seem right to do the usual *Oh my God are you OK?* routine. So we both stay in our respective corners, nursing our wounds.

"We need to talk," I say through gritted teeth.

"I was going to say the same thing," he answers, checking his nose for blood.

He steps back, letting me out of the bus. When my feet

hit the asphalt, I peer up at a sky that looks about as bruised as my eye might be in an hour. The air has an electric feel that makes the hairs on my arms stand up.

"Do you think there'll be a show tonight?" I ask. "This doesn't look good."

"Jack's watching the radar," Griffin responds. "I heard him say there's a storm coming but it's supposed to blow over."

Ugh, are we really talking about the weather? I tell myself to put on my show face. Get brave. Push past the nerves, and do what has to be done.

Griffin follows as I make my way to the edge of the parking lot and pull back the fencing. Overhead, the sky churns. It's probably not a good idea to be outside at all, but finding privacy on a bus or among the pre-concert bustle would be next to impossible.

So we walk.

Rain starts to spit, dampening our shoulders. Lightning strikes nearby, and the thunder that follows seems to open up the sky. We sprint for an empty pavilion at the edge of the fairgrounds, dodging hail the size of peach pits. Once inside, I climb on top of a picnic table and sit with my knees against my chest. Griffin stands in front of me. When I open my mouth to speak, he holds up his hands.

"Before you say anything, I just want to tell you whatever happened in Columbus doesn't matter. OK? It doesn't matter because you and I have *this*." He sweeps an arm out to encompass the rainy fairground, the buses and trucks, the waiting stage. "All those nights after concerts, the music—especially the music—those are ours. And we still have so many of those nights ahead of us. We don't have to be in a hurry..."

"Griffin..." The tears are coming, but before I can say

more, he leans in and rests his forehead against mine. It's the easiest thing to find his lips and forget what I'm supposed to be doing. If we kiss long enough, we could skip the concert. The trucks would load and the buses would pull away, leaving us here in the middle of nowhere. Who would we be if it was just the two of us, no boy band, no internship, no guitar, no music?

Except those are the things that make us who we are; I wouldn't want to know a Griffin and Avery without them.

Pulling away, I tug the hem of my shirt to my eyes. After a couple of seconds, I give up and let myself cry openly.

"Hey. What's wrong?" Griffin smooths my hair from my cheeks, tilting my chin so he can study my face. "Are you still sick?"

I shake my head.

"Just say it," he says. "You can say anything to me."

I let out a choking sob. "Still?"

"Yes. Of course."

I look into his eyes to see love, concern, and complete cluelessness about the bomb I'm about to drop between us. I know I could simply decide, right now, to turn down the Choraliers. I don't have to tell Griffin anything if nothing is going to change. But it feels wrong to keep this from him. If we really can say anything to each other, then I have to be honest.

"There's an opening in Choraliers," I tell him. "It's mine if I want it."

He looks at me blankly. "What does that mean?"

"It means I can go back to Cincinnati and be in the top show choir, like I always wanted."

His brow furrows, scar disappearing the way it always does when he's confused.

"What about L.A.? You were going to move out there."

"But this has been my dream ever since I can remember. I want to go to L.A. I want to be with you. But they need me. Turning down Choraliers would be a really big deal."

He takes my hands, looks deep into my eyes, and smiles a smile that says *Everything will be OK*.

"Then let me convince you to stay. I love you, Avery. I meant it when I said that. You don't have to decide anything just yet. We've got three weeks left of the tour. I'll make them so good you won't even think about going back to Cincinnati."

I fight to keep focus. This is harder than I ever imagined it would be.

"Except we don't have three weeks. If I go back, then I have to be there Monday morning."

He tilts his head, the realization starting to sink in.

"That's the day after tomorrow."

"I know." I bury my head in his shoulder, tears soaking his already damp shirt. He wraps his arms around me, but I can feel tension in them. I lift my head. "Griffin? Are you OK?"

"Honestly?" he says.

"Of course, honestly."

"Then no, I'm not OK." He lets me go and starts pacing the edge of the pavilion, grey sheets of rain behind him. "If you love me, then why would it even matter when they want you back? Why would you want to go? Is it because *he's* there?"

"No." Something about his question makes the tears stop. "This isn't about Hunter. It's about what I want."

He shakes his head at the ground, still pacing.

"How can they ask you to go back there with basically no notice?"

"We have regional competitions two weeks after school

starts. If I take the spot and then I don't know the routines, it hurts everybody. Would you show up to a gig without knowing your music?"

"Well then it's not fair," he says. "How about that?"

"What's not fair is that you don't see my music on the same level as yours." I get down from the picnic table and face him. Something that's bothered me from the beginning of our relationship is snapping into focus. "Choraliers might not be Ariana Grande, but it's still pretty amazing, and it means a lot to a lot of people."

"You're the one who said you didn't want to do it anymore," he reminds me.

"Maybe I was wrong. I got so caught up in all this..." I spread my arms out to encompass everything around me. "The boy band thing, the whole fake romance with Emilio, working, being on the road..."

"...and me?"

"Yes, even you. These past few weeks have been probably the best of my life, but they've also been a lot. You want to talk about unfair? I've got total strangers talking about me, taking my picture, thinking they know who I am and what I want..."

"I get it. Don't think I don't," Griffin says. "But I mean, you kind of did that to yourself, Avery."

We look at each other, stuck. I want everything to be like it was on the Ferris wheel that first time, with the horizon and the entire summer ahead of us. I want the heat of those nights alone after concerts, the music only Griffin and I could hear, and the feeling of being in that little diorama, moving from place to place yet always with each other. Griffin and I have never truly been in the real world together. But sooner or later the real world was going to barge in. Summers have to end. So do boy band tours. Even if I moved to L.A., things would be different.

"You're right, I did do this," I tell him. "And now I'm going to fix it."

He frowns, his eyes dark and intense.

"What are you saying? What does that mean for us?"

Almost as quickly as it started, the rain stops. There's no sun peeking through, no rainbow, just the same blue-black clouds overhead, only they're no longer dumping water. The way Griffin is looking at me ignites a blaze in the pit of my stomach—fear and uncertainty, but also determination. If we really can say anything to each other, then I need to be honest.

"I don't know yet what it means, and I don't have much time to figure it out. But here's what I do know. Right now, you have a show to get ready for, and I've got a fan to talk with."

40

"Avery. Hi." The girl on my screen smiles, open and friendly. "Thanks for making time. I know you're busy."

"No, thank *you* for doing this on such short notice," I say. "I know you're busy too."

I fidget on the couch in the bus lounge, willing myself to relax. When I told Eisha about my plan to do an interview with In Search of True Meaning, she said it was one of the more trusted TM podcasts. Even Emilio knew about it, so I'm probably in the best hands possible, but still. I'm hellaciously nervous. I told Eisha to trust me, now I have to trust Nora.

Nora waves her hand, like it's no big deal to hop online with just a half-hour's notice. Reaching out to her took a massive leap of faith that she'd be available, that she'd still be interested, that she wouldn't be angry with me like all the rest of the fans seem to be. So far, she's been nothing but friendly, nothing but professional.

"So..." she says as she adjusts the angle of her screen. "Before we start recording the actual podcast, let's set some ground rules. There's a lot of sensitive stuff I could ask, and I'm not going to lie; people are interested in what's been going on these past couple of days. But I respect Emilio, and I respect you. I want to make sure you both know I'm not trying to generate traffic with gossip. Unless you want to talk about that stuff, I'll leave it alone."

Relief floods through me. Nora's not angry. She's not going to dig for dirt or try to force me to go places I can't. Tension starts to ease from my neck and shoulders; I sit back, balancing my laptop on my knees.

"I really appreciate that," I tell her. "I'm not allowed to talk about Emilio, for a lot of reasons, but I guess I did want people to get to know me a little better. The only side that's been presented is the one made up from a couple photos, and I guess that's my fault, at least partly, for not letting the real me out. This whole thing has been a completely new experience."

"But what an experience, right?" Nora says. "You even wrote an essay."

She holds up a print-out of the email I sent along with my confirmation of our video chat. The title *What Not to Do on a Boy Band Tour* looks terrifyingly real now that it's in someone else's hands and not in the black and silver journal Mom gave me at the start of everything.

"It sort of started off as a joke," I say. "I was lonely when I started this internship, and maybe a little bitter about some stuff, just trying to figure it all out and work through my feelings. Then I realized it might actually say something somebody might want to read."

"It definitely does, and thank you for trusting me to publish it," Nora says. "But this part... *Don't look down, look up instead* almost sounds like something *to* do on a boy band tour. Are you sure you don't want to take this back and flip some of these *don'ts* into *do's*?"

She's right. Nearly everything I've figured should *not* be done on a boy band tour has an equivalent thing that has added to who I am today.

"I like turning don'ts into do's," I say. "Thanks for being so smart."

"You're the one with the big ideas. And for the record, I especially like this part: *Don't expect people to get it.* I can relate. Not many people understand what being a fan is all about."

"I know I didn't." I hesitate, chewing an already ragged fingernail. "Sorry if this sounds insensitive, but you spend so much time and energy on True Meaning, coming to all the concerts, podcasting about them every week, and some of the people I've met have been... let's just say intense."

"To put it mildly." Nora smiles.

"Right! So when you say you appreciate that I understand, I have to be honest and say that sometimes I still don't. Why do you give this much to just one thing?"

"Developing this podcast has taught me stuff a lot of people go to college to learn," Nora answers. "I've met some of my best friends through TM fandom. Plus, I just love the guys and their music."

"That's obvious," I say, laughing.

"There's no shame in being passionate about something," she says. "What are you passionate about?"

Now I have to think. Right now, the answer to her question is Griffin. But that can't be everything.

"I'm passionate about music, too," I tell her. "And I love the guys. Chase and Landon, Karsten and Emilio, they're some of the most talented people I've ever met. This whole experience has been just incredible."

Nora leans forward, and I can tell she's started recording.

"That's exactly what I want to know. Can you tell me more about what it's like being on the road with them?"

"Well…" I pull my hair away from my face, trying to find the right words. How do you describe the monotony and the constant change? The sense of being part of something special, and yet feeling like one small cog in an ever-moving machine? How do you talk about the horsing around to pass the time, and then time going so quickly that you have to get back on the road before you know it? How do you make someone understand the stress of wondering what comes after, but then also feeling like it could never possibly end?

I tell Nora how I ended up on the tour. We talk about the guys and their personalities, how much I respect their talent and their hard work. We chat about what it's like to live on a bus, going to a different city every day. I even talk a little about what it's like to find yourself attracted to someone in that crazy world—maybe even falling in love.

Of course, I don't tell her Emilio and I were never really together. And I don't tell her I'm with Griffin. I simply say that tours are intense and feelings happen quickly, and that people on a boy band tour are like everybody else—just trying to find their way.

Again, Nora asks what my passion is.

By now, I've talked so much that talking is easy. Without a second thought, I tell her I love to sing. I tell her I love to dance and perform with my friends who also love to sing, dance and perform.

I tell her I am a show choir girl.

41

By the time I'm done with Nora, the storms that threatened tonight's show have passed, and everyone's in full pre-concert frenzy. The VIP tent sits empty. Seats are filling quickly. And from beyond the grandstand come the now-familiar sounds of the fair.

I venture out of the bus, passing Serena, who's all ready in a teal corset and black ruffled skirt, her hair done up in black and blue feathers. She's with Eisha, who has her back to me, talking with someone from a local news station. I point to an imaginary scar just under my eyebrow. Serena nods understanding and creates a distraction before Eisha can rope me into water delivery or replenishing the merch table.

I mime a big *thank you.* Serena gives a thumbs up, and I make a mental note to repay her in some way once all this is over. I've made friends in so many unexpected places these past two months; how weird and amazing is it that one of them is someone as great as Serena Sato?

Next to Eisha on the list of people I'd rather not talk with right now is Mom's new guy, Aaron. The two of them are laughing near the sound truck. My first urge is to go the opposite direction, but if this divorce really is happening, then I'm going to have to get used to her dating other people, right? Dad, too.

I walk over, working hard to look friendly. Aaron shoves his hands in his pockets and gives me an awkward smile.

"Hi, Avery."

I'm pretty sure he's younger than Mom, but his face has the wind-wrinkled look of someone who spends a lot of time outside. And his eyes are kind, which I suppose is all I really need to know at the moment.

"Hi," I say back. I'm sure my smile looks awkward too.

"Are you looking for Griffin?" Aaron asks. "He was here just a minute ago."

"He was moping around and getting in the way," Mom says, pointedly. "I convinced him to find something more constructive to do. He said he'd be backstage if anyone needed him."

"Right." I take a deep breath. I know Mom's waiting to hear what I've decided about Choraliers. I appreciate that she hasn't told me what she thinks I should do—she's letting me make this decision on my own.

"Let me know how it turns out," she says.

"OK," I say. "Wish me luck."

Heading up the ramp behind the stage, I pass June lecturing one of the crew about the high fructose corn syrup in the granola bar he's eating. I slip past Lenny, who doesn't notice, which is a compliment since I now know exactly where not to step, what not to bump, and who not to bother in order to avoid attracting his attention. In one of the trailers at the rear, Jack talks on his phone to someone from Calliope while Claire steams the last few wrinkles from the wardrobe for tonight's concert. The other trailer has been transformed into a makeshift green room, and that's where I find Griffin.

He's bent over his guitar, and I have to take a minute to just stand and watch him. His spiky dark hair, his muscular arms under his black tee-shirt, the way he frowns as he concentrates, closing his eyes now and then as if to absorb the music into his soul. I've never seen anyone so beautiful.

Just as I'm about to let him know I'm here, he looks up.

"Hey," he says.

"Hey," I say back.

"Did you get hold of your fangirl?"

"I did. It helped me figure out a lot of things."

I move to sit next to him, but he stands and meets me halfway.

"Don't tell me yet," he says. "Give me one more chance to either change your mind about leaving or make you glad you decided to stay. Can you come to the concert?"

A warning bell goes off in my mind.

"You're not planning to bring me onstage, are you? I don't think I can do that again."

"No, none of that," he says. "Just please say you'll come. Jack has a ticket waiting for you."

As he speaks, I become aware of a sound in the distance, almost drowned out by the noise of the fair crowd. It's the whir of cicadas, earlier than I'm used to, but it seems fitting —there's an end-of-summer feel to the air. It's the kind of night where I'd probably be out watching the show anyway. And depending what I decide, it might be my last time in a long time to see Griffin play live.

He looks at me with those deep brown eyes. The scar I love so much quirks up as he waits for my answer.

"I wouldn't miss it," I say.

"Turned into a nice night after all, didn't it?" the security guard says as he leads me to my fifth-row seat.

"It really did," I answer. "Let's hope everybody behaves."

We share a smile because even though each city is different, so much is the same. There are the little kids with their parents, the fans with their homemade signs, the fairgoers who don't know much about True Meaning but decided to take in the concert on a pretty night. It's rare for any of these people to truly *not* behave, and if they came close, the guards would just do their best to keep it corralled. Like Eisha said, none of us would be here if it wasn't for them.

Another thing that hasn't changed is how nobody ignores Serena when she takes the stage. As I watch her captivate the crowd, I can't believe she could ever be unsure whether this is something she wants to do. No matter what happens, I hope we'll stay friends so I can see what she decides; I'm pretty sure she'll be great at whatever she does.

Serena finishes her set, and the crew moves onstage to assemble the trampoline for TM. Every now and then, a pyro test sends plumes of smoke into the air. People start to scream before realizing it was a false alarm and going back to their conversations. Then that moment comes when the lights go out and the camera flashes starts. Suddenly everybody's on their feet, ready to go.

None of this is anywhere close to new for me, but it's still impressive: The strobes, the drums, the band on the risers, and the guys appearing out of the smoke. By now I know the order of songs by heart. I could even do most of the choreography if I had to. Here in the fifth row, I've got the perfect spot—close enough to feel like part of the action but not so close as to get swallowed up by the die-hard fans down front. Maybe Nora's podcast will rehab my image, and maybe it won't. For now, I'm happy to be just another face in the crowd.

Like every night, the end of *Party Girl* means it's time for the stools to come out and the guys to bring someone onstage. Tonight's chosen one keeps hiding her face in her glow-braceleted arms. Karsten and Griffin get their acoustics, then settle on their stools next to her with the other guys around them.

"You know, it's crazy," Karsten says. "When you're doing a summer tour like this one, there are a lot of surprises."

"Yeah," Emilio agrees. "You meet people."

"You maybe even date people," Landon adds, eyebrow arched. This sparks a tsunami of screams. The girl on the stool covers her eyes again.

"And then maybe you decide it's not going to work out," Emilio continues. More screams, even louder this time, because they all think they know what he's talking about, and they're glad that's over, because a single Emilio is more fun to fantasize about than one whose photo is all over the place with somebody else.

"Or maybe it does work out," Chase says. He reaches out to fist bump Griffin, who's been busy adjusting the straps of his guitar.

"I think we've all been there," Karsten continues. "Even if you've never been on a tour like this one, you still know what that summer thing is like, right? You meet somebody and you're not sure where it's going, but for that time when you're together, however long it lasts, it's magic. Our guitarist wrote a song about it. What's this one called, Griffin?"

Griffin leans in to be heard over Karsten's mic.

"I'm still not sure about the title," he says. "Right now, I'm calling it *Ferris Wheel Girl*."

My breath catches in my throat. Everything around me freezes as he plays a simple, slightly melancholy chord progression. When Karsten starts to sing, I recognize the melody as a patchwork of the snippets I've heard after all those shows when I thought Griffin was just messing around. They've been stitched together into a song that perfectly captures the feeling of those nights when he and I would escape to our own little world, trying to make every minute count before it was time to get on the road again.

> Taste of summer, the lights of a fair,
> Smell of popcorn in the air,
> You and me with the world beneath our feet.
> You held my hand as we went up,
> Afraid of coming down.
> But the ride had only just begun,
> And soon we were laughing, having fun,
> And being scared has never felt so sweet.

The audience sways along, phones in the air like electric fireflies, as the chorus starts—lush and hopeful.

> Around and around like a carnival ride,
> We hate the heights but we love the high.
> When summer's over you'll go back to your
>   own world.
> But tonight, you're my Ferris wheel girl.

I sit motionless as I listen, letting the music wash over me, watching Griffin play and the guys sing and feeling nearly every emotion one human being can feel at one time.

There are hundreds of people around, but somehow it seems like Griffin and I are the only ones who truly exist.

"Oh my God that was amazing," the girl next to me says as the last chord of his song echoes into the dusk.

"It was so sad!" her friend agrees. "I wonder who it's about!"

Before they can speculate any more, the stools are gone, Griffin's traded his acoustic for electric again, and he's back on his riser while the guys are doing tricks on the trampoline. Later tonight, his song will probably get posted online, and the people watching will get a small taste of what it was like to experience it live. But none of them will ever truly know, and even the people who were here will remember it as just one moment out of a hundred great ones this evening.

But it's one that I will never forget.

~

I DON'T WATCH the last bit of the concert. Instead, I head for the backstage ramp once again. The crowd sounds grow muffled as I re-enter the cluster of buses. In a couple of minutes, the confetti cannons will go off. Normally I love that part, but tonight I can't bear to see it end.

The guys' ATVs are lined up in front of a semi, waiting to be loaded. I sit on the back of one, waiting for Griffin. He's one of the first to come down, all sweaty spiked hair and that perfect smile. I walk straight into his arms, breathing in his summer-salty smell.

"That was beautiful," I tell him. "Your song... it was perfect."

"Yeah?" he says. "For the first time I was actually nervous someone wouldn't like something I wrote. You really did?"

"I loved it. Do you want to take a walk?"

"Not just yet." He pulls away and fans himself self-consciously. "I'm stalling, but I'm also dying in these clothes. Let me change and get my acoustic, then let's go back to the stage."

I follow him to his bus, where he changes into shorts and a fresh tee-shirt and grabs the old guitar. Then I follow him back up the ramp, skirting the crew hard at work, to find a spot away from all the activity. We sit with our feet dangling, neither of us wanting to move or talk. In this moment, I can almost pretend it's any other night after any other show.

Griffin plays softly, pieces of True Meaning songs and fragments of tunes I've never heard before. I lean back on my elbows and close my eyes.

"I could listen to you play forever," I tell him.

"Then don't go and you can."

I look up at the stars, searching for the right words. Finally, I say, "I watch you up here onstage, and you're doing what you love. If I went to L.A. I'd spend most of my time waiting for you to come off tours, working at Calliope and maybe starting to resent you because I missed doing what *I* love. I never want to feel that way about you."

"You could sing in L.A.," he tells me. "If you're serious about it, if you think that's what you want to *do*, then that's the place to be."

"I've seen how hard it is, though. There are no guarantees. But I do have a guarantee in Cincinnati. I always dreamed of being in Choraliers." One of the crew guys pushes a cart close by. I move in to rest my head on Griffin's shoulder. "And it doesn't matter *when* they wanted me. What matters is that I love show choir and I love them."

He puts his guitar down and wraps an arm around me.

Here, next to him, I am worlds away from where I was with Hunter. Hunter is a friend I could never replace. But Griffin is the key to a world I've only begun to explore. No matter where I am, I can't lose that.

"I'm happy for you," he tells me. "Even though it doesn't seem like it, I really am."

"And you don't have to worry about Hunter," I assure him. "He's part of my past. You're my right now, and I hope maybe you'll be my future, too."

I feel Griffin's chest rise and fall with a little shudder—a sad sigh that turns into a chuckle.

"But just so we're clear, I also am the better kisser," he says. "I am, right? The better kisser?"

The only way to answer that is to demonstrate just how much of a better kisser Griffin is.

It takes a while.

"And your hands," I say as I rub my thumb over the calluses on his fingers, trying to memorize how they feel against my skin. "I've always loved them. They're musical hands."

"So are yours." He takes both of mine and brings them up, spreading them wide so that the palms are out, framing my face. He gives them a little shake. "Jazz hands!"

I laugh. "Everything's better with jazz hands."

Griffin leans in, resting his forehead against mine.

"When do you leave?" he asks.

Now it's my turn to sigh. I don't want to do this, but I have to.

"Tomorrow. I'm riding on tonight's bus to Lansing. Mom's staying on to the end of the tour, but I'm flying out of the airport there. My flight leaves around 4 in the afternoon."

Griffin swallows and pulls in another shuddering breath.

"I just can't believe I'm not going to see you every day," he says.

"The Ariana Grande tour comes through Cincinnati. Remember?"

He cracks a smile. "And Indianapolis. And Cleveland."

"If it's within driving distance, then I'll be there. I'll be a groupie."

He raises an eyebrow, his scar creeping adorably up his forehead.

"A fangirl?"

"Yes. And maybe you can come see me if the Choraliers make nationals. Nationals are pretty much always in New York City. You can find a reason to go there for a gig or something, can't you?"

Now, his scar disappears completely as his forehead crumples. He swipes away a tear, trying to look brave.

"I really hoped I could change your mind," he says. "I wrote that song for you weeks ago, before I knew how true it would be."

I reach up, wiping his cheeks dry, trying not to cry myself.

"That song is everything. It's the best gift you could have ever given me. And I can still come to L.A. for college, maybe, or even to work, if..."

I can't say it—the possibility that it won't be true is too hard to think about. So Griffin says it for me.

"If we're still together?"

"Yes. I hope we are."

A chorus of shrieks goes up behind us, at the barricades. Emilio, Karsten, Landon and Chase must have made a surprise appearance to sign autographs.

"What do you think will happen to True Meaning after all this is over?" I ask.

Griffin shrugs.

"Rumor is Calliope's planning to cancel the show after this next season. Emilio won't have time for it once *Dead at Dusk* starts filming, especially if they do more movies, and the ratings for last season were pretty crappy."

I frown. "I thought the tour was supposed to help with that."

"That's how this business is, unfortunately. At any minute, all this could all get taken away. But would that mean we didn't have an amazing summer? Would it take away from how great it feels to be onstage, or all of the people we touched? All we ever really have is right now."

"That sounds like another song," I tell him.

"Maybe you *are* a muse," he laughs. "A muse with jazz hands."

He kisses me again. It's going to be so hard giving this up. But I know he's right: What matters is now. So we have our *right now* until we hear the buses start up, and my phone starts buzzing with texts from Mom, and I half expect to see Lenny's face poking around the scaffolding of the now-deserted stage, yelling at us to get our butts in gear, get up, and get out.

Griffin walks me to my bus. Then we wring out a couple more moments together until Mom orders me inside. Even then, I linger up front, watching out the driver's window as Griffin boards his own bus, giving one last wave before he disappears inside. The buses start to roll, one by one, out of the parking lot and then onto the highway, all of us traveling on to our next destination.

ABOUT THE AUTHOR

Sara Wealer grew up in Manhattan, Kansas (the "Little Apple"), and majored in voice performance at the University of Kansas before deciding she had no business trying to be an opera singer. She transferred to journalism school and became a reporter covering everything from house fires to Hollywood premieres.

These days, Sara works as a copywriter while the sun is out and writes novels by night. She lives in Cincinnati with her husband, two daughters, two dogs and four cats, and still sings sometimes when her schedule allows. When she's not writing, you'll find her at the ballet, or obsessively watching ballet online.

You can find Sara and her books at sarabennettwealer.com

9 798218 903992